GET BACK

The Extraordinary Adventures
of Desmond Jones

By

Michael Leavy

ISBN-13: 9798839469068

To all my friends and family who have had to put up with me banging on about this book for years.

CONTENTS

ACKNOWLEDGEMENTS

Over many years I have gained the knowledge and inspiration to write this book from several sources. They include, among others:

The Beatles Recording Sessions, The Complete Beatles Chronicle, The Beatles Tune In, all by Mark Lewisohn

Shout! The True Story of The Beatles by Philip Norman

The Love You Make, An Insider's Story of The Beatles by Peter Brown & Steven Gaines

The Beatles Anthology by The Beatles

www.beatlesbible.com

www.everyhit.com

I would also like to thank my friend Jim Parks from the USA for the cover design inspiration.

CHAPTER 1

Bath, England, May 1980

"Here comes the sun," said Desmond Jones to himself as he emerged from the University of Bath's canteen one sunny afternoon, having eaten a quick lunch following his morning lecture. Feeling the warmth, he flicked back his dark brown, shoulder-length hair and was about to remove his denim jacket when his attention was drawn to what he perceived as a vision of loveliness walking towards him. On seeing this perfect picture before him, he stopped and stood staring, open mouthed. This was because he initially thought, just for a second, that it was actually Stevie Nicks, singer from one of his top five bands, Fleetwood Mac.

He quickly realised that it wasn't Stevie Nicks but thought that she did look a lot like her, dressed in a long, black, flowing, silk-like dress. He wondered who she was smiling at as she proceeded towards him. He glanced over his shoulder but was puzzled to see no one there. He turned back towards her and smiled as she reached him and stood directly in front of him. Desmond assumed she had mistaken him for someone else as he was certain he had never met her before. She also looked a bit older than the average student and Desmond assumed she must either be a new lecturer or a more mature student.

"Hello, you look like Stevie Nicks," he blurted out before

he could stop himself.

"So I'm told," she responded in a non-descript accent. "I'm Molly. You're Desmond Jones."

"Yes, yes that's me! Desmond Jones. And you're Molly? Wow! Desmond and Molly. Here we are." Desmond was getting a little carried away with the fact that he had finally met someone called Molly, not realising that not everyone would get the connection. "Desmond and Molly Jones, wow!"

"I'm not Molly Jones, just Molly. Who's Molly Jones?" she asked.

"Sorry, sorry," said Desmond. "I got a little excited," he conceded, embarrassingly. "Do you know the Beatles song 'Ob-La-Di, Ob-La-Da'?" he asked. "Well," he continued, without waiting for a reply, "Desmond and Molly Jones are the central characters in the song. I just thought it funny that I should actually meet someone called Molly. Because my name's Desmond. What a coincidence."

"Well how funny," said Molly, a little patronisingly.

"How did you know my name?" asked Desmond, suddenly remembering that she knew who he was.

"Oh I've seen you before. You wouldn't remember though. Anyway, it's great to see you again," she said before he could butt in. "I just thought it would be nice to say 'hello'."

Desmond was a little confused, wondering where he may have met this lady before. "Why don't I remember you?" he asked. "Was I very drunk?"

"Yes," responded Molly quickly, grasping the opportunity. Alcohol-induced amnesia was not uncommon for Desmond in his university days.

"Would you like to go for a drink?" asked Desmond suddenly, surprising himself with his forwardness. He considered that he must have created some sort of impression if Molly had taken the trouble to approach him in the first place. "I mean, you know, if you're not doing anything else," he continued. "But I understand if you don't want to, after all, we've only just met. Or at least I've only just met you. You've met me before but I can't remember that."

"Yes, okay. And do shut up!" interrupted Molly. "Where shall we go?"

"Oh, right!" said Desmond. "Great. When are you free? I'm free now if you are."

They both agreed that they were free to go straight for a drink. After some deliberation Desmond suggested they go for a coffee in the University bar. "That way I won't forget who you are like I did last time, apparently. Maybe we can go for a stronger drink next time," suggested Desmond, rather presumptuously.

They proceeded to the bar and ordered their coffee and took a seat at a table in the corner. It wasn't the most salubrious of surroundings. The lights were bright, the tables were bare, and the wooden seats not particularly comfortable, but it was quiet and it was close and Desmond had wanted get to know the lovely Molly before she changed her mind.

They chatted for a couple of hours whilst getting through two more coffees and a cake each. Desmond did most of the talking, perhaps through nervousness or the fear of any awkward silences which he thought Molly may jump at as a reason to leave. He continued to surprise himself at his ability to converse with Molly.

In fact, Molly was gently manipulating Desmond in order to ensure he was relaxed. She was enjoying his company and didn't want him to feel awkward and think he ought to leave.

She knew that he was a Beatles fan so continually maneuvered the conversation towards his favourite subject. During the course of the afternoon Desmond provided a comprehensive history of his favourite band starting with when Paul and John first met at St Peter's Church fete in Liverpool where John's group, the Quarrymen, were playing. He told her about the various names they were known by before they eventually settled on the Beatles, names such as Johnny and the Moondogs and the Silver Beetles. With a little prompting he continued to inform his avid listener about when the Beatles played in Hamburg; he knew that they performed at the Indra, Kaiserkeller, and Top Ten clubs but was a little unsure of dates. Molly appeared to be impressed enough for Desmond to continue, although Molly's knowledge was somewhat more comprehensive than Desmond's, lyrics to 'Ob-La-Di, Ob-La-Da' notwithstanding, having thoroughly researched the subject prior to arriving in Bath. There were a few times when she had to stop herself from correcting Desmond's occasional omissions or errors, but, on the whole, she was impressed with his knowledge. He further surprised himself by remembering more than he thought he knew. He talked about the Cavern in Liverpool and how the Beatles dominated the Liverpool music scene and he mentioned how he would have loved to have been a teenager in those days in the early sixties, but of course he was only born in 1960 so that was impossible. At this point Molly made a mental note – *maybe one day Desmond will be able to visit the Cavern in the 1960s.*

Desmond was on a roll and he next went on to inform Molly of Brian Epstein's involvement with the Beatles; how he became manager after his interest was sparked by a young man by the name of Raymond Jones ("No relation," he added) when he walked in to Epstein's family store in Liverpool and asked for a copy of 'My Bonnie', a song recorded in Hamburg by the Beatles, backing Tony Sheridan under the name of the Beat Brothers. Suspecting that he might be beginning to bore his 'date', as he liked to think of her, he realised that he would need to cut out some of the details of his Beatles history lesson so he decided to just run through the Beatles UK album and singles releases, ending with the 'Let It Be' album ("Although it was recorded before 'Abbey Road'").

Molly was actually quite happy for Desmond to do all the talking as she knew she would need to make up more than a few things when talking about herself. Molly held a very important position in the secret world of time travel; she was the Time Peacekeeper, looking after timelines and ensuring, with the help of her time agents, that there were a minimum number of parallel existences in the already fragile world of timelines. She was reluctant to discuss time travel unless she deemed it absolutely necessary.

Desmond concluded his Beatles story by confiding in her his belief that the Beatles will one day get back together. "John, Paul George, and Ringo," he said, "surely they'll resolve any differences and get back together. So how about you, Molly?" asked Desmond, catching her on the hop. "Tell me a bit about you. Where are you from?"

"Do you mean spiritually or geographically?" she asked mischievously, hoping to buy a little time. "And anyway," she continued, without waiting for a response, "you haven't really told me anything about you, apart from the fact that you're obviously a big Beatles fan."

"Oh, right, yes," replied Desmond. "In answer to your question, I mean geographically although you can talk about what you want. And yes, I am a Beatles fan. I don't really know how much you already know about me though. After all, I must have been pretty drunk last time I saw you as I can't remember a thing!" he joked. "Okay, what can I tell you about me?" he asked rhetorically.

Desmond continued with a neat summary of his life so far, much to Molly's relief. The more Desmond talked about himself, the less time she would have to talk about her. It took less time than she'd hoped, however, as it seemed that Desmond had had quite an uneventful life thus far. Molly learned that, until moving away to university, he had always lived at home with his parents and brother Michael. He also mentioned his Uncle Ernie and how he introduced him to the music of the Beatles. He'd been on a few family holidays, most often to Devon and Cornwall. Apart from that there was very little else to report.

Well, your seemingly uninteresting life will get more interesting, Desmond, she thought to herself.

It was at this point that Molly started thinking about the future Desmond and how he came to start his time travelling. She liked Desmond and although his time travelling caused additional risks as far as the timelines were concerned, she really wanted him to experience what it was like to actually be there when the Beatles were around. She was aware that even this meeting with him could potentially alter his timeline even though it worked out fine as eventually, in the year 2000, he would find himself thrown into a world where time travel becomes a reality. *I must remember to speak to Lord Woodbine,* she thought to herself.

"So who are you and where are you from, Molly?" asked Desmond, breaking her train of thought.

"Oh, I'm Molly Parks and I'm from, er, Chicago," she responded immediately. "I'm a journalist and I'm here doing some research for a book. I thought I'd come to Bath University to see how people feel about the world. You know, pollution, global warming, the environment, and all that kind of stuff."

"Wow, global warming. That sounds serious. Is it? I've never heard of it."

Molly had to pause for a moment while she reminded herself which time period she was in. *Of course,* she remembered, *environmental awareness was in its infancy. Global warming had barely been heard of in 1980.* "Er, yes, I think it is. I think in the next ten to twenty years or so we'll see a big change in the way people think about the planet."

"So what's global warming?" continued Desmond. "Is the planet warming up? Is that a bad thing?"

"Yes, to both of those, but let's not talk about that now," said Molly, wishing she'd thought of another reason for being there. When she'd decided to visit Desmond, she had thought she would be able to just make stuff up. She wasn't planning to stay long so she was sure she would be able to bluff her way through a conversation.

"Oh, okay," said Desmond, much to her relief. She was now feeling less confident about her global warming knowledge. "And you came all the way to Bath in England to research it," Desmond stated. "It must be an important project."

"It is but let's talk about something else."

"And how will it affect us, this global warming thing?" he

continued, oblivious to Molly's unease.

"Well Desmond," she resumed, ignoring Desmond's puzzled expression, "the weather for a start, and all the knock-on effects. Growing crops and things. Oh, and the ice cap. That's going to melt."

"Goodness me!" said Desmond. "You sound very knowledgeable. So the sea will be warmer. That's good, isn't it?"

"No, Desmond. Now can we talk about something else?"

"Where are you staying?" Desmond asked next, having finally taken the hint regarding Molly's reluctance to continue with the global warming conversation.

'I'm staying in a guest house in the town," she continued confidently. "Would you like to meet tonight?" She was as surprised as Desmond at the forwardness and suddenness of the question. "Where's a good pub?" she asked, confident that Desmond would agree to meet her later.

"The Pepper Pot on Prudence Street is a good pub," answered Desmond.

Molly had felt it was a good time to halt the conversation as she needed time to get her story together. She didn't like to deceive Desmond and wanted to be as honest as possible. But this is difficult when you're the Time Peacekeeper and you didn't want to give any secrets away. Providing Desmond with too much information could affect the timelines. *It's already precarious and I'm probably not helping things by meeting with Desmond,* she reminded herself. *But a girl's got to have some fun, hasn't she?*

They agreed to meet at the pub that evening. Desmond couldn't believe his luck. He'd been approached by a beautiful woman, a few years older than him who apparently had met him before. They seemed to get on really well and, he reminded himself, it was Molly who had suggested they meet in the evening.

*

Desmond arrived at the pub early as he allowed extra travelling time in case of delays. The house he shared with four other students was in the city centre and only ten minutes' walk away but even so, he didn't want to take any chances and risk Molly arriving before him. He convinced himself that if he wasn't there when she arrived, she would assume he wasn't coming and leave, and he would never see her again. Molly had a similar thought and also left plenty of time to arrive at the pub. She would hate to think that Desmond thought she wasn't going to turn up.

"Hi Des," said Molly, feeling more comfortable with the less formal version of Desmond.

"Hi Moll," chanced Desmond.

"It's Molly actually," she replied, giving him a mock stern look, enough for Desmond to realise she wasn't fond of the abbreviated version.

Following this gentle verbal sparring they carried on where they left off earlier that day and began to feel very comfortable in one another's company. Molly had used the break to formulate a convincing back story whilst attempting to be as honest as possible with Desmond. She talked about her interest in science fiction and even broached the subject of time travel and whether or not it was possible.

"I believe that time travel is possible," she boldly claimed, which started a whole hour of discussion using her real-life experiences to provide possible explanations to Desmond's constant *but what if …?* or *how do you explain that?* It turned out that Desmond really wanted to believe but his logical reasoning constantly raised objections.

For his part Desmond realised he couldn't talk about the Beatles all evening so introduced other aspects of his life into the conversation, including his generic love of music, his attempts at learning to play the guitar, his indulgence in board games, crosswords, and his prevailing thirst for knowledge. He talked about his friend and fellow student Nigel who had abandoned his course and went to live in Middlesham in the southwest and work for the Inland Revenue. A couple of years later, when Desmond had graduated in Mathematics, he would follow in Nigel's footsteps and join him in Middlesham and the Inland Revenue after Nigel had informed him of job opportunities.

At the end of the night, they agreed to meet again the following evening, Desmond suggesting they try the Indian restaurant that he and his housemates would occasionally visit.

They continued to meet every evening over the following week and then, all of a sudden, Molly broke the news that she had to go. She told Desmond, with much sadness, that she wouldn't be able to stay in touch for reasons she would hopefully get to explain one day. It broke Desmond's heart and he rarely spoke about it again.

CHAPTER 2

Somewhere near Middlesham,

England, November 2000

Slightly off key, Desmond sang the opening line to 'The Long and Winding Road' as he drove along a meandering stretch of road on his way back from visiting his younger brother Michael.

He was driving through torrential rain. It was a dark winter's evening, and he was getting a little anxious about getting back to the Admiral Nelson at Middlesham for the pub quiz. His brother lived about twenty miles away, in a thatched cottage in a small country village. Desmond enjoyed his occasional visits, keeping up to date with events in his brother's world. Michael was thirty-two, eight years younger than Desmond, married to Angela. Desmond was not married, to Angela or anyone else. Maybe he was waiting for Molly to come along. At least that's what he told anyone who asked. He generally kept quiet about the fact that he had met Molly back in 1980, before she abruptly disappeared.

Desmond had spent the afternoon showing Michael his new book 'The Beatles Anthology' by The Beatles. A book which Desmond had recently bought himself as a present. A book he had been waiting for five years since the Anthology TV series in 1995 and the three accompanying albums,

'Anthology 1', '2' and '3'. He was eternally grateful to his Uncle Ernie for introducing him to The Beatles.

Earlier Desmond and Michael were sat at the dining room table, the book ceremoniously laid out before them. "'Here, for the first time in print, is the history of The Beatles by The Beatles'," Desmond proudly recited to Michael; the first words on the inside cover of the book.

"You're not going to read me all of it, are you?" asked Michael with a slightly worried look on his face.

"No, he's not!" shouted Angela from the kitchen behind them. "He'll want to get back for quiz night, and it's a big book."

Angela was busy looking after their toddler, Desmond's little nephew, Josh, whilst also preparing their Sunday afternoon late lunch, something Desmond looked forward to each time he visited. He rarely had the inclination to prepare a proper balanced meal and Angela's food, along with spending time with his nephew, was his chief incentive for visiting. But today was different; an opportunity to share with brother Michael the contents of the book, and maybe even get him interested.

Ignoring Michael's question and Angela's answer, Desmond turned to the inside back cover. "And look, look," he excitedly pointed out to Michael, "artwork by Klaus Voorman. You know, Hamburg, Revolver, Manfred Mann, Plastic Ono band." A bunch of words which Michael nodded at, but Desmond had his doubts as to whether Michael was really that interested, or even if he knew who Klaus Voorman was.

He continued by opening random pages, each one being a treasure trove of stories, images, snapshots, pictures, quotes from 1960s Hamburg through to the split in 1970.

"Oh look, that chap looks a bit like you," said Angela, jokingly, as she peered over Desmond's shoulder whilst he was showing an increasingly bored-looking Michael some of the old black-and-white pictures of the Hamburg days.

And that was his afternoon. He loved his new book.

*

He was beginning to wish he'd invested in one of those mobile phones that more and more people were owning. He didn't really see the point in it as none of his friends believed in them either and he didn't think they would catch on; and he had a landline. However, had he had a mobile phone he could have rung the Admiral Nelson and asked the landlord to assure 'Le Beats' that he was on his way. The quiz was due to start in about thirty minutes' time and he was already regretting the decision to extend his visit to his brother's house. On a normal quiz night (a normal quiz night being one where he doesn't visit his brother with a big book) he would leave the house at about 8 o'clock to get to the Admiral Nelson in plenty of time for the start of the quiz.

He shared a three-bedroomed house with Nigel and Penelope; number eight Cavendish Crescent, Middlesham. Nigel, Desmond's friend from university, was of similar age to Desmond and they both still worked at the Inland Revenue. His long, bushy brown hair made him easily recognisable by everyone in Cavendish Crescent, a cul-de-sac of ten houses all very similar to number eight. Although Desmond considered him a bit of a know-it-all and could sometimes be annoyingly arrogant, they had remained good friends over the years. Nigel was knowledgeable about The Beatles but was more of a Stones fan which occasionally irritated Desmond. Penelope referred to herself as a mature student, studying English Literature, although she could probably get away with calling herself a student. She certainly didn't look mature, more like an oldish teenager, and thought of herself as a child of the sixties, even though she was born in 1970. She liked things to be done properly and would constantly berate Nigel for being ridiculous.

*

Desmond's anxiety increased when he saw up ahead a long line of red rear lights, obviously the result of some sort of holdup. *Probably flooding,* he thought, *or maybe even a sinkhole.* He had recently watched a television programme about the alarming increase in the number of sinkholes in the UK and had visions of his 1990 red Ford Fiesta hanging precariously on the precipice of a newly formed hole in the ground. After crawling along for about five minutes he decided that the holdup was caused by a bit of flooding. He was heading downhill, and the traffic was a least moving. "Come on, come on," he pleaded to the traffic up ahead, "it's only a bit of water."

Looking over to his right he saw the entrance to a small country lane and wondered if there was a possible short cut. He quickly dismissed the thought, justifying his decision with the conclusion that it would be ridiculous to go blindly chasing a short cut in the dark and wind and rain just to save a few minutes in order to get to the quiz on time. He was also a bit scared of driving down a dark lane and getting lost.

Just at that moment the traffic came to a complete standstill. The line of vehicles stretched downhill towards a bend to the right, after which he had no idea how much further it continued, his vision obscured by numerous trees, their dark outline swaying wildly with the wind. After a couple of minutes of going nowhere, Desmond glanced to his right and once again began to consider taking a chance on the country lane. With this, an old jeep poked its nose through the entrance. He watched with interest as a shadowy figure emerged from behind the wheel. It was difficult to make out any detail but, based on the stereotypical outfit and what at first looked to Desmond like a piece of straw sticking out of his mouth, his guess was that it was a farmer. He wound down his window and shouted across to him, asking if he knew what the problem was.

"Flood," came the response.

He could see now that the farmer was of a dark complexion, possibly West Indian, and was smoking a cigarette, kept dry by the rim of a small hat. "Yes," said Desmond as if confirming the farmer's correct answer.

"You can miss that bit out if you follow me," said the farmer, nodding towards the dark country lane from which he had emerged.

Against his better judgement, with quiz night beckoning and before he could stop himself, Desmond heard himself responding, "Great! Show me the way."

The farmer nodded, returned to his vehicle, got behind the wheel, and swiftly turned the jeep. Desmond turned right and followed him down the dark, country lane and started nervously singing the Peter Frampton classic, 'Show Me the Way.' He was still slightly off key. As his visibility was impaired by the heavy rain and the dark, narrow way ahead, he quickly stopped singing and concentrated on the taillights of the jeep. With a bit of effort, he managed stay within thirty yards of the jeep.

After a minute or so, as the lane grew narrower and darker and the branches of the trees overhead grew closer together, like a giant pair of hands shielding the rain, he started to imagine all sorts of ghastly outcomes of his decision to take the farmer's advice. *Was he even a farmer? Maybe he was a serial killer, luring his next victim to a dark, isolated farmhouse where he would be strangled or stabbed to death, then hung up on a meat hook to be discovered by some innocent passer-by.* How he wished he was back home wading through 'The Beatles Anthology'.

He wondered what his mum and dad would think when they read the news 'Man found stabbed and hanged in a field'. He was thinking that he should have made an effort to visit his parents more often. They only lived a couple of hours' drive away further up the country. His mind wondered back to his childhood and teenage years and how he frustrated his parents by researching and listening to The Beatles rather than spending time on his schoolwork. *If I get out of this alive,* he thought, *I'll definitely visit my parents more often.*

He was brought back to the present when, after negotiating a few tight bends and unexpected turnings, he saw the jeep come to a halt up ahead at a T-junction and then turn to the left. As Desmond approached the junction, he saw a sign on the opposite side of the road ahead indicating to the left, a single destination, a place apparently called Wormle.

"Never heard of it," said Desmond out loud, believing the sound of his own voice to be a comfort in what could turn out to be a stressful situation. "Must be a place on the way back to the main road," he told himself.

As he turned left, he realised that he couldn't see the red lights of the jeep. He wasn't too bothered, however, as he guessed there were probably a few bends in the road, and he would eventually catch up. To his dismay, before he could catch sight of any lights, he came to another junction. He stopped and peered both right and left but could see no sign of the jeep. A few seconds passed and, thinking that he had better soon make a decision to give himself at least a 50/50 chance of catching up, decided to turn right.

Driving with extra care, peering through the windscreen past the wipers and trying to pick out the verges through the torrential rain, he followed the road for a good ten minutes and, after driving under a low bridge, he came to another junction. As he was going under the bridge he heard a sound, not unlike the sound he associated with the pop noise you can make by putting your finger in your mouth and pulling it out against your cheek, but much louder. He quickly dismissed the noise after thinking it may have come from the engine. He preferred not to dwell on engine noises, hoping they would go away and not bother him again. It was a subject he knew little about. At the junction he turned left, mixing it up a bit after turning right at the previous junction.

After another two or three minutes the road came to a dead end. In front of him was what he guessed was some sort of farm building; a large lean-to containing various bulky objects. Objects Desmond assumed were something to do with farming, another subject he knew little about. He couldn't see anything else either side or beyond the building. It seemed to be shrouded in the rain, mist, and darkness.

"What on Earth?" whispered Desmond to himself. The object of his surprise, picked out by his headlamps, was an old, green Austin 152 campervan at the front of the lean-to. It was the type of iconic transport he'd always admired and imagined himself driving around the country in if he was rich enough and brave enough to give up his job at the tax office. He once enquired about one that had been advertised in the local paper as a possible replacement for the Ford Fiesta but decided against it owing to the excessive road tax and the meagre miles per gallon. By this time, he had forgotten his apprehension over what he was beginning to think was his final destination, and was now focused on the campervan.

*

Nigel and Penelope were getting anxious.

"Go outside and see where he is," demanded Penelope, her anxiety resulting in uncharacteristic assertiveness. Brian looked at his watch.

"He'll be here. He's probably been reading his big new book to his brother and forgotten the time."

Brian was the fourth member of 'Le Beats', the name being a source of constant amusement to Nigel and Desmond who never tired of congratulating themselves in creating what they considered an imaginative pub quiz team named derived from an anagram of Beatles.

"It should be '*The* Beats', we're not French you know," protested Penelope.

"Oh really, Pen, pardon moi," Nigel had replied, French grammar not being his strong point.

"Well, it starts in fifteen minutes, and I know he likes to get in the zone. Go on, Nige, go look for him," demanded Penelope again.

"Okay, back in a tick. Get the drinks in, Brian."

Brian reluctantly shuffled to the bar and ordered three pints and a double vodka with diet coke; Penelope's concession to a healthy lifestyle.

*

Ignoring the severe rain, Desmond slowly opened the door of his Fiesta and tentatively stepped out, straight into a large, deep puddle. He didn't seem to notice his wet feet as he crept carefully across to the campervan. He put his hood up in a futile attempt to keep his hair dry but by this point he didn't care about the rain. He had noticed a faint, bluish light coming from inside the campervan. On reaching the van, Desmond flung back his hood and stopped to admire the way in which the windscreen wipers were attached to the top of the windscreen. "Fascinating," he whispered. The van was just under the cover of the lean-to, but with the wind forcing the rain in, the roof didn't provide much in the way of shelter. He peered into the front passenger window and concluded that the interior looked in very good condition considering it dated back to the 1950s. He noticed a cigarette packet in the area next to the gear stick.

"Woodbines," he whispered. "They haven't been around for years." His attention was then drawn to the light he had noticed earlier.

"What on Earth?" he heard himself ask for the second time in as many minutes. The reason was that the light was emitting from a radio. A radio that was on and producing a sound he could just make out through the window. Desmond couldn't help but sing along to 'Tell Laura I Love Her'.

"This must date from about 1960 if I remember rightly," he said, hoping to be awarded an imaginary point. "Sung by Ricky Valance," for a bonus point.

He wondered how the radio could be on and looked around for someone who may have perhaps been listening to it before vacating the vehicle.

Maybe it was the scary farmer, he thought to himself, but there was no sign of anyone. He was thinking that he really ought to be getting to the quiz and reminded himself that he couldn't let the team down. He had, fortunately, dismissed the prospect of his untimely death.

"Another two minutes, then I'm off," he told himself out loud before deciding to try the passenger door. To his surprise it opened. He realised he was getting quite wet at this point, being only partly sheltered from the unrelenting weather, so decided to slip inside the door on to the passenger seat. On closer inspection, the interior was a bit smelly but still in a reasonable condition for its age. He touched the dial on the radio and a few seconds later the whole of the campervan lit up with a blinding white light; and then he was somewhere else.

CHAPTER 3

Hamburg, November 1960

Desmond scrambled to his feet.

"What?! How did I get here? What's going on?" he asked himself out loud whilst performing some kind of shaky dance movement.

He was in an alleyway between two tall buildings. There was traffic noise coming from a few yards away from what appeared to be a busy, brightly lit street. He wandered out to investigate.

Night-time, bright lights, and lots of people, but not people he was used to. They were speaking a different language. Maybe it was foreign tourists. *Where am I?* he asked himself. Desmond certainly wasn't familiar with his surroundings. What had happened to the campervan, the dark country lanes, the weather (it was a little damp here but no torrential rain); this was definitely not anything like Middlesham. His next thoughts were about the pub quiz.

I'm needed, he thought. *How will they manage without me? I'll need to get back.*

He was not sure how to go about that though. He looked around. The bright lights were nothing like what he had seen before. Apart from 'Coca Cola' all of the other neon signs were in a foreign language. More tourists walked past, giving him an odd look. He realised he had been standing with a strange expression on his face like someone who had been asked to explain the meaning of life.

Germans, he realised. *They're speaking German. Why are they speaking German?*

"Why is everyone speaking German?" he asked no one in particular.

No one answered. Just more looks. Looks which said, "Please don't involve me in your situation."

Well, it's no good standing here listening to Germans. I'll need to find someone helpful, he thought. He looked at his watch. The face was broken, and the digital display read 8:88.

"What time is it please?" he asked the nearest passer-by and was completely ignored.

"Ah, German," he remembered. "Vot is de time?" he enquired in his best German accent to the next person who walked by.

"8.15," was the response. "And it's okay, you don't need to use that stupid accent, I speak some English." She was in her early twenties. Dressed all in black and wearing a leather jacket with a long black scarf contrasting with her short blond hair. She was also very attractive. Desmond realised his expression must have looked unusual, eyes wide and open mouthed. He closed his mouth and composed himself.

"Where am I?" he asked "And why is everyone speaking German? Are you German?"

"On the corner of the Reeperbahn and Grosse Freiheit. Because you are in Germany, Hamburg to be precise. Yes, I am German. Do you have another question, or can I go now?"

Desmond didn't seem to take any of the information in.

"No, don't go. Can you help me?"

"I doubt it, but what is it I can do for you?"

"Well, it's quiz night and I need to get to the Admiral Nelson in Middlesham in a hurry. I don't know how I got here but if you could point me in the right direction, I would be eternally grateful. My 'Le Beats' teammates are depending on me."

"I understand what a quiz is but I do not know what a quiz night is. There is nothing like that around here. I'm more into music than quizzes. I assume the Admiral Nelson is some kind of hostelry as I believe *the* Admiral Nelson is no longer with us. I have no idea where Middlesham is and therefore would have difficulty in pointing you towards it. I could make out 'teammates' but what was it you said before that? 'Le Beats'? No idea what you are on about with that one. Are you French?"

"Well, that's not much help really, but thank you for trying. I wouldn't want to seem ungrateful. Do I sound French? I'm English actually. Wait a minute … did you say I'm in Germany? That can't be right. There must be a mistake. And why are people driving old-fashioned cars?" he asked as a 1950s VW drove past, on what he considered was the wrong side of the road, blasting its horn at him indignantly. He noticed he was standing in the gutter and quickly hopped on to the pavement alongside the mystery blonde.

"Not another question," she stated in an exasperated manner. "I am going to have to limit you to three more questions. I have to be somewhere."

"Where do you have to be?" asked Desmond, extravagantly.

"One."

"No, really, where do you have to be?"

"Two."

"Well, are you going to answer?"

"Three, goodbye."

And off she strolled down Grosse Freiheit without another word.

"Well, how rude!" Desmond realised that he was owed at least one more answer having asked one question twice. He started after her, determined not to be short-changed. He was having difficulty keeping up but managed to eventually reach her speed albeit with a slight limp which he guessed he had picked up whilst being transported to this strange place.

"I think I've been kidnapped by a farmer," suggested Desmond. "Drugged and somehow transported to Germany."

"Maybe you're dreaming," she offered, still strolling briskly towards her destination with what Desmond perceived as typical German efficiency.

"If I'm dreaming, wake me up, hit me or something," demanded Desmond, closing his eyes tightly shut in anticipation of a right hook.

Closing his eyes was a mistake. It was a busy pavement, and the bus stop sign was one of several obstacles to be avoided, sometimes difficult for a fully sighted person, let alone someone whose eyes were voluntarily closed awaiting an impact of a different sort.

After the blonde German lady had helped him up, she answered his earlier question. "I'm going to the Kaiserkeller."

"Great, my favourite," replied Desmond, sarcastically.

"It's a club. They have a band; English boys, rock n' roll. You'll understand what they're singing."

In Desmond's mind, this implied that he would be hearing this English rock n' roll band and therefore he would be accompanying her to the club. Suddenly the quiz night at the

Admiral Nelson seemed less important. Perhaps if he accompanied her to the club, he might get more answers to what had happened to him. And he might get to know his companion a little better.

Desmond's head was spinning. Apart from the recent, unfortunate event with the bus stop and the ridiculous notion that he had somehow been transported to Germany, he was beginning to decipher the information that the German lady had given him. He recalled that the Kaiserkeller was the nightclub that The Beatles played in when they first went to Hamburg in 1960. They had started at the Indra, he recalled, and moved to the Kaiserkeller a little later on. He appeared to be in Germany, according to the German lady anyway. *Surely the English rock n' roll band couldn't be The Beatles? No, that would be ridiculous*, he thought. *Next she'll be telling me that she's their friend Astrid.*

"I'm Des, by the way." He never referred to himself as 'Des'. He was unsure why he introduced himself by that name now. Perhaps he was hoping to impress this young lady with what he considered a cooler-sounding name. He soon realised his error and corrected himself. "Well Desmond actually. What's your name?" he asked as he followed her towards the Kaiserkeller.

"Astrid," she replied immediately.

CHAPTER 4

Middlesham, November 2000

"Well, where is he?" asked Penelope.

"No sign," replied Nigel, apologetically. "I've been down as far as the roundabout, and to be fair he can't really go far wrong. After all, it's only seven minutes' walk."

"That's very precise," replied Penelope. "Have you timed it?"

"Of course," responded Nigel a little sheepishly.

Desmond and Nigel both had the kind of personality that regarded accurate estimates of walking time between point 'A' (e.g., home) and point 'B' (e.g., the pub) as worthy of recording.

"He was sure he'd be back in time," said Nigel. "He's only gone to see his brother."

They were aware that Desmond was always a big advocate of getting in the 'zone'. He also needed to make sure he picked up his lucky pen, a Beatles ballpoint he bought for what he considered a bargain from The Beatles shop in Baker Street, London. Whenever Desmond went to London, he always made a point of visiting the Baker Street shop as well as going to Abbey Road to gaze at the EMI studios and to make the obligatory walk across 'the most famous crossing in the world'.

Brian returned from the bar with the drinks. He was twenty-nine and lived in the same village, a few streets away from the rest of the team. He wore an air of inevitability about him, always expecting to be the one to get the drinks, as Nigel, Penelope, and Desmond often assumed greater knowledge of the questions and were constantly in close conversation with each other. In reality, Brian often came up with the right answer to a question, but credit was rarely given where due.

"He'll be here in minute. Desmond won't let us down," said Nigel reassuringly.

"I'm sure you're right," agreed Penelope. "We might as well get ready. We'll have to carry on whether he's here or not."

"Don't worry, he'll be here," came a voice from behind them.

They looked around only to see a darkly dressed figure disappearing out through the door of the Admiral Nelson. The three members of 'Le Beats' simultaneously shrugged their shoulders, settled down, and awaited the start of the quiz.

CHAPTER 5

Hamburg, November 1960

"Are you following me?" Astrid turned and asked as she noticed Desmond was still with her.

"What a coincidence. Your name, Astrid," remarked Desmond. "Yes. I mean no. I'm not following you, I just thought I would tag along."

"Well, I can't stop you coming into the club, but I'm not sure it's your cup of tea, as I believe you say in England. Is that right?"

"Yes, that's right, but I'd like to think it is my cup of tea, as we say in England," added Desmond.

"Why am I a coincidence?" asked Astrid, referring back to earlier in the conversation.

"Oh never mind, I'll probably wake up in minute."

They carried on down Grosse Freiheit, past the Top Ten club on the right.

"Hmm, the Top Ten Club. That sounds familiar as well," said Desmond.

"More coincidences?" asked Astrid.

"Yes," replied Desmond wearily, now convinced that his dream or whatever he was experiencing would produce further remarkable revelations.

Grosse Freiheit was full of life at this time of the evening. There were motorcycles and scooters speeding up and down, cars driving a little too closely to the kerb for Desmond's comfort. There were a group of men, sailors Desmond assumed, shouting at each other and pushing each other around as they spilt out of a doorway.

Soon they arrived at number 36, an inauspicious entrance to the Kaiserkeller.

"Are you really coming in?" asked Astrid.

"Yes, I need to. Definitely. I need to see what happens next."

They passed through the cloakroom area, without leaving their coats. Desmond in particular wanted the security of his coat in case he suddenly ended up at some other unfamiliar location.

"Are you from anywhere near Liverpool, in England?" asked Astrid as they entered the main club area. "You may know these groups if you are."

"Nowhere near," replied Desmond. "But I think I may know them."

"I doubt it. Outside of Liverpool they are not very well known."

"Maybe not yet," said Desmond under his breath.

*

Desmond was immediately struck by the noise. Not just from the band, who he was disappointed to see weren't The Beatles after all (he began to think that he had let his imagination run away with him). There was also the noise of the club generally; shouting, cheering, loud conversation, clinking of bottles and glasses, and the occasional fight. The clientele was certainly not what he was used to at the Admiral Nelson. There were several round tables, each with a half dozen or so people at them. Near the front, next to the stage, was a table which accommodated three people. Three people who looked different from the rest of the clientele. Whilst the rest of the club seemed to be made up of mainly noisy men who Desmond assumed to be sailors, the occupants of this table were young, dressed all in black with different haircuts; a bit like the early Beatles' look. Astrid, he noticed, was making her way towards this table. Not waiting to be asked, Desmond followed.

"That's Rory," Astrid mentioned over her shoulder as they approached the table.

"Good evening, Rory," said Desmond, offering his hand to the nearest young man, sitting at the table.

"I'm not Rory, I'm Klaus, Klaus Voorman," replied the young man, shaking Desmond's hand. "Pleased to meet you."

"No that's Rory; on stage; with the band; up there," Astrid informed a confused-looking Desmond.

"Got it," said Desmond whilst dealing with the news that he had just shaken hands with the young Klaus Voorman. The man who he had only been talking about that very afternoon whilst reviewing his new Beatles Anthology book with his brother.

"Another coincidence?" asked Astrid, noticing the widening of the eyes and opening of the mouth displayed by Desmond.

"Maybe," replied Desmond, regaining his composure and slipping into a chair next to Klaus.

"And this is Desmond Actually, he's French." Astrid's mischievous introduction to everyone was quickly corrected by Desmond.

Next to Klaus, on his left, was another young man introduced by Astrid as Wilhelm, and next to him was Jürgen Vollmer, another name that rang a bell from something

Desmond had read or seen at some stage during his Beatles education.

*

Desmond was impressed by this group of young people, all in their early twenties. They seemed genuinely friendly and made him feel very welcome. Whilst a little reluctant to give too much information away for fear of alienating himself with tales of time travel from the end of the century, he was happy to learn about them. They explained that they were art students and were known as 'Exis', short for the existentialist's movement which was derived from the 'Swing Kids' of the 30s who were influenced by the jazz movement of the time. He learned that the 'Exis' were influenced by the American rock and roll culture of the 50s but were intent on creating their own, unique image, not wanting to copy the American rock and roller's dress. This explained the dark clothes worn by Astrid and her friends.

He also learned that the area they were in was St Pauli and, being in the north part of the port of Hamburg, was frequented by sailors. The Reeperbahn, as it turned out, was the street on which Desmond had 'landed' following his experience in the campervan. They also told him how Klaus had happened upon the night club which imported groups from Liverpool in England and in particular how they had befriended a group called The Beatles. They had been struck by the 'rocker' appearance, the leather jackets, and in particular the bass player's posed, moody look based on James Dean, with his shades and quaffed-back hair and of course the rock and roll music of this group of young men from England. He was informed that they had first of all played at a club further down Grosse Freiheit called the

Indra. A fact Desmond knew well but, out of politeness, made out that he was learning this for the first time.

The Beatles, he 'learned' were made up of five members: Stu Sutcliffe, the moody-looking bass player, John Lennon, Paul McCartney, and George Harrison who all played guitar (although George was lead guitarist, apparently) and Pete Best who was the drummer. The songs they played were mainly the rock 'n' roll songs of the time, songs by Elvis, Chuck Berry, Gene Vincent, as well as a long, long version of Ray Charles' 'What'd I Say' and the occasional ballad like 'A Taste of Honey'. And they were soon to be on stage for the third time that day.

All of this, although some of it he knew about, Desmond found fascinating. Here he was, in Hamburg, sitting at a table in the Kaiserkeller talking with Astrid, Klaus, Jürgen, and Wilhelm, who had just arrived back from outside, his jacket and hair soaking wet. An appearance that led Desmond to assume that the rain was now much heavier outside.

For some reason, Desmond could not get to grips with how to pronounce Wilhelm and he asked if he could call him 'Bill'. Much to Wilhelm's amusement, he said that he had no problem with 'Bill'. "Most people call me 'Bill'," he conceded.

During the discussions Astrid frequently took pictures of the band. Desmond remembered that Astrid was a photographer and had taken many pictures of The Beatles in their Hamburg days. In fact, some were featured in 'The Beatles Anthology'. He also saw the camera pointing in his direction a couple of times which he tried not to notice but secretly wondered if his face could possibly appear in any of the pictures he had looked at of The Beatles in their Hamburg days. Then he decided that it was probably unlikely.

The conversation took place during the set of Rory Storm and the Hurricanes. A fact Desmond realised a few minutes after his misunderstanding of who Rory and Klaus were when sitting down with his new friends. Of course, he remembered, The Beatles and Rory Storm and the Hurricanes took in turns to perform at the Kaiserkeller. Another fact he remembered was that the drummer with Rory Storm and the Hurricanes was one Ringo Starr and he could barely contain his excitement on seeing a bearded Ringo in the flesh, at his drum kit at the back of the stage.

Desmond had, by this time, accepted that all of this could not be a dream. He couldn't comprehend how it could be possible, but he had to accept the fact that he was here, now, in Hamburg in late 1960 at the Kaiserkeller, talking with Astrid Kirchherr and friends whilst being entertained by Rory Storm and the Hurricanes.

"What time are The Beatles on?" asked Desmond to anyone who was listening

"Hello, I'm Alan," said Rory. "In about ten minutes."

"Oh! You're Alan, I thought you were Rory."

"I am."

And this is how Desmond met Rory Storm, real name Alan Caldwell. Rory had noticed Astrid and friends and had also seen a new, older face had joined them so thought he would introduce himself as he came off stage. He asked Desmond if he had seen The Beatles play, to which Desmond replied, "No, not live."

This brought strange looks from the rest of the group, but Desmond managed to gloss over it by quickly moving the conversation on by asking how long his band had been playing in Hamburg. "Since October," was the response, having completed their summer season at Butlin's Holiday camp in Wales.

During this interval Desmond thought back to something that was niggling him from his earlier conversation. Something that Bill had said. It registered as a bit odd at the time but there was so much going on and so much information coming his way that he put it to the back of his mind. Then it struck him. Bill had made a reference to 'The Fab Four'. He had said something about how exciting it must be to be seeing 'The Fab Four' for the first time.

Well, thought Desmond, *two things. One: why would I be excited about seeing an unknown band from Liverpool, England?* It just seemed a strange thing to say but could just be plausible, he supposed, as they had been bigging them up so much. But point two was not so easily explained. Why would he refer to the five-piece band as 'The Fab Four', a name, as far as Desmond knew, was not used until they really hit it big in 1963?

He decided to approach Bill about this. They were all still sitting around the same table, chatting, smoking, and drinking. He tapped Bill on the shoulder and asked if he could have a word. Without hesitating Bill got up and said, "Sure Desmond, let's go outside where it's a bit quieter."

With that, he sprung out of his seat and Desmond followed him through the crowd towards the street.

*

It wasn't much quieter in the street but at least they had a bit of privacy for Desmond to tackle Bill about the 'Fab Four' comment. And the rain had stopped.

"So what did you mean by 'The Fab Four', Bill? Everyone was telling me there were five Beatles: Paul, John, George,

Ringo, er I mean Pete, and Stuart. You called them 'The Fab Four'. What did you mean by that? Eh? What did you mean by that?" asked Desmond, aware that his nervousness, uncertainty, and an element of excitement was making him repeat himself.

"I must have miscounted," explained Bill with a mischievous smile on his face. "Yes, you're right, there are definitely five. The 'Fab Five'; that's it. Definitely five."

"Not four. Not the 'Fab Four' then?" confirmed Desmond.

"No, five, definitely," confirmed Bill.

They looked at each other, Bill with a slight smirk and Desmond with a quizzical look that formed deep furrows on his forehead. This unusual staring contest went on for half a minute before Desmond broke the silence.

"How do you know about the 'Fab Four'?" asked Desmond, completely ignoring the previous conversation.

"Do you mean the 'Fab Five'?" asked Bill in response.

"No, I mean the 'Fab Four', as well you know." Desmond's expression now changed to a slightly more aggressive look whilst retaining the furrowed brow.

Bill nodded, accepting that Desmond had won, an outcome Bill had actually intended all along. "Okay, I give in. I know that there are five but there will be four. I know that for the same reason as you. And the reason you said Ringo instead of Pete just now. I'm also from the future. At least I mean I've seen the future.'

*

Back inside, Astrid, Klaus, and Jürgen were enjoying the next act on stage, The Beatles, playing their fourth set of the evening. Klaus enquired of Astrid what had happened to Desmond, expecting him to have been back to see The Beatles.

"Oh, I'm not sure it's his cup of tea," responded Astrid as the sound of 'Roll Over Beethoven', with George singing lead, threatened to drown out their conversation.

"What is he talking to Bill about?" asked Jürgen.

"I'm not sure but he seems to be experiencing a lot of coincidences since I met him, poor man. Maybe he's experienced another one. Anyway, why are we talking about a confused man from England? I'm listening to the music." Astrid then looked up to the stage just as Stuart, the bass player, with his back to the audience, looked over his shoulder and gave her a smile.

*

Outside, Desmond continued his conversation with Bill, oblivious to the fact that his all-time favourite band were playing, live, inside the Kaiserkeller. To Desmond's continued astonishment, Bill explained that he was a time agent, and it was his role to ensure that this particular part of history was played out exactly as it should be in order not to create too many different timelines. Different timelines, he explained, were created every time someone did something to change the course of history, and everyone would continue to exist in these parallel timelines. So, if this happened, each version of Desmond's life would be referred to as an 'existence'. This meant that a parallel version of events would need to take place alongside what already existed and that the new version would need to start from the moment that someone interfered with what was supposed to happen. Desmond nodded occasionally whilst Bill explained this, but his expression didn't really change much. Bill could tell there were bits that Desmond didn't understand but carried on as he felt he could always fill in the gaps later on.

Only Bill and others like him could set the course of history, he explained. For example, he was able to ensure that John Lennon met Paul McCartney on that historical afternoon in July 1957 at the St. Peter's Church garden fete, Woolton, but only because the future hadn't happened. But when others accidently travelled back in time, as Desmond had ("I'll explain later," he assured Desmond, having seen Desmond raise a finger, about to ask a question), he needed to protect the course of history as much as possible. The reason, he summarised, was that too many parallel versions of history running simultaneously will eventually cause fractures within the timelines and the universe would become unstable.

There were several others like Bill. He didn't know exactly how many, but each had responsibility for following time travellers like Desmond. Bill and the others like him would respond each time someone time travelled and were in danger of changing the path of history. Bill's responsibility was firmly in the world of music, and he explained to Desmond how, on various occasions, he had to step in to prevent major changes to the course of history such as the overzealous autograph hunter who almost ran Elvis over as a thirteen-year-old, shortly after he had moved from Tupelo, Mississippi, to Memphis, Tennessee. The autograph hunter had managed to transport to Memphis in a similar fashion to Desmond ("I'll explain later," Bill assured, again anticipating Desmond's question), and, after having been convinced that he really was back in 1948, set about driving to Elvis' house. He wasn't expecting the thirteen-year-old Elvis to run out in front of him but fortunately, for the sake of the history of rock 'n' roll, Bill managed to arrive on the scene and whisk Elvis back to the safety of the roadside, preventing the fateful occurrence that would have created a whole series of new parallel existences.

"He's still out there somewhere," said Bill. "The autograph hunter, I mean. We lost track of him and for some reason we haven't been able to trace him. He disappeared in the white van he was driving," he added, biting his lip and looking thoughtful for a moment.

How often people like Desmond were transported back in time was also a vague statistic. "Oh, there's a lot of variables," explained Bill, hoping that would satisfy Desmond's curiosity, at least for the time being.

"But the future hasn't happened yet!" Desmond protested.

"Then explain how you exist," responded Bill.

"But it's 1960 and I'm hardly born!"

"Yet you're here," responded Bill.

"So how could you influence things at St. Peter's Church fete in 1957 without changing history?" demanded Desmond.

"Because it hadn't happened yet, at least not in the way you perceive time, and no one had been back there to change it," responded Bill, patiently.

"So, if I'd have gone back to 1957, at St. Peter's Church fete, you would have had to go along to check I didn't change things?"

"Correct!"

"So, what happens if I change things?" asked Desmond.

"Like what?"

"Like, er, I don't know. What if I accidently prevented John and Paul meeting, or George joining the group, or Ringo leaving Rory Storm to join The Beatles?"

"Why on earth would you want to do that?"

"I wouldn't. But suppose I did."

"Then history would change and there would be a parallel timeline, or several parallel timelines depending on how many things you fucked up." Bill smiled and remained remarkably calm, confident he had already made this point clear on at least two occasions.

"In theory," he continued, "you could be creating new timelines by being here now. That's why it's best to observe rather than get involved, however tempting it may be. Sometimes though it's difficult to tell if you were meant to be involved. In other words, your interference is not actually interference, it's what actually happened. But let's assume for now that you're not meant to get involved."

"Right," said Desmond, unconvincingly.

"That's why I'm here now, actually," said Bill, hoping to conclude the question-and-answer session. "To make sure you don't do anything silly with The Beatles."

Desmond sighed. "Well, Bill, I'm not sure that I believe all this. This must be some kind of elaborate joke. A bit like that new film where it's Michael Douglas' birthday and different things happen to him which aren't real."

"Is it your birthday?" asked Bill.

"Well, no, but it might just be a special treat," responded Desmond, grasping at straws.

"Yes, a special treat, that's it, obviously," came Bill's sarcastic reply.

"So how do you explain yourself to Astrid and friends?" asked Desmond, shifting the subject.

Bill sighed inwardly in preparation for the next set of questions. "Oh, they just know me. This is my favourite place, so I hang out here when I'm not anywhere else. Even if I am somewhere else, I can always get back to the same time as I left, so they don't miss me. And my control room is here, in Hamburg."

"And how did you know I was coming?" asked Desmond, not hearing the control room bit.

"I've got a special radio. A time radio. I get a warning. My radio reacts to the change in the timelines. I think you encountered a time radio recently, right? Well, in the cases I deal with they are triggered by certain songs. When you came across the radio in the old campervan which was, by the way, the van The Beatles used to travel to Hamburg, driven by Lord Woodbine, and that song was on, it raised a warning that there could be an incident. The time travel destination is triggered by the radio, and what was happening around the time of the song, 'Tell Laura I Love Her' was released. In your case it was number one in the UK during a time that The Beatles were playing in Hamburg. Having found the radio, the chances are that you were going to be transported back to the time that that record was around, so the Beatles in Hamburg seemed the most likely. But it's not only that. You also have to be the right type of person. To be honest I'm not quite sure what the right type of person is. All I know is that it only works for certain people. Someone else could easily have come across that campervan and radio and that's all it would be – a campervan and radio with no time travel. It's to do with your DNA and the way you're wired. That means, of course, that if you were to somehow change, it may affect your ability to travel."

"Oh, I see," said Desmond unconvincingly. "So, if I come across that radio, or something similar again, I could be time travelling to somewhere around the time the song was in the charts?"

"Yes, that's about it. Most likely something to do with The Beatles because that's what it does you see, Desmond. It takes its energy from you and what with you being a big Beatles fan, that's where you're going to end up. If it happens again that is. You were helped by Lord Woodbine this time. He led you in the general direction of the campervan. He can be a bit of a nuisance like that. He was probably put up to it by someone."

"Oh, I see," repeated Desmond, still not totally convinced. "So will I be able to choose the time I travel to?"

"I'd rather you didn't travel at all," said Bill, "in case you do something silly. But in answer to your question, yes, to a certain extent. It's a bit limited but you could possibly find a few different songs when tuning in but once the same song has been playing for sixty seconds that's it, you're on your way."

"Oh, I see," said Desmond again. Bill was beginning to think Desmond really did see by this time. "And this thing about me changing and not being able to travel. What does that mean exactly?"

"It means that if, for example, you stayed in a different time for too long and you got older, or maybe you had some kind of accident, then your biological make up may have changed sufficiently to prevent you from travelling."

Bill could see that alarm bells were ringing in Desmond's head at this revelation. "Don't worry, Desmond, you would need to be away for three or more days for it to cause any problems. So you're okay for a couple of days yet."

"And who else is there?" asked Desmond. "You mentioned there were others like you. Are they here?"

"Goodness me, no!" responded Bill. "I sometimes work with Matt Black, who lives in the 1980s and we report to

Molly who oversees everything. But she's scary and I don't like to talk about her. Perhaps I'll tell you about them some time."

Desmond's ears pricked up momentarily at the mention of the name Molly, but his train of thought was just as quickly interrupted by a voice from behind them.

"*Kommen Sie zwei herein, um die Beatles zu sehen?*" Astrid appeared at the entrance, reminding Bill and Desmond that they were missing the Liverpool group's performance. "Klaus thinks it would be good for you to see them, although I don't think it's your thing Des."

"Desmond actually," advised Desmond again.

Desmond suddenly realised what Astrid had said. "Blimey, how could I forget about what's been going on in the Kaiserkeller, let's go. And, I'll have you know, Astrid, it is my thing. Very much my thing. Deffo."

"But you haven't even heard them yet." Astrid pointed out as they followed her back into the club.

"Oh, er, yes, I know, but I can tell I'll like them based on what you've said about them. Anyway, I can hear them now and I like them."

Astrid carried on back into the club, shaking her head as she went. "Deffo!" Desmond heard her muttering to herself.

Bill followed behind and took his seat next to Desmond. Bill had, in fact, been happy to keep Desmond out of the club, thinking that the longer he was out of the way of The Beatles, the less chance of him causing an upset, but he decided he was fairly confident that Desmond would behave himself. At least on this occasion.

*

And what an occasion it was for Desmond in particular. He

sat transfixed through most of the performance, not even pausing to see what he was drinking. Not having any Deutschmarks with him, Bill had bought him a couple of beers during the evening. He promised to get him a pint next time he was in Middlesham. Although he had missed the first half hour or so, he remained transfixed for the next hour. John, Paul, and George all shared lead vocals on the rock 'n' roll classics, some of which were to be much better known later, on the first Beatles album 'Please Please Me'. Desmond noted that George sang 'Matchbox', later sang by Ringo on the 'Long Tall Sally' EP. Paul took lead on several others including 'Long Tall Sally'. And as for John Lennon, *well thank goodness I witnessed 'Twist and Shout'*, thought Desmond. John turned out to be exactly the same John he had read about in the many accounts of The Beatles in Hamburg. He continually shouted insults to the watching crowd, was constantly larking about on stage, and tried anything to liven up the atmosphere including, at one point, wearing a toilet seat over his head. It worked; the atmosphere was electric and intoxicating. On hearing this wonderful music, he could feel the hairs on the back of his neck rising. *This is it*, he said to himself. *I'm witnessing the genesis of The Beatles. It can't get any better than this, can it?*

*

Watching The Beatles play live was such a magical experience for Desmond and he was already thinking how difficult it would be to describe to his friends back in Middlesham once he had got past the not insignificant point of explaining the time travel element of his adventure. Although they were all Beatles fans to a certain extent (despite Nigel insisting that the Rolling Stones were better) and regularly talked about their songs and performances, nothing could have prepared him for this and to try and put it into words was going to be a challenge.

Deep down, Desmond couldn't really understand why everyone was not a Beatles fan. They didn't have to be as committed as he was, but they should at least accept that they were the best band in the world. They could even have a favourite band other than The Beatles, if they must, as long as they accepted that The Beatles probably influenced their particular favourite in some small way. Or maybe a larger way if their favourite band happened to be Oasis or ELO. He said 'probably' as Desmond accepted that there were some bands who were so completely different in style that even he would find it difficult to make a connection.

From his point of view, and that of many others, he suspected, there were two distinct phases of the Beatles. There were the early days of rock 'n' roll covers, their own rock 'n' roll songs (examples of which he was currently witnessing), their early ballads and just 'Fab' Beatles songs, in fact everything they ever did up to 'Rubber Soul'. Then there was the second phase where, in Desmond's opinion at least, they created even more magical sounds from 1965/66, ever expanding right up to the end. If he had to choose, which he would fight against in fear of giving the impression that the other period was less than brilliant, he would choose the later period. But, on the other hand, to see the old footage of their performances, and indeed watching three quarters of The Beatles he knew and loved performing in front of his eyes, maybe he should not put their music into periods but acknowledge that this group of friends from Liverpool, England, were responsible for a perfect phase of the evolution of popular music from where he was right now in the early sixties until 1970 and beyond.

But what was it that put them 'streets ahead of their rivals' (according to Desmond's recollection of a review of 'Hey Jude' in the NME in 1968 which his Uncle Ernie had kept and showed to him)? This was a difficult one for Desmond to come to terms with because what he hears is music that has a profound effect on him. Yes, there is plenty of great music around and others apparently get a similar effect from other music, but he can only describe it as a strange magic. Ringo's two enormous drumbeats followed by George's exquisite slide guitar which kicks off the eagerly awaited 'Free as a Bird' single in 1995 was to Desmond's mind a perfect example of the magic. *It's actually The Beatles after all this time*, he thought on hearing it for the first time, and, for that matter, every other time he heard it.

*

It was over all too quickly. At least for half an hour while they had a break before coming on again, according to Astrid.

"I think we need to think about getting you back, Desmond," whispered Bill.

"Really? But they're on again later, and I missed the first bit," pleaded Desmond.

"Desmond needs a bit of fresh air," Bill said to his friends as he grabbed Desmond's arm, guiding him towards the exit.

When they were outside the Kaiserkeller, Bill gave Desmond his view on what he thought should happen next.

"We need to get you back for the quiz, Desmond. It's been quite an experience for you, I'm sure, but there's only so much I think you can take in on one trip. Maybe next time you can stay a bit longer, but I would be happier getting you back fairly soon. Also, the longer you stay, the more likelihood there is of something going wrong with the timeline."

"You mean the more chance there is of me saying or doing something I shouldn't," stated Desmond, nodding his head.

"Well, yes, that is a consideration."

"So, when you said that maybe I could stay longer next time, you mean I can come back?"

"If you like." Bill was beginning to warm to Desmond. He could see that he was not the sort of person to deliberately change things and he could tell how excited he was about seeing his heroes in the flesh. "It doesn't have to be Hamburg. It can be any time you like. Have a think about it. But in any case, you shouldn't stay longer than a day or so. Just to be on the safe side."

Bill smiled, patted Desmond on the back, and said, "Maybe you can stay until the end of their performance tonight. Then we must go."

"Yes, yes please, that would be great," said Desmond gratefully. "Anyway, I've missed the quiz now. I've already given up on that."

"No, you haven't, Desmond. You'll be back in time for the quiz. Don't forget, it doesn't start for another forty years. Let's get back in and see The Beatles."

*

All too soon The Beatles had played their last song of the night, John Lennon had shouted his last insult to the punters and they had shuffled off the stage. Desmond wasn't sure of the time but knew it was the early hours of the morning. Out of habit he had referred several times to his 'futuristic' digital watch but each time it still read 8:88. What happened next was yet another defining moment for Desmond. Stuart Sutcliffe and John Lennon appeared from behind the stage and jumped down to join Astrid's group of friends (of which Desmond considered himself a part, at least for the time being) and started chatting, apparently making plans for what was left of the night.

"Who's the weird-looking old boy in the leather jacket?" asked John Lennon. Although Desmond was wearing a short leather jacket, that's where the similarity ended as far as dressing like The Beatles was concerned. The fact that he was about twenty years older than the rest of the group and had longish, slightly curly and unkempt hair was also a factor in prompting the question.

Astrid introduced Desmond in her usual manner. Desmond didn't really say anything, just mumbled something about being pleased to meet them and that he had heard a lot about them.

Bill whispered in Desmond's ear, "We have to go, Desmond."

"I know," replied Desmond reluctantly.

They followed Astrid, Jürgen, Klaus, Stuart, and John out of the Kaiserkeller into the still bustling street where they were joined by Paul McCartney and George Harrison, Desmond again found himself searching for words after being briefly introduced.

Astrid explained that Paul and George were just going back to their digs to pick up a few supplies and the rest of them were heading back to her parents' place.

"I have to go," stated Desmond, somewhat reluctantly. "Thanks for bringing me here. I'll never forget it."

"Goodbye Dessie," said Astrid, giving him a kiss on the

cheek. They headed off down Grosse Freiheit followed by Klaus, Jürgen, John, and Stuart. "See you again soon, maybe. Hope you find your way back to Admiral Nelson."

"Bye-bye, Dessie," came a chorus from the others.

"We'll need to walk this way for a while, Desmond," said Bill, pointing down the road to where Paul and George had already set off.

"Fair enough, Bill," agreed Desmond.

Bill was still trying to ensure Desmond kept out of trouble, so he made sure they kept their distance from Paul and George who were heading back to their accommodation at the Bambi-Filmkunsttheater. Bill watched them turn left at the end of Grosse Freiheit into Paul-Roosen Strasse and then turn into the cinema. Despite the distance, Desmond overheard them talking about needing to see a lady about 'prellies'. The cinema, well, the room at the back where the toilets were, Desmond recalled was where The Beatles slept. He also recalled that the reason George was eventually deported was that he was discovered to be underage following a fire incident at the cinema.

"Let's go," said Bill.

"Goodnight Beatles. Be careful about, you know, safety, fire, etcetera," shouted Desmond.

"No, no, Desmond," chided Bill. "They shouldn't be careful, should they? Because that might make them avoid things like accidently starting a fire at some stage in the future. Mightn't it, Desmond?"

"Oh yes. Ignore me," he shouted after the two Beatles.

"Don't worry, we will," came the response.

"So how do I get back?" asked Desmond.

"Well, although I can travel using the device in my control

room, to get you back we need to use my radio," responded Bill. "I just need to tune in to the right record. Something popular that can be associated with the time you came from and something you like or have a connection to. Any thoughts?"

"Mmm," pondered Desmond. "Not much that I like around at the moment. My mate Brian likes 'Out of the Silent Planet' by Iron Maiden if that's any help."

"What about the Spice Girls?" asked Bill, ignoring Desmond's suggestion. "I think they're still quite popular in the year 2000."

"Nope," Desmond tartly replied.

"I know, Westlife, 'My Love'."

"Nope. Now if it was the Wings classic number one from 'Red Rose Speedway', 1973, that would be a different matter. Can we go for something else?"

"Yes, we need to. There needs to be some emotional connection to the record to generate the energy for travelling. I can see Westlife and the Spice Girls aren't doing it for you. But they were big in 2000."

"Okay, I've got one," said Desmond. "'Beautiful Day' by U2. I quite like that. In fact, I think it would be a good theme tune to something. Maybe a football programme."

"'Stomp' by Steps? Only joking, let's go with 'Beautiful Day'," agreed Bill.

"What if someone went back to a time that was before the radio?" enquired Desmond.

"Well Desmond, the time travel we look after only started after the radio was invented. There was something in the radio waves that interfered with the time signals. So, I'm only able to travel using the radio and we can't go back to pre-radio days. It is possible though, but I don't have such a device. Only our Time Peacekeeper has one of those. The problem is the further back you go the longer the parallel timelines will be if history gets changed."

"Oh, I see," was Desmond's incongruent reply. "I've got another question," said Desmond suddenly. "What if I'm transported back to the wrong place, or the wrong time, or the wrong parallel existence, universe, timeline or whatever the technical term is?"

"You can only go back to where you came from, Desmond. Well, you shouldn't be able to go anywhere else anyway. That can't happen, not really. And if it does, it's very rare. You, I mean you as you are now, don't exist in another existence. If you changed things now, the baby Desmond back in wherever you lived in 1960 will grow up in another existence from the one you're going back to. And things are very fragile at the moment. Get it?"

"Yes," said Desmond, although worried about the less than convincing 'not really' and 'if it does it's very rare' part of Bill's answer. "So how do I get back?"

"The radio. I've just told you that!"

"No, I understand that. But what happens to me on the way? Where do I go, through a tunnel or something?"

"You mean a time tunnel?"

"Yes, yes, that. A time tunnel," said Desmond enthusiastically as if he was finally beginning to understand the time travel thing. "Is that where I'm going?"

"No," was Bill's disappointingly abrupt response.

"What, no tunnel?"

"No tunnel, Desmond."

"Well, what then?" demanded Desmond.

"Well, you know in quantum physics," commenced Bill,

"where the electrons in an atom just appear in a different orbit without travelling between the orbits? It's a bit like that. You just appear in one time and then reappear in another without travelling in between. No tunnel."

Desmond's expression remained puzzled.

"Got it," he lied.

Bill suggested that they would go back to his flat for a cup of coffee before tuning in to his radio and getting Desmond home. They hopped on a bus and five minutes later they were sat in Bill's surprisingly small, one-bedroomed apartment. Desmond, for some reason, expected a 'Time Lord', as he thought of Bill, to live in much more salubrious surroundings.

Bill had retrieved a very ordinary-looking, 1950's-style radio from what Desmond assumed was a small utility room. Out of curiosity, Desmond tried to look into the room as Bill came out and caught a glimpse several screens and what appeared to be some sort of huge computer which looked to be the height of the room.

"What's in there, Bill?" he enquired.

"Control room," answered Bill. "You can't go in there," he added sternly. "What goes on there is highly complex and intricate and can't be interfered with."

Desmond got the message and turned his attention to the radio. It was one of those big ones with a dial towards each bottom corner and a whole list of countries going across the width of the radio between the dials. The rest of the front was taken up with a big speaker, hidden behind the plastic casing. Bill placed it on the only table in the room and walked into a small kitchen area to make the coffee. On his return he explained that he also had a portable radio which he produced from his coat pocket. It had a very inconspicuous look to it. It was small and black, about eight inches by four, with two green dials peeking out of the top. One for volume and one for tuning, he guessed. On the front was written 'AM/FM Rave Radio'.

"This is for when I'm out and about. You know, in other times, other places," explained Bill.

"Yes, I see," said Desmond. "So, it's for getting you and anyone else back to where they came from," he added. "Make sure you don't lose that one. Or break it. That would be disastrous."

"Yes, it would," agreed Bill.

"How did you get it? Where did it come from?" asked Desmond.

"This one came from another time, another place," answered Bill, vaguely, pointing to the big radio with the dial. "And I made this one," he added, proudly displaying the 'AM/FM Rave Radio'.

Whilst they drunk their coffee, they chatted about the performances they had seen at the Kaiserkeller, with Desmond more than happy to relive the experience. Bill then went on to ask Desmond about his obsession with The Beatles. "After all," he pointed out, "you were a very young child in the sixties so how did you get interested in them?"

Desmond explained how he was first made aware of the band by his Uncle Ernie. Living only a few streets away, Ernie would regularly call in to their house for a chat and a cup of tea with his older sister, Desmond's mother Mary. He would sometimes bring his portable tape recorder along and urge Mary, Desmond, and his father Harry, to listen to the latest Beatles songs which he had recorded from the radio. Desmond particularly remembered hearing 'Hey Jude' for the first time and how blown away he was by it, even at the tender age of eight. This, he thought, was probably what encouraged him to research and listen to all of The Beatles' back catalogue once he was old enough to appreciate the true enormity of what had happened during the sixties. Throughout his teens, whilst his contemporaries were listening to Queen, David Bowie, Fleetwood Mac, and, later, punk and new wave, Desmond's first love was always The Beatles. Each album would be listened to over and over again. Lyrics on the cover or inside the albums of the seventies were fairly commonplace but Sgt. Pepper from 1967, as far as Desmond was aware, was the first album to display the song's lyrics and so learning these became a major project for Desmond.

"If only you put as much effort into your schoolwork," his mother used to chide.

After a while Bill reminded Desmond that he had better be getting back and turned towards the big radio. After a little fiddling with the dial, he tuned it in to what appeared to be a pop music station just as 'Blue Suede Shoes' by Carl Perkins was finishing. Next, to Desmond's amusement, he heard the unmistakable opening to 'Beautiful Day' and then the voice of Bono, who Desmond calculated was probably about eighteen months old in 1961. By this time, he had given up being amazed and surprised. There had been far too much to take in during his visit to Hamburg and he was now in a very accepting frame of mind and was determined to just go with the flow.

Realising that 'Beautiful Day' was his cue to getting back, he tightly grabbed the arms of his chair and braced himself.

"Don't worry, Desmond, it won't hurt," said Bill

reassuringly.

"Wait. I've got another question. You said I could come back. How?" asked Desmond.

"Just go back to the van and tune in to a suitable song. Lord Woodbine chose the last one and set the time travel to touch, so when you touched the dial, off you went. But you can choose one you want from whatever songs you can find. Remember it needs to be associated with the time you want to go back to, and you get sixty seconds. The quantum process gets you to a safe place, somewhere in the vicinity of the action you're looking for. I'll look out for the signal and meet you there."

As he said this Bill was wondering if he had done the right thing in inviting Desmond to time travel again. *Oh well, too late now*, he thought as Desmond disappeared.

CHAPTER 6

Middlesham, November 2000

"Right then! Round one: General Knowledge," commenced Murray, the enthusiastic quiz master.

"Sorry I'm late," came a shout from the doorway, much to the annoyance of Murray, about to ask the first question.

Desmond was soaking wet, his hair and clothes dripping over several people as he hurriedly bundled his way through the dozen quiz teams towards his 'Le Beats' teammates.

"Sorry I'm late," he repeated. "Just back from Hamburg."

"What?!" replied the other three 'Le Beats'.

"I'll explain later," replied Desmond with a slight smirk on his face. "What have I missed? Fill me in. How can I help?"

"Nothing, we haven't started yet," shouted Murray, indignantly, across from his stool at the bar. "If it's okay with you, I'll carry on."

"Yep, off you go, Murray," said Desmond, helpfully.

With a shake of his head, Murray started again. "Right then! Round one: General Knowledge."

*

Two and a half hours later, the quiz had finished. 'Le Beats' were triumphant and gratefully accepted their prize of four bottles of ale from Murray.

During the quiz Desmond started to tell his teammates about where he had been. How he had met Lord Woodbine who appeared to be a farmer and how he had been mysteriously transported back in time to Hamburg in 1960.

As he expected, the response from Nigel, Penelope, and Brian was incredulous to say the least. They didn't believe a word of it and were thinking that Desmond had had some sort of accident which had affected his self-awareness, in particular his ability to understand what an idiot he sounded like when recounting tales of Hamburg, Astrid, Bill, Klaus, Jürgen, Rory and, of course, The Beatles.

They had remained at the Admiral Nelson for half an hour following the quiz after which they were politely asked to leave by Alan, the landlord, who wanted to go to bed. Desmond continued to talk about his experiences all the way back to Cavendish Crescent. Brian joined the three of them as they entered number eight.

"Okay, just go through it one more time," demanded Penelope, much to the annoyance of Nigel and Brian.

So Desmond did, answering questions along the way. Because he didn't understand it himself, he dealt with the time travel element in much the same way Bill had done with him, giving vague responses about parallel existences and the need to keep these to a minimum. He was also quite proud to recount the 'conversations' he had had with The Beatles and was particularly keen to let them know that they had referred to him as 'Dessie' even though he would have hated to be referred to as 'Dessie' by any of the three 'Le Beats' team members.

"Okay, you've convinced us," exclaimed Penelope after another half hour when she couldn't think of any further questions.

"Really?" responded Nigel.

"I agree, really?" chipped in Brian. "I'm not sure you speak for all of us, Pen."

"Look," responded Desmond. "Why don't you come out to the campervan with me next Sunday afternoon and I'll show you." Desmond knew that they rarely had other plans on a Sunday afternoon as they liked to keep Sundays free to avoid complications in getting to the quiz on time. This Sunday was, however, an obvious exception in Desmond's case.

"Bill said that I could time travel again and he would meet me, whenever or wherever I go to. He wants to make sure I don't change history. And I need him to get me back."

"Let's just be clear on this; you want us to come out with you to some old farmer's campervan to see you time travel?" said Nigel.

Brian nodded in agreement with Nigel but then, having thought about it for a few seconds, added, "Well, I haven't got anything better to do on Sunday afternoon."

"Seriously?" said Nigel. "What do you think, Pen?"

"Yes, let's do it. I told you, I'm convinced," responded Penelope.

Nigel looked at them all in turn, threw up his hands, and said, "Okay, I'll come."

"Right. Brian, meet us here at two o'clock next Sunday," ordered Desmond.

"I'll be here. Now I need to go home and get some sleep," he said. And off he went back to his flat, a five-minute walk through the village.

"See you in the morning then," said Desmond to his two housemates. "Don't forget, I've had a much longer day than you two."

"Yeah, right," said Nigel, sarcastically.

CHAPTER 7

Somewhere near Middlesham, November 2000

It took them a little longer than expected to reach the campervan. Brian turned up at Cavendish Crescent right on time at two o'clock the following Sunday and the four of them climbed into Desmond's Fiesta with Brian in the front passenger seat and Nigel and Penelope taking the rear seats. He took the route that he would usually take to visit his brother and after about fifteen minutes started to look for the entrance to the narrow country lane on his left. He knew roughly where it was but as it was dark and raining the previous Sunday, he almost took a couple of wrong turns.

"All these country lanes look the same to me," he said, getting his defence in before Nigel could complain.

"How difficult can it be?" was Nigel's back-seat-driver's view.

Once Desmond had found the correct country lane and turned into it, his next thought was *where do I go from here?* It had seemed easier going this way on the previous occasion he was there when he was following Lord Woodbine. He eventually reached the T junction and saw the sign to Wormle and he turned left as he did previously. This, he remembered, was where he lost the jeep up ahead so he was on his own from here apart from Nigel, Penelope, and Brian who were no help at all. Nigel even suggested which way to go at the next junction, right, which as it happened turned out to be correct. Desmond also remembered the low bridge and, coincidently, the same popping noise as he drove under it. *Mmm*, he thought, *must be something to do with the time travel thing. Probably entering some kind of time travel port like you do with an airport. I think I'll call it a time dimension portal.* "We've just entered the time dimension portal," said Desmond, knowingly. "That was what that popping noise was about."

No one questioned Desmond's confident statement. He just heard a communal, "Oh."

Desmond remembered to turn left at the next junction and a short time later they had arrived at their destination. They were at the dead end in front of the lean-to, and the old, green Austin 152 campervan was still there.

"There it is," said a relieved Desmond, stating the obvious. "I told you. And you lot didn't believe me. Well, except Penelope."

"Well, that doesn't prove anything, does it?" said Nigel.

"Agreed," agreed Brian. "It's just an old campervan."

"They *are* right, Desmond," added Penelope seriously. "We need to see further evidence," she added, as if she was some kind of detective.

Fortunately, the weather was better than the last time Desmond was there. It was sunny and fairly mild for November. On his return from Hamburg the weather was exactly the same as when he left the campervan. It was also exactly the same time as when he left. Having realised he could still make the quiz if he hurried, he had quickly exited the campervan, jumped in his car, and drove, eventually finding his way back to the main road via a different route having avoided the flood. *So, Lord Woodbine was right after all, I did manage to avoid the flood,* he had thought as he looked in his rear-view mirror at the trail of cars behind him, carefully negotiating the flooded road.

"Right, follow me," said Desmond. They all piled out of the Fiesta. "This is the campervan. The time machine or whatever you want to call it."

"Is there a time tunnel?" asked Penelope, hopefully.

"No," answered Desmond abruptly, in much the same manner as Bill had replied to Desmond's question regarding the time tunnel. "It's a bit like quantum physics," he added, hoping they wouldn't ask him to expand.

They didn't. They all stood next to the passenger door where Desmond had entered and exited the van previously. After about a minute, Nigel spoke.

"So what happens now? How long are we going to stand here? Are you expecting to get beamed up or something?"

"Oh, sorry," said Desmond as if waking from a dream. "No, of course I don't get beamed up. That would be ridiculous. As I've already explained, it's all to do with the radio."

"Are you going in?" asked Penelope, as if they were standing at the edge of the sea, wondering whether or not to go for a swim.

"Yes, are you going in?" prompted Brian.

"Does it only work for you?" asked Nigel.

"Yes, I think so," responded Desmond. "I was especially chosen by Lord Woodbine. It's only certain people with a particularly strong intelligence that are able to do this," he added, slightly exaggerating Bill's explanation.

"Oh, I see," said Nigel. He was actually slightly relieved as, although he still had huge doubts about Desmond's story, he didn't fancy taking the risk of time travel, even if the opportunity was there. Neither Penelope nor Brian, although keen to see if Desmond really could travel in time, expressed any kind of interest in doing the same.

Desmond realised he was a little nervous about getting back into the campervan. Last time he didn't know what was about to happen and therefore had no doubts about his safety. This time was different; he knew he would be transported to somewhere back in time, assuming it still worked, and he wasn't one hundred percent sure that Bill would be there to get him back. However, he had come this far and didn't want to look foolish in front of his friends. He needed to convince them and there was only one way to do that, he conceded.

"Right, off I go then," he said enthusiastically. "I'll just go in now then," he said but didn't actually move.

"Go on then," encouraged Nigel.

"Yes, off you go," agreed Brian.

"Can we see you tune the radio?" asked Penelope.

"Yes, I think I'll leave the door open so you can share the experience." Desmond thought that he would feel more confident about the experience with his friends in attendance.

"So do we just wait around for you to get back then?" asked Penelope.

"We shouldn't have to wait at all, should we?" answered Nigel. "Desmond said he got back at exactly the same time as he left, last time."

"Oh good," said a relieved Penelope. "I didn't fancy just waiting around, not knowing what had become of Desmond. If something went wrong, we could be waiting for ages. And even then he may not come back at all."

"Yes, he could get trapped in the time tunnel," interjected Brian. "It might collapse or something and leave Desmond trapped for all eternity in between time." Brian permitted himself a congratulatory smile for coming up with such a scenario.

"Or," added Nigel, rather enjoying the discussion, "he might just get stuck back in time, never to return. He would grow old before all of us."

"Or," chipped in Brian with a chuckle, "he might get stuck for ten years and come back ten years older."

"Or, or," said Nigel, desperately searching for another scenario, "he might get sent ten years into the future and we won't see him for ten years, and he'll look the same as he does now!"

"Or he may get stuck halfway between time zones and only half of him may come back," added Brian.

"Now you're just being silly, Brian," said Nigel, seriously.

"Boys, boys!" interrupted Penelope. "He's right here you know. I don't think now is the right time to talk about what might go wrong, do you?"

"You started it. But yes, you're right," said Nigel. "Where is he?"

Nigel said this as they all looked around and noticed Desmond was not, in fact, right there.

They found him sat back in the Fiesta, staring ahead with a blank expression.

"Maybe I shouldn't make another trip after all. You're right. It's too risky. I don't want to get stuck."

He started the engine and told the three of them to get in. But they had come all this way and were keen to see what happened when Desmond entered the campervan.

Nigel, Penelope, and Brian then spent a few minutes apologising and assuring Desmond that he would be fine and that they had just got a bit carried away. Eventually, Desmond turned off the engine and got out of the car.

"There's no time tunnel, Brian," he said as he walked back to the campervan.

He waited for several seconds before speaking again. "Right, this is what I'm going to do. I'm going to go for it because, to be honest, who else is going to get such an opportunity? Right, I'll just go in now then," he said for the second time.

He opened the passenger door half hoping it would be locked this time, but it opened with no problem. He left the door open and slid across to the radio while the others looked in expectantly. This time the radio wasn't already switched on, so he turned the dial until it clicked, and slowly increased the volume. At this point it was just static noise that you get when in between stations. He reached for the other dial to attempt to tune into a suitable song. Strangely enough, he hadn't actually thought about which time period he wanted to visit. He had been more concerned about convincing his friends about his time travel, and now, following their recent discussion, about whether or not he was going to get back from wherever he goes.

After a brief pause, he decided that he was just going to find a song he liked and then consider if that was the era he would like to visit. Once he had found a song, he knew he had sixty seconds to make his mind up before finding an alternative.

He had explained the sixty second rule to his friends and they had agreed to count down as soon as he found a song so that he could change his mind within the allotted time.

He turned the tuning dial a few degrees in a clockwise direction until he heard a song playing. It was the unmistakable voice of Neil Diamond singing 'Love On The Rocks'. Although he loved the song, he quickly decided to continue searching as he realised, if he were to continue with these trips, he would like to experience more of the early years before jumping too far ahead, and this song would send him to a much later time, after The Beatles had split in fact. *Maybe another time*, he thought.

He continued to turn the dial before sixty seconds had elapsed. Immediately upon hearing the next song he exclaimed, "Yes, this'll do. This is the one." The song they were listening to was 'Help!' a song Desmond knew was released in 1965 so he would have a rough idea what was happening in the world of The Beatles at this time. The others had already started the countdown when they first heard the music, referring to Brian's watch which had a second hand, so Desmond braced himself and waited to be transported. He heard "Five, four, three, two, one." Then there was the blinding flash of light, and he was somewhere else.

CHAPTER 8

New York, 15 August 1965

Desmond hit the carpeted floor in what appeared to be a corridor of a hotel. He realised he had left the campervan in a sitting position and therefore arrived at wherever he was in the same position but, with there being no seat, he found himself on the carpet. He quickly scrambled to his feet, not wishing to be discovered on the floor by anyone who happened to come along at that moment. *At least it was a carpet, and it's not raining,* he thought, remembering his Hamburg landing. He decided to walk the way he was facing as there didn't seem to be any indication of where to go. He could see from the room numbers on the doors that he was possibly on the third floor as they all began with three.

As he passed room 333, a smartly dressed man, wearing what looked like a chauffeur's cap, who Desmond thought was probably about his age, emerged from the room.

"Ah, you're here," he said in what sounded to Desmond like a fake American accent.

"Er, yes I'm here," replied Desmond. "And what exactly am I here for?" he asked.

"Didn't the agency tell you? You've got a very special job today; helping transport some VIPs to Shea Stadium. The Beatles. Probably not your thing but the young people love them."

"Oh yes, they did say, now you mention it," lied Desmond, his mind working overtime in taking in the information about Shea Stadium and The Beatles and also deciding whether or not to go along with the charade.

"We're getting a ride to the helicopter pad and then we're taking them across New York to the World's Fair building in Queens, showing them a few sights on the way and flying over the stadium. Then they get a Wells Fargo truck to the stadium. We were hoping to land them at the stadium, but we're not allowed."

"So, you're the pilot of the helicopter?" asked Desmond, looking for clarification. *Wow! This is a lot to take in in one go*, he thought.

The man who Desmond had mistaken for a chauffeur, but was in fact a helicopter pilot, nodded with a puzzled look on his face.

"Yeah, that's right. To be precise it's a New York Airways Boeing Vertol 107-II but I call it a chopper. And you're the security guy, right?"

"Yep, sure am," answered Desmond in what he considered was an American accent.

"I thought they'd send someone a bit, you know, beefier I guess, but you'll have to do."

Desmond wasn't quite sure how to take this so stuck his chest out, nodded, and said, "Oh yeah, I'm used to this kind of thing. No worries there. Security's my game." As he said it, he was thinking, *'Security's my game!' What am I saying?* He decided, however, that he was in too deep now to back out.

"You English?" asked the pilot. Desmond had already forgotten his American accent.

"Yes, but I'm good at security," he replied, as if being

English put his security credentials in doubt.

"Great!" replied the pilot. "I'm Chuck, by the way,"

"I'm Dessie," replied Desmond. "Well Desmond actually but everyone calls me Dessie," he lied, again. Somehow he thought Dessie and Chuck sounded like a good combination.

"Dessie huh. Haven't we met before?" he added with a frown.

"Nope, definitely not," replied Desmond confidently.

"Well, don't stand out there in the corridor, Dessie, come on in," said Chuck.

"Don't you have a uniform?" he asked as Desmond followed him into what turned out to be a huge, beautifully decorated room. The theme was floral. As well as the settee and two chairs next to the full-length window, there was a circular table in the middle of the room adorned with a huge bouquet of flowers. The king-size bed occupied the left side of the room

"Ah, yes. I left it down in reception," Desmond lied. Then he wondered why he had said that as Chuck would, no doubt, expect him to get it.

"Right. Why d'ya do that?" asked Chuck.

Desmond responded saying something about making sure he had the right details about the job before changing. Chuck, who had acquired a puzzled look, said, "Look, I'm just going to the bathroom. Why don't you go get your uniform and I'll meet you back here in a few minutes?"

Desmond opened the door and stopped. There was Bill, holding a baseball-style hat with the word 'Security' across the front.

"Your uniform, sir," said Bill.

"But, what, how, why?" was all Desmond could say at this point.

"I saw the real security guy in reception and persuaded him to part with his hat," replied Bill.

"How?"

"Well let's just say I found out something that he wouldn't want to make public. It involved moving forward in time and him spending money he shouldn't have had. Let's leave it at that. Is 'why' your next question?"

"Why?" asked Desmond.

"As you know," Bill started, "I need to keep an eye on you to make sure you don't, you know, change things and I could see you were in an awkward situation so thought I would help. And I'm sure you would enjoy a trip in a helicopter to the Shea Stadium."

"Yes, that would be great," he whispered to Bill. "I'm sure a hat with 'Security' written on it will be an acceptable disguise," he added sarcastically.

"I've got you his I.D. badge as well," said Bill, waving it in front of Desmond's face. "He looks a little bit like you."

"Oh," said Desmond, apologetically. "Great," he continued, feeling slightly more confident. "Hang on, let me come out there with you in case Chuck comes out of the bathroom."

Desmond left the door ajar, and they continued their discussion out in the corridor. Desmond was torn between the excitement of taking a helicopter ride with The Beatles and the fear of being found out and what consequences that would bring. He also pointed out that security wasn't really his 'game', despite what he had told Chuck, and wondered what he would do if he was called into action. Bill tried to reassure him that history showed that there were no major incidents during the trip to the stadium and that he should just go along with it and enjoy the ride. After thinking about it, Desmond seemed to accept this as a convincing argument and felt a little more confident.

"Will I actually be able to go to the stadium?" asked Desmond, his fears being forgotten with the thought of seeing his heroes make history by performing at the first ever stadium gig.

"I expect so," said Bill. "Just go along with it and I'll see you at the stadium."

"Where am I, by the way?" Desmond asked Bill. "I didn't feel I could ask Chuck as I'm supposed to know where I am," he explained.

"You're at the Warwick Hotel, Manhattan. Near 6th Avenue," Bill added unnecessarily.

"Who's that you're talking to?" came a voice from the bathroom.

"Oh, it's the staff. They've just brought my uniform up," replied Desmond.

"See you later," whispered Bill. "'The staff', really," he muttered to himself.

"Wait," called Desmond in a loud, panicky whisper. "Shea Stadium is a big place with lots of people. How will I find you?"

"I'll find *you*. Don't worry," said Bill as he hurried off down the corridor.

Desmond popped the cap on and fastened the clip of the I.D. badge to his jacket.

"What do you think?" he asked Chuck, hands open, as he re-entered the room.

"I think you're wearing a hat and a badge," Chuck responded.

"This is what our people wear these days," said Desmond.

"We like to keep it low key. You know, not to make a big thing of it," he added, almost convincing himself.

"Whatever," said Chuck. "We need to get movin', Dessie. Come with me."

Desmond followed Chuck to the basement car park of the hotel where they were confronted by a large group of people surrounding some other people. It turned out that The Beatles had been taken down to the basement in preparation for their journey to the heliport.

"You wait here by the limo," said Chuck, "and I'll get the passengers."

Chuck promptly walked over to The Beatles. Shortly afterwards Desmond realised that Brian Epstein and The Beatles were actually walking towards him.

"Pleased to meet you, Mr Epstein," said Desmond confidently, offering his hand. Following his Hamburg experience, Desmond was beginning to control his astonishment at meeting anyone connected to the famous band.

Brian Epstein shook his hand, smiled, and politely asked, "Who are you? You look familiar."

"Desmond Jones, security," replied Desmond confidently, dismissing Mr Epstein's comment about looking familiar as Desmond knew he hadn't met Brian Epstein before. He was careful not to show too much of the badge he was wearing with the name and photograph of someone called Ian.

"Come on, boys. In we get," said Brian to The Beatles who followed him into the limousine. John Lennon stopped as he was about to get in, looked at Desmond, and said, "What's your name? You look familiar. Have we met?"

"Er, no," replied Desmond nervously. "I'm Dessie."

"Oh," replied Lennon. "If you say so, Dessie."

Desmond jumped in the front and took his seat beside Chuck and the driver of the limousine.

After a short drive they arrived at the heliport where they boarded the helicopter and were joined by a film crew. Desmond had seen 'Sullivan Productions' on the name badges of the crew. He discovered that they were briefed to film the next stage of the journey involving a sightseeing tour over the Manhattan skyscrapers and landing on the World's Fair building.

Desmond's head was spinning. There were two reasons for this; firstly, he wasn't keen on flying, particularly in a helicopter; and secondly, he was in a helicopter with Brian Epstein and The Beatles on his way to the Shea Stadium to see the biggest concert that had yet to happen. Above the noise of the helicopter, he was able to listen to the comments and the banter coming from the VIP passengers and the astonishment of exactly how big the venue was when flying over the stadium.

"Look at that, isn't it great?" shouted Chuck.

It's a long way from the Kaiserkeller, thought Desmond.

They landed on the roof of the World's Fair building and were hurried to the waiting Wells Fargo armoured van, their transport to the stadium. Chuck remained with the helicopter, and, for a moment, Desmond wondered if the was expected to remain with Chuck now that they had finished the flight. He decided that he had better stick with the group as he didn't want to miss the action, and he had to meet up with Bill somehow. He was half expecting to be stopped as he entered the Wells Fargo van but nonchalantly pointed to the word 'Security' on his cap and took a seat in the van.

"Come on in, Dessie," said John as he made space beside him.

"Have we met before?" asked Paul this time.

"Er, no," lied Desmond again.

The rest of the short journey to the stadium passed quickly. Desmond kept quiet but listened in fascination to The Beatles nervously chatting amongst themselves whilst they prepared for the biggest gig of their lives.

*

On arrival at the stadium an army of police and security guards ensured their safe entry whereupon the band were rushed out of the van by another huge entourage. They then ran off to prepare for the concert, without having time to say goodbye to Desmond. Desmond had followed The Beatles out of the van and found himself alone as the van reversed into a three-point turn. He started to panic, thinking how he was going to find Bill in a stadium containing 55,000 screaming Beatles fans. He then felt a tap on his shoulder and turning around was relieved to see Bill smiling broadly at him.

"Bill, Bill, it's you."

"Yes, it's me."

"How did you find me?" asked Desmond excitedly.

"Oh I knew where you'd be," answered Bill. "I need to make sure you get back, after all."

"Oh, of course. I need to get back," said Desmond somewhat disappointedly.

"Shall we get you back now or do you want to stay for the concert?" asked Bill.

"I think you know the answer, Bill," replied Desmond, giving Bill a disapproving look.

"Okay Desmond. Come with me, there's someone I'd like

you to meet."

"What? Who? Who do you know that would want to meet me?" asked Desmond, incredulously.

"She doesn't want to meet you. She doesn't know you. But you may want to meet her," responded Bill.

"She? She?" said Desmond.

"You're repeating yourself, Desmond," chided Bill.

With a few exceptions, such as Molly from twenty years ago, Penelope, and Astrid from Hamburg, Desmond had generally been a little nervous in the company of women and he wondered who this mystery person could be. *Maybe one of Bill's fellow time travellers. Or perhaps Bill had found someone called Molly and thought it would be a good idea to get us together. But if we did get together there'd be no point as I have to time travel back to where I came from.*

"Who is it?" asked Desmond again.

"Oh, you'll see. Just come with me. We need to get back up to the main stadium. You'll still need to wear your cap and badge in case we're challenged on our way."

They were at the other end of the stadium from the makeshift stage, way beneath the terraces where all vehicles coming to the stadium entered. Desmond followed Bill up to the terraces, climbing endless steps. Occasionally Desmond would flash his badge, not too closely, to enquiring security guards. As they approached the crowd, they could hear music which Bill informed Desmond was coming from the King Curtis band who were on the tour with The Beatles. They emerged near the top of the stadium just as the King Curtis band finished their set. Desmond gasped at the enormity of it all and could see the tiny stage in the distance down at pitch level. Deciding that now would be a good time to lose the cap and badge, he swiftly removed them and stuffed them into his jacket pocket. After all, he didn't want to cause any confusion.

"So, who am I meeting?" Desmond was getting more nervous.

"Be patient," teased Bill. "All will be revealed soon."

"Do we have time for this?" asked Desmond, looking for a way out of this potentially awkward situation. "We need to get to a good position to see The Beatles."

"Yes, follow me," replied Bill abruptly.

Bill promptly proceeded down some steps separating vast waves of fans. They arrived at the end of a row in the second tier and Bill approached a blonde lady who Desmond guessed was in her early twenties. She was sat at the end of a row, next to the steps, and wore a camera around her neck.

"Hi, we met earlier," Bill reminded her. "I said I knew someone who would be interested in meeting you. He's a big fan of The Beatles."

As he said this Bill opened his hand towards Desmond as if presenting him at an awards ceremony.

"Er, hello," mumbled Desmond. "I'm Dessie ... Des, er Desmond," he eventually arrived at.

"Make your mind up, Desmond," said the young lady with a puzzled look on her face, thinking *who the hell is this old guy and why does he want to meet me?* "I'm Linda. And this is David," she added quickly, pointing to the man sat next to her. He had a camera bag on his lap and appeared to be in the process of making adjustments to his camera.

"Hello Linda and David," blurted out Desmond.

David nodded and carried on adjusting his camera, occasionally holding it towards the stage as if to check its suitability.

"To be honest, I'm not sure why Bill here wanted to introduce me to you but it's nice to meet you all the same," said Desmond, having calmed down a little from his initial nervousness.

"And it's nice to meet you, Des," said Linda.

"Are you looking forward to seeing The Beatles?" asked Desmond nervously, grappling with ways of conversing with Linda.

"Oh yeah, that's why we're here," she said.

"Oh yeah, of course," replied Desmond, trying to sound cool. "Yeah, yeah, yeah," he added embarrassingly. Thinking that he had made a bit of a fool of himself he decided that he should leave Linda alone now. "Anyway," he said, "as I say, I'm not sure why Bill has introduced us but it's nice to meet you."

"Yeah, you've said that already but that's okay," replied Linda.

"Oh, yes, sorry," said Desmond.

"It's allowed," Linda responded.

"This is Linda Eastman, Desmond," interjected Bill.

"Yes, I know, and what is your point? ... Oh, Linda *Eastman*." Desmond suddenly realised what Bill had said. "Linda *Eastman*," repeated Desmond. "Linda Eastman." He then turned to Bill and whispered in his ear, "The future Mrs McCartney."

"Yes Desmond," Bill whispered back. "Why do you think I introduced you to her?" he added with more than a hint of exasperation.

"Yes, Linda Eastman," confirmed Linda.

"Yes, Linda Eastman," added David, momentarily looking up from his camera.

"Do you know me somehow? Have we met before?" Linda asked Desmond, wondering where this was leading.

"Not exactly, not yet anyway," was Desmond's reply, resulting in a puzzled look from Linda and a worried look from Bill.

Linda turned her attention to Bill. "So, remind me, Bill, why would Dessie want to meet me?" She had decided to settle on the least formal version of Desmond's name.

"I can't really say but it will all become clear one day. He's a big Beatles fan, you see," answered Bill.

"Yes, you mentioned that. Well, I don't really understand but never mind," she replied.

"And I'm sorry for any confusion, Linda," said Bill.

"So am I," said Desmond. "But I understand now."

"Well, I'm glad somebody does," said David, again momentarily looking up from his camera.

"Well, we must be off to find our seats," said Bill. "Goodbye. May see you again sometime. Come on, Desmond."

He grabbed Desmond's arm to encourage him to go with him. He was starting to get a little nervous about him saying something he shouldn't.

"Who's your favourite Beatle?" spouted Desmond suddenly. "I bet it's Paul."

"Desmond!" said Bill, in a loud whisper. "We need to go now."

"I'm thinking Ringo, actually," replied Linda.

"No, I think you'll find it's Paul," said Desmond, ignoring Bill's protestations.

"Okay," she replied with a frown.

Desmond was about to turn and leave when he saw a discarded 'New York Times' on the steps. He grabbed it quickly, held up the front page, and asked Linda if she would take his picture.

"Okay," she replied and immediately snapped Desmond holding the paper. Desmond thanked her and stuffed the paper into his inside pocket.

In the background was the empty stage awaiting the arrival of the Fab Four.

"We have to go now. It's been great to meet you. Cheerio," said Desmond.

"Yeah, I know!" said Linda. "Cheerio," she added in a mock English accent.

And with that Bill pulled him away and they headed back up the steps to find a place to see The Beatles.

"What was all that about? 'Who's your favourite Beatle?'" mimicked Bill as they were moving towards their seats.

"Oh, just a bit of fun. No harm done."

"Let's hope not," said Bill, shaking his head. "And the photo? You'll never see it, you know. It's not like she can send you a copy when she gets it developed."

"I know," said Desmond. "But just think, there's going to be a picture of me in 1965 at the Shea stadium. And Astrid took a few as well back in Hamburg. How did you know it was Linda Eastman?" Desmond asked Bill next. "And how did you find her?"

"Well, I knew she was here, at the stadium when The Beatles played. I was able to locate her with my radio using the locater device; it's a kind of add-on. I also use it to locate you when I need to."

"And how did you get to meet her once you found her?"

"Not everyone is as socially awkward as you, Desmond. I just started asking about her camera, if you must know."

"They're ready for you. Are you ready for them?" came the announcement from the stage as anticipation was building to fever pitch. Next, four tiny figures were seen running across the pitch towards the stage. And there they were on stage about to start. And there was Desmond, in the audience, preparing to be amazed yet again. He knew the sound would not be brilliant and he knew most of the music would be drowned by the screams of the audience. However, he listened intently and soaked up the experience as they stormed through their twenty-five-minute set of: 'Twist and Shout', 'She's a Woman', 'I Feel Fine', 'Dizzy Miss Lizzy', 'Ticket to Ride', 'Everybody's Trying To Be My Baby', 'Baby's in Black', 'Act Naturally', 'A Hard Day's Night', 'Help' and 'I'm Down'.

*

"Time to get back, Desmond," said Bill when it was all over and they were making their way up the steps out of the stadium.

"Wow, what an occasion!" said Desmond, ignoring Bill. "I didn't hear too much, what with all that screaming, but what an occasion," he repeated.

"Yes, but it's time to go," insisted Bill. "Follow me."

Desmond followed Bill until, twenty minutes later, they were outside of the stadium and making their way to a suitable place to time travel back to their respective destinations. As they were making their way through the crowd, Bill mischievously called out, "Hello Barbara" as they passed a group of young fans, then ensured they hurried on past. A puzzled Desmond looked around and saw an equally puzzled young lady clearly thinking *who is that and how does he know my name?*

"Who's Barbara?" Desmond asked as they sped on ahead.

"Never mind," said Bill. "Let's just say Ringo's her favourite. I think I'm spending too much time with you, Desmond; maybe I should have kept quiet!"

"Okay," replied Desmond, thoughtfully.

On the way Desmond told Bill about how he almost decided not to time travel this time, following his friends kindly pointing out a number of scenarios that could result in him being either stranded or, worse still, stuck between times for all eternity.

"I know they were just making things up, but I think they had a valid point in some ways," said Desmond.

"Yes, I know what you mean, Desmond," conceded Bill as they turned into the side street. "I realise you are relying on me to a certain extent to enable you to get back."

"To a complete extent, I would say."

"Well, yes but I'll always find you, you know."

"Yes, but what if—"

"Oh, here we go," interrupted Bill.

"What if," Desmond continued, undeterred by Bill's interruption, "what if an accident should befall you or you lost the radio, or someone stole it? I'd be stuck."

"You have a strange turn of phrase sometimes, Desmond," replied Bill with a smile. "But don't worry about it. If an accident should befall me, as you put it, there are others, other time agents who will be able to help you. My friend Matt Black for example."

"Oh, Matt Black. You've mentioned him before. Matt Black; that's a funny name. Okay, thanks Bill. Do you know what I would like to see?" asked Desmond, changing the subject completely.

Bill rolled his eyes and said, "What now?"

"The Ed Sullivan Show," Desmond answered.

"The Ed Sullivan Show," repeated Bill.

"The Ed Sullivan Show," repeated Desmond.

Desmond was referring to the ground-breaking first appearance of The Beatles on the Ed Sullivan Show in February 1964 when they first hit America. He had seen the black-and-white footage of it many times and had also read several accounts of the historic event which led to the start of 'Beatlemania' in the USA. His most recent reference to it was when he read it to his brother Michael in 'The Beatles Anthology' the previous Sunday back in 2000.

"Well, if we're going, let's make it quick as I've got other time agent duties to attend to. We don't want any fractures in the timelines, and I've got to keep an eye on things," said Bill, sounding important. "Give me a minute to research it. Wait here, Desmond." Bill then hurried out of the side street.

After a few minutes Desmond's mind started to wonder and he was again recalling the comments of Nigel and Brian about getting stuck in the past. *What if Bill doesn't come back?* he thought. *He could get run over, or shot, or he could fall down a hole, a sinkhole! I wonder if they had sinkholes in the sixties. What if he gets mugged and loses his radio?* Desmond was beginning to regret mentioning the Ed Sullivan Show.

After ten minutes Bill returned, none the worse for wear, clutching a brown carrier bag.

"Thank goodness, Bill," said a relieved Desmond. "You didn't fall down a hole or anything, did you?"

Bill didn't answer, he just shook his head and opened the

bag. He handed Desmond a cap, a name badge, and a hot dog.

"Here you go, Desmond. We need a reason for being there so I'm hoping the cap and badge will help. And I thought you might be hungry."

Bill was right about Desmond being hungry. He ate the hot dog in three bites. The cap had the word 'Staff' across the front and the badge, printed on a card behind a piece of clear plastic, read 'Des Jones – Ed Sullivan Show, 9th February'.

"Thanks Bill," he said. "I prefer Desmond, but this will do. What does yours say?" He studied Bill's badge as he was pinning it to his jacket. It read 'Bill Brown – Ed Sullivan Show, 9th February'.

Bill donned his 'Staff' cap, reached into his pocket for the radio, and said, "Right, let's find a song."

After a bit of twiddling the sound of the Dave Clark Five singing 'Bits and Pieces' emanated from the radio.

"Come on, Bill," said Desmond. "I think you can do better than that!"

Bill sighed, twiddled again, and out came 'I Want To Hold Your Hand', The Beatles' first US number one which had ironically been knocked off the top of the UK charts by the Dave Clark Five.

"Will that do?" he asked.

"Excellent," replied Desmond. "How do we both travel together?" he added in a bit of a panic, aware that the sixty seconds were in progress.

"Just grab hold of me," said Bill, expecting Desmond to maybe put his arm around his shoulder, but was shocked when Desmond took a running jump and gave him a massive bear hug with arms and legs wrapped around him, as if he was greeting him like a long-lost friend.

CHAPTER 9

CBS Television Studio 50, New York, 8 February 1964

There was a certain amount of navigation to ensure they arrived at the right place. After all, there was a lot of Beatles-related activity going on around this time in New York what with all of the publicity the radio stations were hyping up. Somehow the radio managed to land them in the right place. They were, however, a day earlier than the actual performance. They had arrived in CBS television studio 50 on West 53rd Street, Manhattan, during rehearsals for the following day's Ed Sullivan Show.

During Bill's absence back outside the Shea stadium, his research informed him that the only seats available had been snapped up by the 700 or so people attending the show. There were around 200,000 applications for tickets for the event. Bill surmised that this was as close as the time radio's safety device would allow them to get the actual event.

"Are you guys okay?" came a voice from along the passage in which they appeared. Bill quickly disengaged Desmond and noticed that the question came from a man in a brown coat and a baseball cap, the front of which bore a badge depicting wings. The man was about Desmond's age, apparently part of some crew or other. He also looked familiar. Desmond quickly dismissed this as a coincidence as they couldn't possibly have met before.

"Oh, yes, fine thank you," replied Desmond. "Just having a group hug before the show tonight."

"Right," said the brown-coated man slowly, with a perplexed look on his face. "But you know it's rehearsals today, the show's tomorrow."

"Oh yes, of course. Of course we did, didn't we, Bill?" said a disappointed Desmond.

"I'm Chuck," said the brown-coated man. "Are you here to—?"

"Yes, just a few last-minute checks," interrupted Bill. "This is Des and I'm Bill."

"Yes, look," interrupted Desmond, proudly showing his name badge to Chuck.

At this point Bill hit his forehead with his hand. Desmond had also realised that they had met, or will meet in the future.

"You *are* Chuck. Aren't you a pilot?" he blurted out before Bill could stop him.

"What? How, how do you know? Actually, I'm in training for my chopper pilot's licence. Why did you ask?" He was about to ask if Desmond could predict the future but decided against it.

"It's those wings on your cap," said Desmond, thinking quickly, imagining Bill's exasperated expression.

It turned out that this was indeed the very same Chuck who Desmond would meet, or had met, in eighteen months' time. Chuck, it transpired, had taken a job working at the CBS studio and was currently working with the team making preparations for The Beatles' appearance on the Ed Sullivan show the following day. His real passion, however, was flying and he was due to take his final test in a few days' time.

Once they had completed their introductions and Desmond had managed to avoid more questions from Chuck, they parted company, but not before Desmond made Bill cringe on two more occasions.

"Good luck with the piloting, maybe we'll see you again in eighteen months or something," said Desmond. "Oh, and would you like to take our picture?" he asked pointing to the camera that he had just noticed Chuck was clutching in his hand.

"Sure. Smile," said Chuck.

Desmond duly obliged, once again embracing Bill, much to his annoyance.

They proceeded along a corridor, past what Desmond guessed were dressing rooms, towards what sounded like rehearsals going on. In fact, what they heard was a song Desmond recognised as 'Consider Yourself' from the musical 'Oliver'. They emerged in the main part of the studio where they saw a group of people on the stage rehearsing. Taking the lead on 'Consider Yourself' was a young man whom Desmond thought he recognised but couldn't quite place. Before long, a break was called for and the young singer was heading straight for them. Bill grabbed Desmond by the arm, saying, "Best not to get noticed; we don't want to be attracting any unwanted attention."

But Desmond wasn't going anywhere. He had suddenly realised who the young man walking towards them was.

"Hello, it's Davy Jones, isn't it?" said Desmond before Bill could do anything about it.

"Er, yes," responded Davy Jones. "Have we met?"

"No," interjected Bill quickly before Desmond could do

any damage. "We just like the song and knew you were starring in 'Oliver' at the moment."

"Yes, and I'm big fan of the M—"

Desmond, who was about to tell Davy Jones that he was a big fan of his future group, the Monkees, was immediately interrupted by Bill. "Musical. He's a big fan of the musical."

"Great, good to hear it. Say, you're from England, right?" asked Davy Jones of Desmond, in his best English accent.

"Yes, how did you know?" replied Desmond.

"Because you're speaking with an English accent? It's a nice change to hear someone from back home. What brings you here?"

"Oh yes, of course. What brings us here?" said Desmond, repeating Davy Jones' question, trying to buy a little time. "What brings us here, Bill?" he added, passing the buck. He realised Bill was probably already nervous about the conversation and would no doubt give a more convincing answer than he could think of.

Bill stepped in. "Oh, um, we were just visiting New York, and a friend asked us to help out today. Extra staff needed and all that what with The Beatles being here."

"Oh yes," responded Davy Jones. "They're big in England, aren't they? And big here of course. I think everyone in America is going to be watching tomorrow! You're from Germany, right?"

"Wow, you're good at accents," said Bill, slightly patronisingly. "And yes, it's a big occasion for The Beatles. Anyway, we should be getting on, lots to do and all that."

But before Davy Jones could slip away, in jumped Desmond. "Do you know when The Beatles are rehearsing, Davy? We'd like to get a sneak preview if possible."

"Yes, they're here and on next. Just hang around for a few minutes and they'll be on the stage. I think they're in the dressing rooms the other side of the stage. Anyway, must nip to the loo. What are your names, by the way?"

Desmond ignored the question. He was gazing back at the stage area where The Beatles had just arrived and were setting up their equipment.

"Don't be rude, Desmond. Davy asked our names," said Bill, interrupting Desmond's concentration. "I'm Bill, and this is Desmond, or Des as he sometimes calls himself, pointing to their name badges."

"Oh, yes, sorry Davy I was distracted by The Beatles. I'm Des and this is Bill," added Desmond, causing a little unnecessary confusion. "I'm a bit of a daydreamer sometimes. Do you believe in daydreams?"

"Bit of a strange question," replied Davy Jones, "but yes I suppose I do."

"Don't say it, please don't say it," whispered Bill under his breath.

"Ah yes," continued Desmond knowingly, completely ignoring Bill's pleas. "I thought you were a daydream believer."

"Right. Anyway, see you later," said a confused-looking Davy Jones as he went off down the corridor.

"Are you nuts?" asked Bill. "Daydream believer? Really?"

"Look! The Beatles," continued Desmond, nodding towards the stage, again ignoring Bill.

They somehow managed to avoid the attention of anyone who seemed to be in charge of proceedings while they stood in the shadows watching The Beatles preparing for their rehearsals.

*

The rehearsal appeared to be going well with everyone in good spirits. Although they were also due back the next day for final rehearsals, they were intent on getting it right during this afternoon's session. As well as some standard rock 'n' roll jam sessions, The Beatles ran through the songs they were planning to play during the live show. The songs were 'All My Loving,' 'Till There Was You', 'She Loves You', 'I Saw Her Standing There' and 'I Want To Hold Your Hand' with each one being given a warm round of applause by all who were there: staff, technicians, sound engineers, camera operators, producer and, of course, Bill and Desmond. After each song, The Beatles would go up to the control room and chat with the engineers. Desmond strained to see if he could get an idea of what they were talking about but couldn't quite make it out from their position. He also noticed them leaning over the console as if noting the position of the dials and knobs for each song. Desmond concluded that they were very meticulous in their preparation. *I'd love to know what's going on up there*, he thought.

About halfway through the session, everyone stopped and went for a break, leaving Bill and Desmond alone in their spot near the stage. The Beatles headed off in a different direction and the engineers left their control room, presumably to go for a coffee or a smoke. His curiosity getting the better of him, Desmond suddenly saw this as an opportunity to find out what had been going on in the control room.

"Won't be a minute, Bill," Desmond informed him and, before Bill could stop him, off he went towards the steps to the control room. Bill desperately wanted to shout to him to get him back but thought better of it. Bill cringed as he saw

Desmond enter the control room. What he was expecting to find, Bill, or Desmond for that matter, had no idea.

What he did find was a control console with a glass of water precariously positioned on the side. He saw several chalk marks with numbers beside them against the various sliders and knobs. He concluded, correctly as it happened, that the numbers referred to the songs and the marks represented where the controls should be for each one. *Mmm, interesting*, he thought. He then proceeded to knock the glass of water over the console.

What happened next was a sheer panic-driven attempt to repair the damage. He found a few tissues in various pockets of his jeans and jacket and a scarf on the back of a chair. With these he managed to mop up most of the water but also removed the chalk marks. Bill looked on in horror, not daring to join Desmond for fear of them both being discovered. He urgently motioned Desmond to get back down to their relatively safe hiding place. After what seemed an eternity, Desmond made his way back, bringing the scarf and tissues with him. Just as he was out of sight, the engineers re-entered the studio and made their way up to the control room.

"Desmond, you really need to control yourself," admonished a more than slightly irritated Bill. "What happened up there?"

Desmond explained about the chalk marks on the console and how he suspected they were to do with the levels for each of the songs The Beatles would be performing on the show.

"So now you've changed history, Desmond," said Bill resignedly.

Desmond was silent. Not because he had been

admonished by Bill but because something was whirring around in his head. After a few seconds his eyes widened, and a smile came across his face.

"No, no, I was meant to do it! I read about it in 'The Beatles Anthology' last Sunday, or sometime anyway." Desmond had lost track of time with all the excitement of his latest exploits. "The chalk marks; they had been wiped during the rehearsal. They thought it was the cleaners, but it was me. I was meant to do it," he repeated.

"Oh," said Bill with a puzzled look on his face. He was trying to make sense of what Desmond was saying. He was working through the thought process: had they not time travelled to this rehearsal, the chalk marks would not have been removed and therefore things would have been different. Maybe not much different but different all the same.

"So sometimes," Desmond continued, "I'm meant to be a bit irresponsible."

"What? No; well, maybe. I don't know," Bill replied. "If that's the case, how do I know when you're changing history or just making it happen as it was supposed to?"

"Dunno," shrugged Desmond.

Back on the stage The Beatles were plugged in and ready to continue. One of the sound engineers was on stage explaining that their meticulous planning had been thrown into disarray by the cleaners who had apparently wiped their chalk marks. A few arms were thrown into the air followed by some grumbling and mumbling. Then they continued.

They listened intently to the remainder of the rehearsal. Maybe it wasn't exactly what Desmond had intended, witnessing the rehearsal rather than the actual appearance on the Ed Sullivan show, but he was elated with the experience all the same. Bill, he couldn't help noticing, was a little pre-occupied but still seemed to be enjoying himself. Desmond ensured he didn't miss anything by occasionally giving him a nudge with his elbow.

At the end of the rehearsal Desmond asked Bill if there was any problem. "You haven't lost the radio, have you?" he asked.

"No, all is fine. It's right here," he answered, tapping his inside pocket. "You seem obsessed with me losing the radio. Don't worry it's not to going to happen. Probably. Time we were getting you back, Desmond."

"Yes, I suppose so," Desmond replied, a little worried about the word 'probably'. "I've been away a long time, and I'm hungry again."

Just at that moment a blonde, middle-aged lady walked past them clutching a banjo.

"Hi Tessie," said Bill.

"Hello," said Tessie, and walked on past.

A confused Desmond alternated between looking at Bill and Tessie, and then asked Bill who it was.

"Tessie," answered Bill. "Tessie O'Shea. Now let's find a suitable tune to get you back."

"Oh. Tessie O'Shea. Goodness me. Two Sheas in one day! Get it? Shea Stadium and Tessie O'Shea," Desmond explained.

"Yes, very good, Desmond."

"Where are you heading?" Desmond asked. "You could come back and meet my friends if you like."

"Maybe another time. I think I ought to get back to Hamburg at the moment. I've got a bit of research to do. I need to find out if you need to be anywhere to ensure history doesn't change. Those chalk marks got me thinking that maybe you're supposed to be at certain places in The Beatles' story. Or maybe not. Maybe the cleaners would have wiped the marks anyway."

"Oh, okay," said Desmond. "Happy to be anywhere you think I should be. I think. So, I'm going first, am I? Oh yes, I'll have to," he continued, answering his own question. "Otherwise I'll be stuck without the radio."

"How about 'She Bangs' by Ricky Martin?" Bill asked.

CHAPTER 10

Somewhere near Middlesham, November 2000

"Wow, I'm back!" exclaimed Desmond, expecting a barrage of enthusiastic questioning from his friends.

"What do you mean, 'I'm back'?" said Nigel. "You haven't been anywhere. We've just been half blinded by the light and there you are saying 'I'm back'."

"But I *am* back," protested Desmond, "I've had the most amazing adventure. I've seen The Beatles. Twice. Three times if you count Hamburg."

It suddenly dawned on Desmond that he had arrived back at exactly the same time as he left so, as far as his friends were concerned, no time had elapsed. He quickly realised he had some convincing to do. He thought the only way was to recount the whole adventure and hope they would believe him.

*

It had been a rather disappointing experience for Nigel, Penelope, and Brian. After all, all they had done was take a drive to an old campervan, watched Desmond tune the radio, and were now being driven back to Middlesham. Desmond had decided not to go into detail immediately but suggested they meet early at the pub for food and drink, at 6.30, which would give them two hours to enjoy the story. All he would say on the car journey home was that he had been to New York twice and met a few people.

"Which I'll tell you about later," he assured them.

This was met with understandable scepticism until Desmond remembered the newspaper he had picked up at the Shea Stadium. He dragged it out of his inside pocket and threw it across to Nigel in the front passenger seat. After Nigel had patiently straightened it out and held it up to show Brian and Penelope in the back seat, they sat in a stunned silence as Desmond, now with a slight smirk on his face, continued driving.

Desmond, Nigel, and Penelope made their way to the Admiral Nelson at 6.23 precisely allowing for the seven minutes' travelling time in order to arrive at 6.30. On arrival back from the campervan, Desmond had managed to get a couple of hours sleep, having been awake for the entire New York adventure. He estimated that he had been away for at least twelve hours in his time frame. Since waking, despite constant nagging from Nigel and Penelope, Desmond refused to discuss his latest adventure until they were all at the pub.

"Anyway, I don't want to have to repeat it all again for Brian. Let's all be patient and wait until we get to the pub," he said.

*

"Get the drinks in, Brian," ordered Nigel.

They were sat around their usual table by the fireplace, customarily reserved for them by Murray. Brain had arrived a couple of minutes after Desmond, Nigel, and Penelope so Nigel had decided it was only fair that Brian got the first drinks. Brian was about to ask why they had waited for him to arrive before getting the drinks but thought better of it, not wanting to listen to Nigel's contrived explanation. He returned with the usual mix of real ales and Penelope's double vodka and diet coke.

"Okay, I'm ready," said Brian, settling into his seat. "I hope you haven't already told these two about your latest trip down the time tunnel," he added.

"No, don't worry, Brian," replied Desmond. "Not a word has passed my lips. My counsel has been kept. Silence has indeed been golden. And there's no time tunnel!"

"Get on with it, Desmond," said Penelope.

And so, Desmond started to recount his tale, starting with his arrival in a corridor of the Warwick Hotel. He told them about Chuck and how he had met him twice, and how Desmond had managed to persuade him that he was a security man thanks to Bill's help. To his friends, this was almost as unbelievable as the time travel encounters but they accepted that it must have happened if the rest of the story was true. He went on to explain how he got to the Shea stadium, by helicopter piloted by Chuck, where he met the future Linda McCartney and later Davy Jones of the Monkees when at the Ed Sullivan studios eighteen months earlier. He described how he was possibly part of The Beatles' story by spilling a glass of water over the mixing console and how this worried Bill.

Desmond's story then turned into a question-and-answer session. Nigel, Penelope, and Brian all fired questions at him about The Beatles, the helicopter ride, the pilot, Linda McCartney, Davy Jones, and various other topics. Desmond was happy to respond following each answer with a "next please!" In fact, he was beginning to see himself as a minor celebrity within his very small circle of friends. Between them they had decided to keep all of this time travelling adventure news to themselves. After all, it had taken Desmond quite some time and effort to convince his friends that he had actually time travelled, and he couldn't face trying to do the same with people he didn't really know. Also, he was quite content to keep it as their own little secret, something only they knew about.

Two hours went quickly, and they were surprised when the quiz suddenly started.

"Right then!" came Murray's usual opening statement. "Round one: History."

Brian groaned inwardly. "Not my favourite subject. It's all questions about before I was born," he said seriously.

The others rolled their eyes and picked up their pens in anticipation of writing down their responses for Penelope to fill in their answer on the answer sheet.

*

"Second place; not too bad," said Penelope as they strolled back towards Cavendish Crescent.

"Not good enough," said Nigel. This was his usual reaction when they didn't win. Despite Brian not being born at the time the history questions related to, he managed to answer all of them correctly. Unfortunately, they failed to score enough points on the music round, usually their strongest subject. Desmond put this down to tiredness after his adventures in New York.

"Shut up, Nigel. We all did our best," said Penelope.

"Yes, shut up, Nigel," chipped in Desmond. This was followed by an expectant glance from Penelope and Desmond towards Brian.

"Yes," added Brian, half-heartedly.

CHAPTER 11

Middlesham, November 2000

It was the following Saturday and Desmond was making himself busy with his cleaning duties. They had a rota organised by Penelope which Desmond adhered to religiously. This morning was his turn to clean the kitchen. He glanced up at the clock above the cooker and wondered if Nigel was going to surface any time soon. It was 11.30 a.m. Penelope had been up for some time and was lounging about in the lounge on their battered old red sofa watching a film on BBC 2 which was even older.

They had invited Brian around for twelve o'clock to watch 'Football Focus' and suggested he bring them all fish and chips for lunch. The plan was then to play a board game and also discuss what they think Desmond should do next as regards time travelling.

Brian arrived at 11.59 complete with fish and chips for four. One minute later Nigel made his way down the stairs, having smelt lunch.

"Great," he said. "Well done, Brian. Just in time."

Penelope organised the condiments and they all sat around the lounge table eating lunch whilst watching the discussion on whether or not Leeds were capable of beating Arsenal that afternoon.

Following lunch, Desmond fetched the Monopoly and

issued a warning to Nigel not to cheat. Nigel took his usual offence to this and then volunteered to be banker.

"You're always banker, Nige," said Penelope. "It makes it too easy for you to cheat."

"I don't cheat," protested Nigel.

"Let's toss for it," suggested Desmond before any further animosity broke out. He then proceeded to organise the coin tossing. It was decided they would have a semi-final where Brian and Nigel tossed a coin and the winner would then toss a coin between the winners of Desmond and Penelope, the other semi-finalists. Nigel won.

After about an hour of playing the game, they decided to have a break. Brian got up to make the drinks, even though he was the only one of the four who didn't live there. Whilst drinking their beverages, Penelope opened the time travel discussion by asking Desmond where he was going to go next.

"Well, I'm not sure. I'm not sure if I'm going to go anywhere. I don't want to push my luck."

"Don't be silly, Desmond," answered Penelope. "You've got the opportunity. You've got to use it. Hasn't he, boys?" she added, looking to Nigel and Brian for support.

"Yes," agreed Brian.

"Yes," agreed Nigel.

"Well, if I do agree to it, where should I go?" asked Desmond. "What do you think, Brian?"

"No good asking Brian," interrupted Nigel before Brian could open his mouth. "Here's a man who's ambivalent about Marmite. How can you expect a decision about your next trip?"

"Abbey Road. 'Sgt. Pepper'," suggested Brian. "And I'm not ambivalent towards Marmite, Nigel. I just don't mind it one way or the other."

"Good idea, Brian," said Penelope, not getting into the Marmite discussion. "What do you think, Nige?"

"Sounds good to me," answered Nigel.

"That's it then," said Penelope. "Abbey Road it is."

"Hang on, hang on," Desmond interjected. "Do I get a say in this?"

"Nope," replied Nigel. "I think we know best."

"Well, I would've chosen Abbey Road anyway. If I'm going anywhere that is. I haven't decided yet," said Desmond with as much authority as he could muster.

"Yes, you have, you know you have," said Penelope. "We just need to decide when you're going."

"How about tomorrow?" suggested Nigel. "We're all around and we don't want to leave it too long. The campervan might not be there forever."

"Good point, Nige," said Penelope.

"Yes, good point, Nige," said Brian.

"So tomorrow it is then," said Nigel, glancing at Desmond for confirmation.

"Okay, okay, I'll do it," agreed Desmond. "But I'm not sure how many more of these trips I want to do. What if something happens to Bill and he doesn't turn up? Or what if he loses his radio? I'd be stuck that's what. Stuck forever. I'd never be able to get back. I'd never see you again."

The others fell silent, staring at the floor, pondering on what Desmond had said. Nigel broke the silence.

"Oh, you'll be fine, Desmond."

"Yes, you'll be fine," agreed Penelope and Brian.

"Right, whose go is it? Oh, mine I think," said Nigel, looking towards the Monopoly board.

"And don't cheat, Nigel, I saw you 'accidently' miscount your £200 for passing 'Go'," warned Penelope.

CHAPTER 12

Somewhere near Middlesham, November 2000

The following morning they set off from Cavendish Crescent and headed to the campervan. During the journey Desmond was quiet. He was a little nervous and part of him was hoping the van would be gone which would put an end to his worries about being stuck in the past. A bigger part of him, however, was looking forward to being at Abbey Road, actually witnessing the making of Sgt. Pepper. Much to the amusement of his friends he was dressed in an evening suit complete with bow tie, hoping that he could arrive in Abbey Road studios at the time the orchestra were recording their contribution to 'A Day in the Life'. He had also grabbed his old folk-style guitar on the way out of the house, explaining that he might need a prop as he reasoned it would help explain his presence there. At least if he was holding a guitar, it would look as though he was some sort of musician. The fact that he couldn't play it very well, never having the patience to spend the time practising, seemed less of a problem at this time.

"The way I understand it," explained Desmond, "is that the orchestra and other musicians all turned up dressed like this," pointing to himself as if he was some sort of male model. "And all of the other invited guests were dressed in fancy dress or such like."

"So you'll blend in," confirmed Brian.

"Yes, that's the idea."

"I wonder if you're in the photos, you know, like the ones in your book 'The Beatles Anthology'," suggested Penelope.

"I've had a look," confessed Desmond, "but couldn't see me. So it's probably not one of the things I influence," he added, as if he in some way played a part in shaping the future of The Beatles. "At least Bill will be happy if I don't need to do anything to ensure continuity of the timeline."

"'Continuity of the timeline'," mimicked Nigel. "Get you!"

*

A few minutes later they arrived at the campervan. Desmond was not altogether ecstatic about it still being there but concluded that, as it was there, he was meant to travel again. He had already been to the library and researched possible songs that were around at the time of 'Sgt. Pepper' and more specifically at the recording of the orchestral section of 'A Day In The Life'. There was only one choice as far as Desmond was concerned: featuring his recent acquaintance, Davy Jones, 'I'm A Believer' by the Monkees happened to be number one at the time.

"Off you go then, Desmond," said Nigel as soon as Desmond pulled on the Fiesta's handbrake. Desmond gave him a look, shook his head slightly, and took a couple of deep breaths.

"Right, I'm ready," he said, and was out of the car and strolling purposefully towards the campervan before the others started undoing their seatbelts. He reached the campervan, immediately turned around, and walked back to the car. The others thought for a minute that he's changed his mind, but he headed straight for the boot, picked up his guitar, and strolled briskly back.

His friends quickly followed, having made their way out of the car, and joined him at the passenger door of the van.

"Off you go then, Desmond," repeated Nigel.

"See you soon," added Penelope.

"Bye Desmond," said Brian in a tone which suggested he may not see him again.

"I'll be right back," said Desmond, opening the door and sliding into the passenger seat. He turned on the radio and within seconds the sound of 'I'm A Believer' was oozing through the speakers. After sixty seconds he was gone.

CHAPTER 13

EMI Studios, Abbey Road, London,

10 February 1967

Desmond arrived in a corridor of number three Abbey Road in Northwest London.

"Are you here for the recording for 'A Day in the Life'?"

Desmond heard the question, and it took him a few seconds to realise the voice was coming from behind him. He turned around to see a young man, smartly dressed in a shirt and tie with a beige jacket. *'A Day in the Life,'* he heard in his head, *oh yes!*

"Er, yes," he hesitantly replied, much less enthusiastically than the reply in his head. Desmond suddenly wished he had brought something more 'orchestral' rather than the old folk guitar he had tightly gripped by the neck in his right hand.

"Okay follow me," the young man ordered. "I'm Richard and I'm helping out with the organising of this," he explained. "We're going along here to studio one."

"So what instrument do you play?" he asked Desmond who was following a few paces behind. "Only joking," he continued before Desmond had chance to answer. "I can see you've got a banjo in your hand."

"Well, it's a guitar actually," replied Desmond.

"I know!" said Richard. "You musicians, what are you like?"

Desmond followed Richard to the studio. As he entered, he was struck by a seemingly chaotic scene. There were several musicians tuning up their instruments wearing full evening dress. Some wore additional novelties: hats, clown noses, and even a gorilla's paw. Members of the Abbey Road staff were milling around, moving seats, setting up microphones, and running cables to and from speakers.

"I'll leave you to it then," said Richard. And off he went.

Desmond was well aware that he had to somehow avoid meeting up with the members of the orchestra. He assumed that they probably all knew each other so he wanted to ensure that he wasn't questioned by anyone.

"Who are you and what are you doing here?" came a demanding voice from behind him. The question took Desmond by surprise and when he turned to look over his left shoulder, he saw the famous Beatle's producer George Martin awaiting an answer.

"Oh, er, I'm a friend of Jack's," Desmond responded, thinking fast and plucking a name out of nowhere, hoping there might possibly be someone called Jack in the orchestra. He immediately regretted it and accepted that he was going to be ejected from the studios. He was aware that in the early days fans would occasionally somehow find their way into the studios, so surely everyone would be suspicious of anyone they didn't recognise.

"Jack Brymer, the clarinettist? Oh right. He's not here yet but you're welcome to have a seat and wait. If you're hoping to play that thing," he said, pointing to the guitar, "you won't get paid you know. We've got a budget for forty musicians and no more."

An awestruck Desmond thanked George Martin and walked to the back of the studio, behind the orchestra, and found an empty chair. He looked from side to side to see if anyone else was about to challenge him and sat down, not realising that the looking from side to side in itself would have caused suspicion had anyone seen him.

After a few minutes Desmond relaxed a little. He had got this far without being found out, he reasoned, so it should be fine from now on as long as he didn't draw attention to himself. He was looking down at the floor, attempting to be inconspicuous, when a pair of shoes appeared in front of him. The shoes were multi-coloured with bright yellow laces. Just above the shoes were the ends of a bright red pair of what Desmond understood to be bell bottoms; they were very wide at the bottom but became tighter towards the top end. Continuing his gaze upwards, above a large, shiny buckled belt, was a purple paisley design shirt decorated with a string of beads hanging from the owner's neck.

"Hi man," came a greeting from the owner of the sixties hippy outfit.

"Oh, hi Bill," replied Desmond, looking up and seeing Bill sporting a false moustache, a pair of shades, and a wig of shoulder-length black hair.

"Oh, I thought you wouldn't recognise me," said Bill disappointedly. "Thought I'd make the effort to blend in, like you did," he added.

"Sorry Bill. Would you like me to feign surprise that it's actually you underneath that lot?"

"No need, Desmond. It's too late now," said Bill, pulling up a chair and settling down beside him.

As they chatted, various people entered the studio and wandered around, stopping here and there to discuss the exciting events that were about to follow. There seemed to be quite a lot of hugging, kissing, and nodding of heads. They saw a man giving directions to others who were holding cameras. Desmond couldn't remember his name but decided that this must be the chap he had read about in his 'Beatles Anthology' book and was responsible for making a film of the orchestral element of the evening. As others came into the studio, Desmond would nudge Bill and point out who they were. The Beatles had yet to appear, but Desmond marvelled at the fact that he was in the same room as Mick Jagger and Keith Richards, plus Donovan and Marianne Faithfull. He also recognised George's wife Pattie who was holding a camera and taking occasional pictures. Desmond even attempted to get himself in one or two of the pictures when the camera was pointing in their direction, much to Bill's annoyance.

Desmond was becoming restless. "Do you think it would be alright to have a word with Mick Jagger? Nigel's a big fan and I'm sure he would love it if I could report back to him that I actually spoke to Mick Jagger."

"No I don't, Desmond," said Bill. "You might say something silly."

"And change history," cut in Desmond. "I'll be careful, don't worry." Then he was up and out of his chair before Bill could stop him.

Bill hit himself on the forehead with the palm of his hand in frustration and immediately hurried after Desmond. There were too many people in the studio to enable Bill to catch up with him and the next thing he saw was Desmond gently tapping Mick Jagger on the shoulder.

Bill decided not to continue the chase as he thought it may cause even more of a disruption but instead stood back and let the interaction play out. He viewed the exchange over the shoulder of a smartly dressed man who was holding a clarinet and wearing a clown's hat. There seemed to be a good rapport between the two of them with Mick Jagger even breaking into a laugh now and again. After a while Jagger introduced Desmond to Keith Richards who also seemed to be enjoying Desmond's company. The conversation continued for a few minutes until someone else grabbed the attention of the two Rolling Stones and Desmond, not wanting to push his luck, turned back towards Bill who was still standing in the same place wearing a worried expression. Desmond was squeezing past the man in the clown's hat in front of Bill and, noticing the clarinet, wondered if this was the Jack that George Martin spoke of earlier. Thinking that George may be watching, Desmond further antagonised Bill by shaking the hand of the clarinettist and greeting him with a "Hi Jack." Bill grabbed Desmond by the arm before he could say anything else and pulled him towards their chairs at the back of the studio, leaving Jack the clarinettist with a puzzled expression.

"What was all that about?" asked Bill when they were in their relatively safe place, settled in their chairs, partly concealed by bunches of balloons attached to two bassoons in front of them.

Desmond recounted his conversation with the two Rolling Stones. He had merely asked Mick Jagger how things were going with the band and had he seen any of The Beatles lately. Mick apparently was happy to share the latest Rolling Stones news with Desmond, presumably because he was in the same room as a very select group of people who were all connected in some way to the forthcoming recording session. It so happened that the Stones latest album 'Between the Buttons' was currently riding high in the album charts which, of course, Desmond pretended he knew although in reality he only had a vague idea of some of the Stones' albums and didn't know precisely when they were released. He did, however, recall that 'Their Satanic Majesties Request' was released after 'Sgt. Pepper' and bore some resemblance to the 'Sgt. Pepper' concept, incorporating unconventional instrumentation and sound effects. The recording of 'A Day in the Life' was still early in the making of 'Sgt. Pepper' so Desmond knew he had to be careful not to talk about tracks that weren't, in some cases, even written yet. With this in mind he asked Mick what he thought the rest of the album might be like and they spent a little while talking about how it was probably going to be the best and most unusual yet. Desmond appeared to impress him with his musical knowledge, surmising that maybe, as they were now using a four-track recording machine, they will be even more expressive and experimental. He also hinted that it would be interesting if perhaps some of George Harrison's newly acquired Indian influences were to find their way on to the album.

"It was good to catch up with Keith too," Desmond added, as if they were long-lost friends. "He asked me if I was in the orchestra, being dressed up a bit like the others, and I told him I was a friend of Jack's who is in the orchestra and I'd met the boys a couple of times."

"Oh good, you told them you've met 'the boys'," said a resigned Bill.

Bill had listened to Desmond's story of his conversation with the two Rolling Stones with some apprehension but was relieved that no real damage appeared to have been done.

"Sorry Bill, I should have known better," said Desmond as if bringing an end Bill's anxiety. "So, who shall we talk to next?" he then asked immediately, straining to see over the orchestra. "Look, there's Donovan."

Before Desmond could make a move towards Donovan, however, he noticed that Paul McCartney was now in the studio, chatting with George Martin. He had read in his new book that McCartney and George Martin shared the conducting of the orchestra during the orchestral build-up. He wondered if he might grab his guitar and join in. Bill noticed Desmond staring at his guitar which was leant against the wall behind them.

"You're not on the list, Desmond."

"I know, but no one will notice if I join in at the back. I know exactly what to do. I need to start at the lowest note and build up to the highest, increasing in volume as I go. And I go at my own pace," stated Desmond proudly.

Just then George Martin and Paul McCartney moved towards the front of the orchestra. By this time the other Beatles had also arrived and there was an almost tangible excitement in the studio.

"Okay everyone," said George Martin, loudly addressing the orchestra. "We have a twenty-four bar gap to fill and this is what I want you to do. First of all, I want you to start playing very quietly and gradually increase your volume as we reach the crescendo. Secondly, I want you to start at the lowest pitch of your instrument and build up to the highest pitch. Thirdly, do this independently of your colleagues. We'll do a few takes and Paul and I will be conducting alternately. Geoff will be looking after things in the control room. Any questions?"

Desmond also heard him mentioning something about clarinets slurping, trombones glissing, and violins sliding. There were a few raised eyebrows and several members of the orchestra looked at each other with a puzzled expression, but these classically trained professionals eventually just got on with it.

Despite Bill's misgivings, Desmond had grabbed his guitar and was poised ready for the first take. He would never get a better chance to play on a Beatles' record, even if no one would hear it, and nothing was going to stop him now. Not even Bill.

After a couple of warm-up sessions, George Martin had called for silence, and they were about to begin the first take. Desmond had his thumb poised on his low 'E' string and was ready to go. And then he was away; watching George Martin indicating the timing of the twenty-four beats from behind the balloons, listening to the Beatles' rhythm track and trying desperately to space the increase in pitch correctly in order to arrive at the highest note at the right time. Just for a moment he had forgotten where he was and that he was participating in a piece of musical history; he just wanted to concentrate on his guitar, and it was as if he was back in his own front room in Cavendish Crescent.

He was quite pleased with the first attempt, even though he had to speed up a bit towards the end in order to fit all the notes in. Bill remained silently resigned to the fact that Desmond wasn't going to stop, so sat there trying to keep his head down and not be noticed. Anyhow, they couldn't move anywhere until there was some kind of break in proceedings as they would stand out like the gate crashers they were. He was secretly pleased for Desmond, however, and at times couldn't help smiling. By the end of the second take Bill was as captivated as Desmond was and joined in with a spontaneous round of applause.

Following the four takes onto all of the tracks of the four-track tape, the orchestra started to get ready to leave, chatting amongst themselves whilst packing their instruments away. George Martin and The Beatles were conversing with various members of the orchestra and the assortment of friends and associates. Bill indicated to Desmond that this might be a good time to slip away.

"Hang on," said Desmond as he made his way towards the front, once again leaving Bill a little panic-stricken.

Desmond had spotted John Lennon chatting to Mike Nesmith of the Monkees. He sidled up to them and started nodding his head as if he was part of the conversation.

"Good session tonight, well done," said Lennon, noticing Desmond out of the corner of his eye.

"Yeah, great job man," agreed Mike Nesmith. Neither of them realising that Desmond's performance was hardly representative of the rest of the orchestra's.

"What did you play?" asked Nesmith.

"Oh, just the guitar," replied Desmond nonchalantly.

"Have we met?" asked Lennon suddenly, Desmond's manner seemingly stirring a memory.

"Yes," replied Desmond before he could stop himself. "We met in America, Shea stadium. Oh and Hamburg."

"We have to go now, Desmond," said Bill who had made his way to Desmond during these revelations about previous meetings.

"What are you saying?" interrupted Mike Nesmith. "You were in Hamburg with The Beatles? And America? Wow, you get around a bit."

"Yep," said Desmond as Bill pulled him away, leaving John Lennon staring, expressionless, after them.

*

"While we're here we might as well cross the road," said Desmond as they were shown out of the front door. With Desmond clutching the neck of his guitar, they crossed the small car park to the gate. "You know; the crossing. Look it's here," he added, pointing to the right.

"Just do it, Desmond." Bill was still miffed at Desmond's blatant disregard of his concerns over the possibility of changing history and the further possibility of more existences being created, putting a strain on the timeline structures.

Desmond was smiling at Bill, walking backwards towards the crossing, hoping his expression would change to one of forgiveness and encouragement.

"Here I go then," he said as he suddenly swung around to his right and stepped into the road, still looking at Bill.

"Wait!" shouted Bill, arms reaching out towards Desmond.

Desmond had completely forgotten to check the road and, in the next instant, the white Ford Transit van was forced to slam on its brakes but could do nothing to avoid knocking Desmond down. He crashed towards the ground and disappeared under the van. The guitar was flung from his grasp and crushed under the front wheels.

Then something really odd happened. Bill ran towards the crossing, shouting out, "Desmond, Desmond!" The driver of the van, wearing a baseball cap and dark glasses, hopped out at the same time and came around to join Bill. The driver muttered something to Bill as they both peered under the vehicle, dreading what kind of sight they would see. They saw a smashed-up guitar and nothing else. There was no one there, Desmond had vanished.

CHAPTER 14

Somewhere near Middlesham, November 2000

"Where's he gone?" asked a shocked Penelope.

"He's gone time travelling. Where do you think he's gone?" answered Nigel.

"No, Nigel," said Brian. "Penelope's right. He comes back at the same time as he goes. And he's not back. Look," he added, pointing to the empty seat.

"Yes. Something's gone wrong, boys," said Penelope.

"Oh, he'll be back," said Nigel, attempting to be reassuring but with his voice betraying a little doubt.

"Maybe he's missed the van and materialised somewhere else around here. I'll have a look behind the lean-to," said Brian.

"Good idea. I'll have a look over there in the next field," offered Penelope, pointing towards a wooden gate to their left. "You look in the field on the other side, Nige."

"Okay, but he won't be there," protested Nigel.

As they all turned away to go searching for Desmond, the door of the van suddenly opened and out came what they could only assume was a hippy from the sixties.

"Who the fuck are you, and where's Desmond?" was Penelope's uncharacteristically brutal opening. Nigel and Brian stood behind her, nodding their heads in agreement of the questions.

"And why are you dressed like a hippy?" she added.

"Does it matter?" asked Nigel, impatiently.

"Everyone stay calm," said the hippy, with a hint of a German accent, making a downwards calming motion with his hands. "Let me explain. My name is Wilhelm but you can call me Bill."

"Oh, Bill. Yes, we've heard about you. You're Desmond's time buddy," said Penelope, beginning to follow Bill's advice and calm down slightly.

"So where's Desmond?" asked Nigel.

"Yes, where's Desmond?" asked Brian.

"We don't know at the moment," replied Bill, removing his wig and sunglasses. "Let me explain."

"Ahh," said Nigel, Penelope, and Brian, before Bill could start, simultaneously realising it wasn't his real hair as the wig came off.

Bill went on to explain the events at the EMI studios. He started by confirming that at the moment he doesn't know where Desmond is, but everything is being done to locate him. He briefly explained the events of studio one and that Desmond had overstepped the mark with his comments to John Lennon about meeting him before and that, when they were outside the studios, Desmond wasn't concentrating before stepping on to the crossing. Mindful of how the next piece of information might be received, he told them about the Transit van knocking Desmond to the ground and finding that he had disappeared when he and the driver peered underneath.

"What do you mean he's disappeared?" asked Penelope. "He can't just vanish into thin air?"

"Well, he can actually, Pen," said Brian, helpfully.

"Yes, thank you, Brian, I know that. What I mean is how can he disappear by being run over by a van? He obviously didn't plan to go anywhere else."

"Yes, I know it seems odd. It hasn't happened before," said Bill, becoming a little uncomfortable with the situation.

They all stood in silence for a minute before Penelope spoke. "So what happens next and what have you done so far to find him?" she asked, continuing to lead the interrogation.

"It's a bit complicated," started Bill. "I'm not sure how much Desmond has told you about me, but I look after timelines; the ones particularly related to the kind of events Desmond has been involved in. That's why I need to keep tabs on him. In case he changes history. The timelines are fragile, and we can't afford to have too many parallel existences running. I need to find him just as much as you need him back here. We don't know what sort of damage he could be doing."

"Or what sort of damage has been done to Desmond," said Penelope.

"As you can travel in time, why don't you go back to before Desmond got run over and stop him stepping into the road?" interjected Nigel.

"It's too dangerous," Bill explained. "If he hadn't disappeared, as a one-off I might be able to do that, but as he's somewhere else, in a different time, I can't risk it. I need to know exactly what has happened and what he may have changed. Also, whether he disappeared or not, that version of Desmond would stay where he is in a parallel existence, and we don't know what he may be faced with. It will be better all round if I bring the same Desmond back."

"Yes, we want the same Desmond back," said Penelope. "So, back to my original question, what happens next?"

"I need to get out of these hippy clothes," answered Bill, looking down at his attire. Penelope gave him a stare.

"Then," he continued quickly, "I'm going back to the control room, which is in Hamburg, to do a more thorough search. He can't be away for too long as his make-up will change, and it will be more difficult for him to travel. One of my colleagues, Matt Black, who looks after other time travellers, is there at the moment. I'll go and see how he's doing."

"Matt Black? Really?" asked Nigel, rhetorically.

"I'll come back and let you know when we've found him," said Bill reassuringly, as he made his way towards the campervan, repositioning his wig and sunglasses. "Although it may take a while, I can come back to you any time from now. See you in a minute or two, hopefully."

"We don't necessarily need to see you, Bill, with all due respect," said Penelope. "We just need Desmond back."

"Yes, I mean you will see me if there's a problem, which there won't be obviously."

He jumped into the van and before long there was a flash of light and he had disappeared.

CHAPTER 15

Control Room, Hamburg, 1960

"Okay Matt, what have we got?" asked Bill.

Matt Black was dressed as he was named, wearing the same black Exis uniform as Bill and his friends usually wore. He was leaning over a desk full of what looked like a recording studio control panel, his longish black hair hiding his face.

"Oh there you are, Bill. How did they take the news? And why are you still wearing that hippy outfit?"

"Okay, I think," replied Bill, ignoring the second question.

Upon his arrival, following Bill's call for help, Matt had suggested that Bill should pay a visit to Desmond's friends just in case the worst-case scenario played out and Desmond could not be found. There was also the fact that, even if he was found, he may not be able to travel if too many changes had taken place. If he were able to travel, the changes could also affect the accuracy of his return, so there would be no guarantee of exactly when he would get back to his own time. It was a very uncertain situation.

They worked together for the next few hours, constantly trying different combinations of dials, knobs, and levers, occasionally referring to one of the half dozen screens spread around the control room. Now and again they would investigate an anomaly in one of the time waves displayed on screen. If a suitable explanation for the anomaly could not be found, either Matt or Bill would pay a visit to that particular timeline and investigate. They had decided straight away to start searching the sixties decade as that seemed to them the most likely period that Desmond would travel to, willingly or not.

"Nothing there," said Matt on his return from a brief visit to Rishikesh in India, 1968, where The Beatles had spent some time studying transcendental meditation.

CHAPTER 16

Tittenhurst Park, Ascot, March 1971

Desmond stirred. He had the worst headache in the world. If it was a hangover, it would have been a ten on his hangover scale. He was lying on what felt like a soft carpet. He didn't feel like opening his eyes but preferred to just lie there for a moment. He couldn't deal with anything else; not while his head was about to explode. He drifted in and out of consciousness for the next few minutes before gently trying to lift his head very slightly from the floor. Upon attempting to do so he realised his head wouldn't move very easily. He determined that it was sticking to the carpet so decided to leave it where it was for a while. In the meantime, he started thinking about the rest of his body. Still not moving and trying to take the focus away from his head, he realised the whole of his body was aching. He tried to narrow it down: *Apart from my head is any area of my body hurting any more than anywhere else?* He decided that it was his left arm. The one he wasn't lying on. *It feels like it's broken. And my ribs; they don't feel too good either.* After a few more minutes Desmond considered opening his eyes. *I can't stay here forever,* he thought. *I'm going to have to see where I am.* Very slowly Desmond opened his left eye. His right one appeared to be stuck shut. He couldn't really see anything. Everything was white. Apart from where he was lying. *A soft, comfortable, cream rug,* he thought to himself. He began to think he was in heaven.

"What the fuck?!" said John Lennon upon entering the room.

"Who are you?" demanded Desmond from his prone, semi-conscious position.

"Robert! Yoko!" shouted Lennon, ignoring Desmond's question. "There's a man in the piano room. Robert! Get in here quick!

Robert, who was Lennon's right-hand man, part-time bodyguard, and general handyman, appeared instantly behind him, wearing a t-shirt and jeans and holding a hammer which he had been using for a repair job in the kitchen.

Lennon's voice was still agitated, "Can you get rid of him? Should we call the police?"

By 'get rid of him' Lennon meant for Robert to remove him from the premises. For historical reasons, calling the police wasn't his first choice. Desmond interpreted 'get rid of him' differently.

"No! no! Please don't get rid of me," he pleaded, quickly regaining his senses and focussing on the man with the hammer.

Still ignoring Desmond, Lennon turned to Robert. "Where's Yoko? She'll know what to do."

"I don't know, John, I think she's in the grounds somewhere with Julian. Do you want me to go look for her?"

They both turned to look at Desmond, considering the practicalities of removing him. He was still lying on the floor, now partly propped up on his good elbow, staring at the hammer with a look of terror.

"He looks harmless enough, Robert. I don't think he's dangerous. You go and look for Yoko, I'll see if I can do something about him."

"Are you sure?" asked Robert. "It won't take me long to get rid of him."

"He looks badly injured. You go on and I'll find out what he's doing here."

Desmond began to relax a little as Robert left the room. "Thank goodness for that," he said. "I thought I was a goner for a minute. Now that the chap with the hammer has gone, could you tell me where I am and who you are?"

"What do you mean, who I am?" came back Lennon. "This is my house and you're trespassing. Who are you? How did you get in here? What do you want?"

Desmond was bamboozled with the questions which came at him like a machine gun from the man dressed in white trousers, white waistcoat, and flowery shirt and spoke in an accent Desmond had interpreted as Liverpudlian. As if his head wasn't hurting enough, he now had to try and untangle the questions and formulate some kind of response. Which was going to be difficult, he realised, as he had no idea what he was doing there or how he got there. As the man asking the questions still seemed irate, Desmond thought he had better say something.

"I'm Desmond and I'm from Middlesham, Cavendish Crescent actually. I'm sorry but I don't know why I'm here or how I got here. I thought you might be able to tell me. I must have been in some sort of accident. I think I've got a broken arm. And my head hurts," he added. "I may have broken some ribs," he further added before Lennon could reply.

John Lennon looked down at the sorry heap of a man lying on his floor in an evening suit and bow tie. His demeanour softened as he remembered Desmond really was hurt and appeared as mystified about his presence as he did.

"Yes, you are hurt, aren't you," said Lennon, almost apologetically.

He walked the five yards or so from the doorway over to Desmond in this largely empty room. The only furniture being a white grand piano, a settee, a couple of comfy chairs, and a coffee table.

"Can you get up?" he asked.

"I'll try," said Desmond, holding out his right hand, the one which didn't have a broken arm attached.

Lennon took his arm and ever so slowly and carefully helped Desmond to his feet. He supported him as they made their way a few paces further into the room to the settee where Desmond plonked himself down. Not being familiar with these kinds of situations, Lennon wasn't sure how to proceed. For the time being he had forgotten about the fact that a complete stranger, with seemingly no agenda for being there, had appeared in his piano room and was more concerned about what to do about his injuries. "What do I do now?" he asked Desmond.

"Well, I think I might need an ambulance if it's not too much trouble. Or at least a lift to the nearest hospital. I think I need to get mended," replied Desmond. "But first can I just sit here for a while?"

"Yes, but I'll get you something," replied Lennon. "A whisky, brandy, cup of tea?"

"In a minute," said Desmond. "Yes. A cup of tea would be lovely. If it's no trouble, but not just yet. Can you stay here for a minute while I get my thoughts together? I think it'll help if I can talk to someone. I might fall over otherwise."

Lennon thought for a moment, weighing up the situation.

He wasn't alone in the house with this stranger, and they'd already agreed he looked harmless. "Sure. It's not every day an injured man in a fancy suit appears on your rug. What do you want to talk about? Anything but The Beatles. I've done enough of that."

"Don't worry I'm not particularly bothered about talking about beetles. Are you some sort of pest controller?" Desmond asked in all innocence.

Lennon stared at him contemptuously, again trying to make sense of the situation. "Yes, very funny, ha ha," he responded sarcastically. He noticed Desmond's puzzled look and came to the conclusion that he may not be joking. "Are you serious?" asked Lennon incredulously. "Not beetles, *Beatles,*" he emphasised, which of course made no sense to Desmond. "B-E-A-T-L-E-S," he spelt out. "Beatles. You know, "The Beatles, John, Paul, George, and Ringo. The most famous group in the world." He threw his arms open. "I'm John Lennon, formerly of The Beatles."

Desmond looked blank.

Lennon paused. "Are you saying you've never heard of The Beatles?" He was still a little sceptical. "Where have you been for the last ten years?" he asked.

"Not sure," was Desmond's response. "Tell me about this band of yours."

Grabbing the opportunity to talk to someone who apparently didn't know who he was, Lennon thought he might as well indulge him. "I'm not talking about the group." Although Lennon understood Desmond's use of the word 'band', it wasn't a term commonly used at this time, so he used the word 'group', being more comfortable with it. "As I've said, I've done enough of that. I'll tell you a bit about my life. Everyone else seems to know it. Except Yoko, she didn't know about it. I'll tell you how I'm feeling now. I'm talking to someone who has somehow appeared in my house. Someone who has never heard of me. I'm not used to that. Several years ago, I wrote a song called 'Help' and it was just that; a cry for help. That's a bit like how I feel now. I've always felt that way. Everything I do I'm not sure where it will lead or what people will think of me. Maybe it doesn't matter, they'll form their own opinion of me anyway. Except you, Desmond, 'cos you don't know me. Imagine what it's like to be viewed as if 'they' know all about you, as if they know how you're thinking. I've been a Beatle and now I'm not. I'm me, an individual. I'm John Lennon. I have ideas of what I want to do but should I be held back by what people think? No, I shouldn't. I've made a lot of mistakes and done things I regret but I've done some good things."

"You seem alright to me," said Desmond, a shade inadequately.

"Thanks Desmond." Lennon paused for a moment then decided to carry on. "I've done some solo stuff since The Beatles. I'm working on an LP now. I'm going to call it 'Imagine'. The Beatles ..." Lennon paused again, realising that he was about to talk about The Beatles after all. "The Beatles," he sighed. "It all got too crazy. We were a simple rock 'n' roll group and it all went mad. We couldn't tour any more. We couldn't connect with the audience. We couldn't hear ourselves through all the screaming fans; so we spent a lot of time in the studio after that."

Lennon was rambling now, picking out random events from his Beatles' life. "We did 'Sgt. Pepper' which took months. We did a song call 'A Day in the Life' and we got a big orchestra in and they all played their instruments, getting higher and higher up the scale. They all played at the same time and then they stopped all of a sudden. Everyone was dressed up. A bit like you, Desmond, with your fancy suit on. We did the 'White Album' after we came back from India. It wasn't the same doing that album. A lot of disagreements. We were all doing solo stuff really. Then, later, there were real arguments, men in suits, Apple, falling out." Another pause and they both sat in silence.

"Have we met before?" asked Lennon suddenly. "You seem familiar."

"I don't know," replied Desmond. "I don't think so. Maybe we have but I don't remember much at the moment. Although when you mentioned the orchestra that sounded kind of familiar, but I couldn't have been there, could I?"

"Seems unlikely. Why would you have been there? There were a lot of people there though. Maybe you were in the orchestra with your suit and all," Lennon joked.

"Who's Yoko?" was Desmond's next question.

"Yoko? You've not heard of Yoko either? Where *have* you been, Desmond? She's my wife. She's an artist, she's a writer, a film maker, a singer, musician. We've done records together. We met in at an art gallery. She changed my life. We've done so much stuff since we met. We got married two years ago, in Gibraltar. I wrote a song about it. Me and Paul did it. Just us. 'The Ballad of John and Yoko'."

"Who's Paul?" Desmond asked. "Is he the Paul you mentioned earlier; one of The Beatles?"

Lennon chuckled. "Yes, that's right, Desmond. Me and Paul go back a long way. We were in the Quarrymen together about fifteen years ago along with some other guys; Colin,

Ivan, and others who came and went. Then George joined. We eventually became The Beatles with Pete and Stu. Stu died then Ringo joined instead of Pete and that was it, the four of us. But we don't exist anymore. In twenty years' time we'll be forgotten. Things change; nothing lasts forever. Seems like you've already forgotten about us, Desmond. Maybe when your head gets better, you'll remember us."

Desmond put his fingers tentatively towards his injured head. "Oh yes, I'd almost forgotten about that," he said. "You know, things are starting to sound a bit more familiar. Some of those names you mentioned. I'm sure I've heard them before. Tell me about some of the songs."

"I will but I think we need to get you looked at, Desmond. Never mind about the hospital, they'll probably ask you a lot of questions you can't answer. I'll get someone around. I'll get Robert to ring a man who knows a man who can get a man around. A real medical man. He's very discreet, and efficient. Wait there," Lennon added unnecessarily. "I'll go find Robert and Yoko then we can talk about the songs."

Lennon left the room as Desmond made himself more comfortable on the settee, closed his eyes, and slept.

127

CHAPTER 17

Control Room, Hamburg, 1960

"We need more help," said Bill, resignedly. He had now changed out of the hippy gear and was dressed in his usual black attire. "How could we have lost him? This has never happened before."

Three more hours had passed with Bill and Matt following several leads regarding the whereabouts of Desmond. Bill was now becoming anxious following his return from Candlestick Park, San Francisco, 1966, The Beatles' last public performance before the Saville Row rooftop session in 1969. It was his most recent false alarm.

"Look," said Matt. "We need to think about this. We know that Desmond's destination is determined by whatever music is playing on the radio. The time radio. How could being hit by that van make him disappear?"

There was a pause while they considered the question.

"The only explanation is that a relevant song must have been playing on a time radio when he was hit," said Bill, attempting to answer his own question. "And," he continued, "the song must have been relevant to Desmond."

"Are you saying that a relevant song was playing on the radio of the Transit van at the time it hit Desmond?" interjected Matt.

"I can't see any other reason he would disappear.

Somehow there was a time radio playing in the van. But how could that happen?" responded Bill. "Unless," he started but quickly put the thought to the back of his mind.

"Unless what?" asked Matt.

"Oh, it's nothing. Right, what's next?"

"We need to get back to the accident and find out more about the van and its driver and have a look at the radio," concluded Matt.

"And find out what it was playing at the time. That way we can pinpoint an approximate time and hopefully a place where we can find Desmond," added Bill. "Let's have a look at the control board to see if we can pick a time just after I left the scene of the accident. We must be careful not to go back while I'm still there. That will cause all sorts of trouble and we're in enough of that as it is. But we can't leave it too late as things will have moved on and the van may not be accessible."

"So what was the situation just before you left the scene of the accident? Did you speak to the driver?" asked Matt.

"Only very briefly," responded Bill. "We were peering under the van, looking for Desmond, and he wasn't there."

"And then what happened?" asked Matt.

"We looked under the van again, just to make sure," said Bill.

"And then what happened?" asked Matt again, patiently.

"When I was sure Desmond was nowhere to be found, I realised he must had been transported somewhere so I told the driver I had to go. And I went. That was it. I nipped back around the corner of the studios and came back here. That's when I contacted you."

"And the driver said nothing?" asked Matt.

"Not that I can remember. No, wait!" Bill thought for a moment as he tried to recall what was said immediately following the accident. He hadn't really taken it in at the time owing to the shock, but he started to recall something the driver had said. "Maybe he did say something. Something about wanting to meet up. Yes! He said something like 'I wanted to meet up with him, not run him over'."

"Why didn't you say that before, Bill? That means the driver knows Desmond."

"Yes, it does, Matt. I'm sorry, I'd forgotten it with all that was going on. And I must have shouted out Desmond's name when he got run over, as I was running towards the van. We need to go and investigate. And why was the driver wearing dark glasses at night? No wonder he didn't see Desmond. And the baseball cap. It's almost as if he was trying to hide his identity."

"Well anyone can wear a baseball cap and there may be a perfectly reasonable explanation for the dark glasses; but this all seems a bit odd," added Matt. "I think it certainly warrants further investigation."

They headed for the control room and started switching switches and turning dials.

CHAPTER 18

EMI Studios, Abbey Road, London,

10 February 1967

"That was close, Matt," said Bill, as they appeared beside the EMI studio building at Abbey Road just as the silhouette of a hippy disappeared in front of them. "The driver should still be there if we hurry. Let's go."

The driver was there, dressed just as Bill had described, wearing a baseball cap and sunglasses. They saw him step into the road, heading towards the door of the van. The road was fairly quiet, being late at night. As vehicles approached from behind the van, they slowed down, their drivers taking a look to see what was going on before carefully negotiating their way around the van, seemingly abandoned, towards the middle of the road, its back half positioned on the crossing.

Bill gave a shout and jogged up towards the driver with Matt following closely behind.

"Can we have a word?" asked Bill as they arrived next to him.

"Yes, of course," he replied. "Who are you? The police?"

"No, I was here just now. When you ran Desmond over. Remember?"

"I remember running Desmond over, obviously. It's just happened. There was a hippy here as well and we looked under the van."

"Yes, that was me," said Bill. "I've changed," he explained, realising he must look completely different.

"Oh, yes, it is you. That was a quick change," replied the driver.

"What was playing on the radio?"

The question came from behind Bill. It was Matt becoming impatient and trying to get to the point of their confrontation.

"Who are you?" asked the driver, peering around Bill.

"My name is Matt, Matt Black," replied Matt, sternly, as if the name should have meant something to the driver.

"Hang on," said the driver. "I'll need to move the van," he added, aware that his vehicle was causing some traffic disruption.

Before Matt could stop him, he had made his way around the front of the van and hopped into the driver's seat. Just as Matt and Bill began to protest, fearing he may drive away, he leaned across and wound down the passenger window.

"The radio wasn't playing, it was a cassette," he said. Then he turned the ignition key and instead of parking the van in a safer position, sped off down Abbey Road.

"Wait! Wait!" shouted Bill and Matt, running after him.

After a few yards they stopped, realising he was gone. They stood there on the pavement, outside the studios, and looked at each other.

"What do we do now?" asked Bill.

Matt said nothing, not able to give a response. They silently turned around and headed back towards the crossing.

"We can't create yet another timeline. It's too dangerous," said Matt as they sat down on the wall at the front of the studios. "There's already a new one because that driver wouldn't have knocked Desmond over if Desmond hadn't come back to 1967. If we come back again and try and stop the driver getting away, or even if we stop Desmond from getting run over in the first place, it's going to cause problems."

They sat there for several minutes, in silence, pondering what to do next. Wondering if they would ever find Desmond and how they would explain it to Desmond's friends if they didn't find him. Bill knew that he could return to the same point in time when he last saw Nigel, Penelope, and Brian but he was also aware that their time to find Desmond was limited. He also knew that if left too long, even if they did find him, Desmond may not be able to travel back to the same time and place where he last saw his friends. Matt was thinking about the further chaos this incident would cause to an already fragile series of timelines. It was his and Bill's responsibility to try and maintain order and they just missed their chance to get a lead on Desmond's existence.

"There's something odd about this," said Matt, stating the obvious. "Even if he was playing a cassette, it still had to be part of, or at least connected to, a time radio. Maybe he had a car cassette player in his van. And how did he get hold of a time radio?" he asked, rhetorically. "And what was playing on his cassette player?" A further minute or two passed then Bill sat up suddenly.

"Hang on a minute. Hang on a minute," he repeated. "A car cassette player?"

"Yes, or a radio cassette player," confirmed Matt, wearing a puzzled expression, wondering what Bill was getting excited about.

"A car cassette player in 1967? Cassettes have barely been invented," stated Bill, becoming more animated and patting Matt on the leg repeatedly. "What's he doing with a radio cassette player in 1967? Who is he?"

"My goodness, Bill. You're right," said Matt standing up. "The first radio cassettes weren't produced until the early seventies. Let's think. How does that help us?"

"Well, we know that if our mystery driver was playing a cassette, the chances are that the music playing is going to be at least from the seventies onwards when the music cassettes started becoming popular. So that must be why we can't find Desmond. We've been looking in the wrong time period. How long were cassettes available for, Matt?"

"If my knowledge of the period is correct, I think they were popular right through the 1980s and into the 90s," Bill replied. "That's still a lot of possibilities to check."

"So what do you suggest? I guess we ought to get Molly on board," suggested Matt.

"What? Molly! No, surely not!" Bill was becoming uncharacteristically animated at the very thought of telling Molly.

Bill thought that Molly, in her position as the overseer of all things time related, should only get involved as a very last resort. Matt and Bill shared similar responsibilities in maintaining order to the various timelines, but the Time Peacekeeper was much more important. Everything stopped with Molly. Bill would see Molly's involvement as a failure on his part. If things went badly wrong it could result in him losing certain responsibilities, even restricting his time travel. He felt that if there was the slightest possibility of fixing things without Molly knowing anything about it, they should do it. Matt had a more relaxed attitude towards Molly and saw her as a source of help when help was needed.

"You said yourself that we needed help, Bill. Molly will help get it sorted. Let me try and make contact with her when we get back to the control room. I'm sure we can find a signal using your equipment."

"Can't we just try searching a bit more once we get back?" pleaded Bill. "After all, it looks like we've been looking in the wrong timeframe so far. Maybe if we can scan the seventies, eighties, and nineties we might have more luck."

"Okay Bill. I can see you're concerned about Molly getting involved but you really don't have to be. You worry too much. She's a pussycat really," said Matt, reassuringly. "Although if Desmond is lost, she'll go mad," he added, completely spoiling his efforts to calm Bill. "Also, do you remember the incident when young Elvis nearly got run over by the crazy autograph hunter? And you saved him? She went absolutely ape shit!" Matt could hardly contain his laughter by this time. "And no harm was done, apart from the fact that the autograph hunter went missing. Imagine what she'll be like if we can't find Desmond."

"Thanks for that," said Bill, "I feel really reassured now," he added, sarcastically. "There is something else actually, Matt," said Bill becoming serious.

Something had been niggling Bill since his discussion with Matt back at the control room and during the last few minutes he had had a realisation about the Transit van, the time radio, and Desmond's disappearance. Many years ago, Bill had acquired a white Ford Transit van for time travelling purposes and had a time radio and other tracking equipment fitted. As a time agent, he was able to add technology which meant the van also travelled in time to the selected destination, unlike the campervan that Desmond had encountered which only transported the occupant. On a trip during 1985 to check out possible suspicious time travelling activity related to the 'Live Aid' concert, he parked the van in a secluded spot in Wembley, North London, while he made his way to Wembley Stadium where preparations were taking place for the concert. It turned out to be a false alarm but when he returned to where he thought he'd parked the van, he couldn't find it. At the time he didn't know whether it had been stolen or he had simply got confused about the location. Either way, after several hours of fruitless searching, he had to eventually return to the control room using his portable time radio. He had reported it to Molly who wasn't best pleased and despite several searches using the equipment in the control room the van couldn't be found.

All this he explained to Matt who nodded throughout the explanation. "Ah, well now I understand about you and Molly," he said. "No wonder you don't want her around. I bet she was livid."

"Well, she was cross about it but I think she accepted it in the end," conceded Bill.

"So you're thinking that the Transit van which ran Desmond over was the one you lost, or had stolen?" summarised Matt.

"Yes, but I'm pretty sure it was stolen," said Bill defensively.

"And the driver," continued Matt, ignoring Bill's comment, "has added a cassette player to the van and somehow connected it to the time radio?"

"Yes," said Bill. "And we know he's been time travelling

because we're in 1967, before vehicles were fitted with cassette players."

They both sat in silence for a while, pondering what all this meant. They suspected that the van was the one 'lost' by Bill. They knew it had a time radio and a cassette player. The driver had been time travelling because he had acquired the cassette player from the future. They didn't really know what he looked like as he was wearing a baseball cap and dark glasses. Unfortunately, they didn't know where he was now. They seemed to be at an impasse.

"Shall we go then?" asked Bill after a few minutes

"Yes, we'd better get back and start looking again." He then glanced towards the crossing, looked at Bill, nodded towards the crossing, and said, "Shall we?"

"I suppose we should. It'll only take a minute," said Bill.

So just as countless thousands of others would do in years to come, Bill and Matt made their way towards the crossing, looked both ways and strolled across to the other side, Matt leading with his hands in his pocket with Bill directly behind him. On the return crossing, Bill took the lead, stepping back on to the crossing after a car had stopped for them, the driver wondering what on earth they were doing, crossing the road only to cross back again.

CHAPTER 19

Somewhere near Middlesham, November 2000

Nigel, Penelope, and Brian stood staring at the campervan as Bill disappeared, wondering if he was about to reappear at any second.

"Well, he's not back yet," said Penelope, impatiently turning to have a look around. "Let's position ourselves around the area like we did just now in case he reappears somewhere else," she suggested.

Brian headed towards the side of the lean-to and Penelope and Nigel headed for their respective fields.

"I'll have a look but there's no point," said Nigel, repeating his earlier protest.

Just as they disappeared from sight, a figure appeared next to the campervan. She was wearing a long black flowing dress with a black shawl. Her long blond hair was adorned with a fake, pink carnation. Her arrival was silent and unremarkable. After adjusting her hair and brushing a few specks of dust from her dress she looked around. "Hello, where are you all?" she called, presumably expecting to have seen Desmond's three friends.

Having heard the shout, Brian appeared from behind the lean-to and was joined by Penelope returning from the field.

"What's Stevie Nicks doing here?" whispered Brian to Penelope.

"Ah, there you are. I'm Molly," she declared, "Molly Parks. Bill and Matt work for me. You've met Bill and he's probably mentioned Matt. Come here and have a chat with me."

Brian and Penelope first looked at each other then edged cautiously towards Molly in a similar fashion to how someone might approach an unexploded bomb. As they reached her, she held out her hand to greet them and they both shook her hand. They visibly relaxed, as if discovering the bomb had been defused. They guessed her age at mid-twenties to thirty. Just at this point Nigel approached from his field, not having heard the arrival of Molly.

"No sign of him," he declared as he rounded the corner and stopped in his tracks. He made his way towards Penelope and whispered in her ear, "What's Stevie Nicks doing here?"

"I'm not Stevie Nicks, I'm Molly," answered Molly. "And I'm not deaf. You're not very good at whispering, are you, Nigel?"

"S-sorry," stuttered Nigel. "I was just a bit surprised to see you. We're looking for our friend Desmond. Have you seen him? He's wearing a tuxedo. Not an ideal outfit for the countryside I must admit but he's been travelling. How do you know my name anyway?" he asked.

"I know all about Desmond and his friends. I'm here to help. In fact, I've met Desmond before," Molly stated.

"When did you meet Desmond?" asked Penelope abruptly. "He's never mentioned you."

"I met him in 1980 at Bath University," replied Molly.

There was a brief pause while they digested Molly's revelations. "Oh, you're Molly! That Molly. I think he did mention you," interjected Brian. "He never said much about it. Only that you suddenly disappeared, and he never saw you again. I think it affected him quite badly at the time, so he probably doesn't like to talk about it."

"Yes, I remember," added Nigel. "He's only mentioned you once that I can recall. A long time ago."

"Well, he never mentioned it to me," said Penelope, indignantly. "I thought he might have confided in me," she added with a little hurt in her voice.

"He probably thought you'd harp on about it all the time, Pen, and he wouldn't want that if he was trying not to think about it," said Nigel.

Penelope shrugged and said nothing.

"Yes, I did feel bad about that," reflected Molly. "I thought it for the best that I kept away. It was all too busy and complicated around the time, what with major interferences to the timelines. He wasn't aware that I was working with timelines. That's what I do you see. I'm the Time Peacekeeper. As in peacekeeper of time, not timepiece keeper," she explained to avoid confusion.

"So what were you doing at Bath University?" asked Nigel.

"Well, to be honest, I'd met him in New York the same year, the older Desmond, your Desmond if you like, but later in the year, and I thought it would be nice to go back and see him in his normal timeline. He hadn't met me of course, when I saw him at university."

Penelope, Nigel, and Brian all held a similarly puzzled expression.

"B ... but Desmond hasn't been to New York in 1980," stated Penelope. "Has he?" she asked, turning to Nigel and Brian. "He's only been there in the 1960s on his time travels. Or is that something else that I've been kept out of the loop about?"

"Nope. Not that I know of. Not been there in 1980," replied Nigel. Brian shook his head in concurrence.

"So, you're saying that the Desmond you know hasn't time travelled to 1980s New York?" asked Molly.

"That's right," they all confirmed together.

"Which means," continued Molly, "that he went there after the accident. So why can't we get a trace on him now?" she asked herself. "Because," she continued to answer her own question with a look of enlightenment on her face, "the accident has caused a change in him. Or maybe he's been away too long. Thinking about it, that explains his appearance; the arm in a sling, the scratches on his face. And he was there with a guy called Chuck. He played quite a significant part in all this."

"Chuck, who's Chuck?" asked Nigel and Brian together.

"Never mind about Chuck," said Penelope, "what about Desmond's injuries? Arm in a sling and scratches on his face sounds bad to me."

"Pen, he's been run over by a Transit van, he's bound to have a few scratches," was Nigel's less than sympathetic response. "At least he's alive by the sound of it."

"I suppose," conceded Penelope. She then recalled something about Chuck. "Do you remember?" she asked Nigel and Brian. "When Desmond was telling us about his trips to New York in the 1960s he mentioned a Chuck a couple of times. It can't be the same one, surely?"

"Yes, you're right," said Nigel and Brian together, again.

They looked to Molly for an answer, who was still working things out in her head. "Well maybe it is. It must be, surely. I'll need to think this through. I need to speak to Bill and

Matt about it."

"So were you close? When you met him at Bath?" asked Penelope, still smarting from being left out of the loop. "I guess he must have liked you a lot if it's affected him so much that he can't talk to me about it," she added.

"We got on really well. He'd could have caused us a lot of trouble in New York, but he did it for the right reasons. I thought it would be nice to meet him again under different circumstances. To see if we got on."

"What on earth was he doing in New York?" asked Nigel at last. A question they were all about to ask eventually.

"Was it in December?" asked Brian, the realisation that December 1980 was quite a significant time in the life of a Beatles fan had suddenly hit him.

"Of course!" said Nigel and Penelope together.

"Yes," confirmed Molly. "December the 8th 1980. The day John Lennon was murdered."

At that moment something vibrated in amongst the various layers of clothing Molly was wearing. She found the vibrating device, the portable control console, and studied it for a few seconds.

"It's from Matt," she said. "He's in 1960. They're finally asking for my help to find Desmond. I'm going to nip back to join them and get the full story. We know he disappeared in 1967 and when I saw him in December 1980 he had already had the accident, but that's all we know at the moment. Don't worry, we'll get him back to you before you know it."

"Why can't you visit him at a later time and ask him where he was after he disappeared? Or even go back to New York in 1980 and bring him home?" asked Nigel.

Brian and Penelope looked at each other and started nodding, surprised that Nigel had thought of something that appeared to be a good idea. Penelope was annoyed that she hadn't thought of it first.

"Yes, good question, Nigel," she said. They all looked at Molly.

"Good question indeed, Nigel, and I can understand why you ask it, but we can't find him. I mean, we can't find any trace of him since the point in the timeline that he disappeared in 1967. There's no trace of him. No impulses, no energy signals, no movement in the quantum void. I received a time signal for New York because there was about to be a possible major disruption. I had no idea it was about Desmond. I'm not even sure the signal came from him. I can't go back there. That timeline is well underway, for twenty years, and I can't risk another one." Molly was aware of a further complication which she chose not to share at this moment. Desmond couldn't come back straight from 1980, he had to go back to an earlier time before he could come home. Until she had more information about where Desmond was before 1980, she had to keep it to herself. She would explain everything later.

"Is he dead?" asked Penelope in a panic.

"I don't think so," answered Molly, reassuringly. "If he was dead, he would have been under the van that ran him over and he wouldn't have been in New York in 1980. The accident has done something to his signals, that's all. Not everyone is easy to trace. We're still looking for an autograph hunter who almost ran over Elvis Presley. But we'll find him. Hopefully before too long if my thinking is right."

"How long have you been looking for him? The autograph

hunter I mean," asked Brian.

"Since 1948," replied Molly. "But don't worry, we won't take that long to find Desmond."

"I certainly hope not," said Penelope.

"So just remind me," said Nigel, thinking things through, "why didn't you ask him in 1980 when you saw him in New York?"

"I didn't know about the accident then," responded Molly. "I'm just finding out about it now. All I knew at the time was that someone was about to change history. And that happened to be Desmond."

"I'm confused again," said Penelope.

"Don't worry, Penelope, it's very confusing, time travel and all that," replied Molly. "Look," she continued, "I have a suggestion. When we're ready to bring Desmond back, we should be able to get him back here, right now, however long he is missing for. But I think it would be better if you make your way back home and then, if it turns out there's an arrival issue, at least you'll all be in more comfortable surroundings." Molly was already feeling the harshness of the cold, breezy November day and imagined Nigel, Penelope, and Brian were too. Although she was determined to remain upbeat about the situation, at least in front of Desmond's friends, she was thinking if the worse happened and he didn't come back it would be better all round if they weren't stuck out in the middle of the countryside indefinitely. At this suggestion the three of them had a brief discussion among themselves and agreed that they would return home without Desmond. Nigel volunteered to drive, having previously insisted that Desmond insured him to drive the car in case he needed it in an emergency situation.

"Wait a minute," said Penelope. "Does this mean you never find Desmond, because if you did, you would have sent him back to here now?"

"Not at all," replied Molly. "We haven't found him yet but when we do, we'll agree now to send him back to his house, assuming that's where you'll be. And you'll need to tell me where that is, by the way, just in case Desmond is unable to tell me or is confused for some reason."

This last statement also worried Penelope but she seemed happy that when Desmond did return, they would all be together at the house. They gave Molly the address and she entered the details into her hand-held portable control console. As Time Peacekeeper Molly wasn't bound by specific equipment such as a time radio, her portable device gave her instant access to time travel wherever she was.

"Anyway, if there's nothing else, I'd better get back and see how the boys are getting on. See you soon."

CHAPTER 20

Control Room, Hamburg, 1960

Back in Bill's apartment, Bill and Matt resumed their search for Desmond. It was a thankless task, and they were getting nowhere. After another hour had passed without even getting the slightest reading on the equipment, Matt again suggested they contact Molly. Much to Bill's reluctance, they finally agreed that it had to be done.

"Right, I'll get started," said Matt. "We should be able to get hold of her on her portable control console, and don't worry, we'll face her together. I'll be right behind you."

Bill's job, and Matt's, was to minimise the effect that time travellers had on events and therefore prevent too many parallel timelines happening. Which is why Bill was wary of Molly. He felt he had failed in his duty by allowing Desmond to have too much interaction with The Beatles and others around them. Had he been stricter in controlling Desmond's travels, and insisted that he was only there to observe, all this wouldn't have happened. He thought by explaining the consequences to Desmond that he would not get so involved but hadn't accounted for his curiosity and enthusiasm. He was sure Desmond hadn't deliberately tried to distort the timelines. After all, how could he be expected to understand the complications of time travel? He knew nothing about it. Bill had been at it for years; and Desmond had been like a kid in a sweetshop, not being able to stop himself dip into the endless possibilities surrounding him. Molly was aware of Bill's commitment to the job and was also aware that he could be a bit lax in his control of the time travellers.

Matt fired up one of the screens in the control room and started typing furiously. After about thirty seconds he stated, "Right that should do it. Not quite sure where she is at the moment, but she knows we're trying to contact her. I'm sure she'll be here soon." They then waited in silence for Molly's arrival.

"I hope she'll be understanding about it all," said Bill nervously, breaking the silence. "She can be a right pain in the backside if she feels like it. And to be honest, I can't really blame her. I was supposed to be looking after Desmond."

"Oh, you worry too much, Bill, she'll be fine with it," reassured Matt.

"Yes, I'll be fine with it," said Molly from Bill's living room.

"Wh … wh … what? How long have you been there?" asked Bill.

"Oh, not long. Just long enough for me to hear you wondering how much of a pain in the backside I'll be."

"Oh s … sorry," spluttered Bill. "I was only joking. Ha ha." The fake laugh was a pathetic attempt at defusing what he considered to be a tricky situation.

Matt, in the meantime, was quietly sniggering away to himself.

"And you can stop sniggering as well, Matthew," said Molly, turning her attention to Matt. "You're not blameless in this either."

"Yes, I am," came back Matt. "Blameless I mean. I wasn't

even there."

"Okay, fair enough," said Molly. "It was all Bill's fault."

Bill opened his mouth in shock and his head gave a series of involuntary twitches from side to side. "Well, thanks for your support, Matt. I'm glad we're in this together!"

"Oh, yes, sorry Bill, but I can't have Molly blaming me," said Matt. "But I am behind you all the way."

"Thanks Matt," said Bill with a hint of sarcasm.

"Don't worry, boys," interrupted Molly, "hopefully not too much damage has been done and we can learn from your mistakes."

"His mistakes," said Matt, slyly pointing Bill. "Yes, let's move on." Matt gave Bill a look as if to say *see, I am supporting you*.

"So, I understand we've lost Desmond Jones. Tell me what you know," demanded Molly.

Bill recounted the details of the visit to the EMI studios. He was clearly embarrassed when explaining the depth of interaction Desmond had with various Rolling Stones, Beatles, and other pop royalty of the era but gave an accurate account of the whole time leading up to the point where he and Matt returned to the scene and the van driver had driven off. He explained their conclusion that the van driver must have somehow gotten hold of a time radio followed by acquiring a cassette player. He also conceded that there was circumstantial evidence to suggest that this could be the same man who stole his van. "If only he had told us what cassette he was playing at the time, we could probably find Desmond within minutes," he added with frustration.

"So, you're saying that when Desmond was hit, you think the driver was playing a cassette which was somehow connected to the time radio in the van he stole from you in the 1985," Molly began to summarise. Bill winced. "The problem is cassettes were produced retrospectively after they became mainstream. It narrows it down a bit but not enough. We need something else."

"Yes. We've now decided to look a little later than the 1960s but still no luck," said Matt."

"Okay, thanks Matt, that's useful," said Molly.

Bill looked a little put out at Molly's appreciation of Matt's comment. "Yes, I've put quite a bit of work in already," he added, attempting to gain Molly's approval.

"Well done, Bill," said Molly. "Well, I've got some information," she continued, "Desmond is still alive. I thought he must be, but I have proof." She explained about her visit to New York in 1980 where she encountered an injured Desmond and her visit to Desmond's friends who confirmed that he hadn't previously been to 1980's New York.

"Oh, so you've been to see Desmond's friends as well?" said Bill. "When I went to see them, I thought I ought to explain the situation, just in case we never found him again. I didn't say that to them though. Just reassured them. And great news that he's still alive."

"Well done, Bill," said Molly. Matt smiled. "Right," she continued, "this is what we're going to do. We need to get a time transmitter to Desmond at EMI studios and we need to do it without creating any more timelines. We also need to avoid any time loops. A time loop, as you know, is what occurs when you meet yourself when time travelling. We must avoid this at all costs. To avoid creating more timelines, there must be no change to the events that have already occurred as a result of Desmond's visit to Abbey Road."

"And the time transmitter will tell us where Desmond is, following the accident," summarised Bill, more to himself than anyone else. He thought for a moment. "But let's say we're successful in getting the transmitter to Desmond. Won't that cause problems?"

"Yes, Bill, it will," said Molly. "It will complicate things because we would expect to pick up the transmitter signal as soon as it's in place and of course we haven't picked it up yet even though, if successful, Desmond will have had it on him when he left the studios. Which is why we need a delay timer on the transmitter. The problem is the longer we leave it until the transmitter starts, the more chance there is that Desmond will unknowingly discard it and move on as he'll be unaware he has it. Another consideration is that I've met him in New York after the accident. That meeting still has to happen, from Desmond's current time position."

"So how long do we set the delay for?" asked Matt. "If it's longer than three days he may not be able to travel at all."

"Exactly Matt," said Molly. "We need it to start transmitting no earlier than when whoever plants it returns back here. I'll set it for three hours from now to allow for any unexpected delays and for anything else that needs doing. That would then cover the fact that we're not receiving the signal at the moment and keep the timeline secure."

"Great. I'll plant it on him," volunteered Bill. "No, I can't," he immediately realised before Molly could object. "I'll already be there, and we'll cause a time loop. Matt, it'll have to be you."

"I'm going to do it," said Molly before Matt could respond. "I think I'll blend in easier."

Sure you will, thought Matt. *That crazy hair and witch's robes will fit in great.* "Good idea," he said.

"And here it is," she said, dramatically producing a small black object from beneath her swirling robes. It was round and flat, no bigger than a large coin, and had a small dial on the front. "I picked it up on the way back from seeing Desmond's friends. My plan is to slip it into his pocket while he's not looking. I'm told he was wearing an evening suit, is that right?"

Bill explained that, as The Beatles wanted that particular evening to be a special occasion, they requested that members of the orchestra wear dress suits so Desmond dressed appropriately in order to fit in.

"Great," said Molly. "I can't remember him wearing the jacket when I saw him in New York, but hopefully it will have been there somewhere. He certainly wasn't wearing the suit trousers though. He was wearing some dreadful loon pants which could date anywhere between mid to late-sixties and mid-seventies. God knows where they came from. When I get the opportunity in the recording studio, I'll put the transmitter in his jacket pocket. Then we just have to hope he doesn't find it and still has it with him when he leaves New York. Okay, let's get an accurate fix of where and when I'm going."

The three of them worked together to arrive at the exact information needed to enable Molly to arrive inside the studios shortly after Desmond had arrived on 10 February 1967.

"Right, I'm ready," declared Molly. She fiddled with her portable device for a few seconds and promptly disappeared.

CHAPTER 21

Tittenhurst Park, Ascot, March 1971

The door swung open and in walked John Lennon, closely followed by a small Japanese lady dressed all in white and carrying a tray with a teapot and three cups. Desmond stirred. He had slept for about ten minutes.

"Here he is, Mother," said Lennon, using his favourite term of endearment towards Yoko Ono. "Desmond Jones from outer space or somewhere else. He just landed here with a broken head and arm. Doc is on his way and tea is served."

"Oh, thanks John," said Desmond, still waking from his nap. He turned his head towards the small Japanese lady "And hello, you must be Yoko. Sorry about dropping in like this. I don't really know how it happened. I have no recollection of how I got here. I've lost my memory. But I think some things are starting to sound familiar."

Yoko Ono nodded in his direction. "John told me. Welcome to our house," she said, succinctly.

"Yes, don't worry, Desmond," said Lennon, "I've told Mother all about it."

Desmond nodded, a little confused about his term for Mrs Lennon but understanding who he was referring to.

"Shall I be Mother?" asked Lennon, picking up the teapot and confusing Desmond a little more. He poured the tea and pulled up a chair opposite Desmond. Yoko took a seat alongside Desmond on the settee. "The doc should be here in the next half hour," he assured him. "He'll get you sorted out and up and ready to go. If you know where to go, that is."

"I've no idea," Desmond answered. "Maybe someone will be looking for me. When the doctor has been and fixed me, can we have a look outside to see if I recognise anything or if we can see anyone looking for me?"

"Sure we can. There might even be a search party, Desmond," said Lennon. "In the meantime, we can talk about The Beatles and our songs. You never know, it might stir a few memories." Lennon had forgotten all about his reluctance to talk about The Beatles. It seemed to him that Desmond was a blank page to whom he could recall anything he wanted to about the last fifteen years of his life without fear of having his words twisted or taken out of context or misquoted. Although he used the media to his advantage when chasing political causes and promoting world peace, he was also very wary of opening up about his life for fear of being misrepresented and misunderstood.

"So how long have you been writing songs, John?" asked Desmond. He was already feeling comfortable in the company of John Lennon. And despite Yoko sitting silently next to him, he found her a calming presence. It was as if Lennon was his only friend at that precise moment.

"I wrote a couple early on, before we were known outside of Liverpool. That's where we're from, Liverpool," he added. "They weren't very good though, the very early ones, but they got better. Once The Beatles started to get bigger, we started putting a few of our own songs into the set. From quite early on, me and Paul agreed that all our songs would be 'Lennon and McCartney originals' whether they were written individually or not. Our first hit was 'Love Me Do'. I played harmonica on that one. Me and Paul sang it. We recorded mostly cover versions in those days, then we started to put more and more of our own songs on the albums."

He continued reminiscing about the songs. Desmond listened intently and, as he listened, he began to realise some things sounded familiar. Not familiar enough to make much sense; just familiar enough to make him think that he wasn't hearing some of these things for the first time.

"Earlier you mentioned a song called 'A Day in My Life'. What was all that about?" asked Desmond.

"No, I didn't," chuckled Lennon. Yoko smiled. "'A Day in the Life' is the one I mentioned earlier. 'In My Life' is a separate song. That's a good song. They're both good songs. 'A Day in the Life' is just about things I read about in the papers, like the number of holes in the roads in Blackburn. That's the one with orchestra. Paul had a separate part of a song and it fitted in perfectly for the middle eight. 'In My Life', that was me reflecting. It started off as a song about Liverpool."

"Yes, the orchestra!" said Desmond with enthusiasm. "Why are bells ringing in my head?"

"Maybe it's your concussion or whatever that knock on the head has done to you," suggested Lennon.

"No, I mean the orchestra. Just for a split second I thought I saw something in my head. Maybe it was nothing. Anyway, the songs. So, you wrote separately?"

"Not always. In the early days we would sit down together with our guitars. Sometimes it was in the porch of Aunt Mimi's. That's where I lived. Aunt Mimi brought me up. We would work out things together, but we wrote a lot of stuff individually later on. Even then we would often contribute to each other's songs. Like I said just now with the middle bit of 'A Day in the Life'. Sometimes me or Paul would get stuck on a song lyric, or a melody, and we would make a suggestion or even say to leave it as it is. On the LPs we did after 'Sgt. Pepper', the 'White Album', as some people call it, those were all written separately, and we weren't all there for the recording of them either."

"Did the others in the band also write songs?" asked Desmond, interrupting Lennon's output of information. "Seems like it's all you and Paul."

"George wrote 'Something'," Lennon replied.

"Can't you remember what?" asked Desmond in all seriousness.

"No, no, that's the name of the song, 'Something'," explained Lennon. "He wrote other songs too, great songs, but me and Paul wrote most of them. Ringo wrote a couple too."

"Oh, sorry John, I understand now. 'Something'," said Desmond. "'Something'," he repeated, pensively.

"Another bell ringing?"

"Maybe."

For the next ten minutes Desmond listened intently as his new friend talked expressively about his group and his songs. He talked specifically about his influences such as Elvis, Buddy Holly, the early Motown artists, and later, Bob Dylan. At the mention of Dylan, Desmond again experienced a momentary sense of familiarity which passed as quickly as it arrived. During this time Yoko left the room, explaining that she would look out for the doctor who was due to arrive at any time.

After a few minutes Yoko returned and following her was an Asian man in his forties, dressed in multi-coloured striped jacket and white trousers carrying a regular doctor's leather bag. He turned out to be Dr Jasper. Yoko returned to her seat on the settee next to Desmond. "Good afternoon, John, and what have we here?" he asked, looking towards Desmond.

"Desmond Jones," answered Lennon before Desmond could respond. "He's lost his memory and can't remember how he got here or how he got into our house for that matter. He's had a bang on the head, we think he's broken his arm and he also thinks he has broken ribs. Is that about it, Desmond?"

"Er, yes, that's it, thanks John," replied Desmond. "I also have had a few bells ringing about stuff John has been talking about. Do you think you can help me, doctor?"

"Yes I can, Desmond Jones." replied the doctor. "From what I hear it sounds as if you have a touch of transient global amnesia, TGA. If you think you have a broken arm and ribs, you probably have. I will examine you and we will take it from there. Please remove your clothes."

"Oh, er, okay yes. Um, would you mind leaving the room, John?" asked Desmond.

"Don't worry, Desmond," chuckled Lennon, "I'm off. Let me know when you're done, Jasper."

Yoko remained seated. "And you, Yoko," demanded Desmond, nodding towards the door, "if you don't mind." Yoko gave an almost imperceptible nod and headed for the door with a faint smile on her face.

Fifteen minutes later Dr Jasper called John and Yoko back to the room. In came John, closely followed by Yoko, and walked towards the seating area. Dr Jasper was in the process of packing up his bag. "I'm going to take Desmond to my hospital for an x-ray and get his arm in a cast. I should be back in an hour or so. We'll check out the rest of him while we're there. Come with me, Desmond."

Desmond obediently followed the doctor out of the room. "See you later, Desmond," said Lennon.

CHAPTER 22

EMI Studios, Abbey Road, London,

10 February 1967

There was a lot of commotion going on in the corridor which ran towards Studio One of the EMI Studios. Molly stepped out into the corridor from an empty side room in which she appeared. She moved swiftly, doing her best to blend in with the various musicians, engineers, and guests walking towards the studio. Gripped tightly in her right hand was the transmitter she had to drop into Desmond's jacket pocket. A task, she reminded herself, which needed to be completed without being seen, particularly by Desmond.

She entered the studio unseen and unchallenged. *So far so good,* she thought. She followed a couple of people wearing tuxedos and carrying musical instruments; a trumpet and something she didn't recognise but which she concluded was some sort of brass instrument, partly circular and with a large end and a bit to blow in, musical instrument knowledge not being one of her strong points. Her knowledge of pop and rock stars of the 1960s was not as comprehensive as Bill and Matt's, but she did recognise a couple of the Rolling Stones when she saw them milling around among the gathering group of celebrities and studio personnel. The next part of her plan was to locate Desmond; not an easy task with members of the orchestra wearing the same outfit as him. She kept moving whilst scanning the room as she didn't want to attract anyone's attention who may notice she was looking for someone. She was keen to avoid any offers of help. She knew Desmond was carrying a guitar and would possibly be looking awestruck.

She was just beginning to wonder how much longer she could risk being there without being challenged when she spotted her target. He was making his way along the fringes of the orchestra area carrying his battered folk guitar. She now had to plan her route to reach him without attracting attention, from Desmond or anyone else. Being careful to avoid eye contact with anyone, she kept her head down, only glancing up periodically whilst edging towards him. As she moved, she began to question her judgement in deciding to carry out such a dangerous operation. After all, she was the Time Peacekeeper and any time anomalies caused by her error would have serious consequences. She really had to be extra careful. After two minutes she was at her destination, just behind Desmond on his right-hand side. She held the transmitter in her hand and was about to drop it into the right-hand pocket of Desmond's jacket when she heard an authoritative voice just to her left.

"Who are you and what are you doing here?"

She immediately froze and was desperately trying to formulate a suitable answer when she heard Desmond speak.

"Oh, er, I'm a friend of Jack's," she heard Desmond say.

It was Desmond he was talking to, not me. I'm still okay. She was impressed with Desmond's quick response and amazed when the authoritative gentleman believed him, mentioning a clarinettist called Jack Brymer. She then acted quickly.

Desmond was about to move so she dropped the transmitter into the pocket and fled. She safely made her way back to the corridor and stepped into the same small room that she had arrived in before tapping some time co-ordinates into her portable device. She was not heading immediately back to the control room, however. First, she decided to pay a visit to Cavendish Crescent, Middlesham, in the year 2000.

CHAPTER 23

Middlesham, November 2000

Nigel, Penelope, and Brian had a sombre journey back from the site of the campervan. They sat in silence for the first few minutes of the journey, pondering what would happen next. After the silence Penelope let it be known that she was very worried about Desmond's situation and wasn't entirely convinced by Molly's reasons for sending them back to the house. Nigel and Brian retained an air of optimism, and both were attempting to keep their group spirits up.

"I'm sure he'll be joining us very soon, Pen," asserted Nigel.

"Yes," said Brian. "I expect Molly and her team will find him soon, and then he'll be joining us."

"Yes, he's probably on his way right now, travelling through the time tunnel," continued Nigel."

"There's no time tunnel," replied an irritable Penelope.

"She's right, Nige," confirmed Brian. "He doesn't use a time tunnel. He said so."

"I know, I know," said Nigel. "I'm just trying to explain the delay. Maybe the transporter or whatever it is he uses has some kind of fault."

"Oh yes, that's it, Nigel," said Penelope, sarcastically, "I expect it's got a puncture and he's waiting for the breakdown truck to arrive."

They sat in silence for the remainder of the drive back to Cavendish Crescent. They let themselves in and Nigel and Penelope made their way to the lounge while Brian put the kettle on. Nigel and Penelope sat either end of the battered old red sofa, leaving one of the two less than comfy chairs to Brian.

"I wonder how long he'll be," said Brian, looking at his watch.

"Oh not long now, Brian," answered Nigel.

"Oh don't start that again, you two. There's only so much of this wondering when he'll be back I can take. I'm hungry, whose turn is it to get food?" She and Nigel looked towards Brian.

"Well, it can't be me," protested Brian, "I don't live here."

"Right, yes, you're right," said Nigel, stalling and waiting for Penelope to offer to get lunch, even though, according to the rota, he was well overdue to do it himself.

"Do I really need to check the rota, Nigel?" said Penelope. "We all know it's your turn. As you well know, the rules are that if two or more of us are here and we're not just making our own lunch, the rota kicks in. And I think you'll find—"

"Alright, alright," interrupted Nigel and he stormed off into the kitchen where he retrieved two large pizzas from the freezer and stuck them in the oven.

"Lunch will be ready in sixteen minutes," he stated on returning to the lounge.

"Thanks Nige," said Brian

"Thanks Nige, not too difficult, was it?" said Penelope, being unable to resist a further dig at Nigel.

Half an hour later the pizzas were gone, dishes were cleared, and the three friends had resumed their positions in the lounge.

The silence was broken by Brian. "Shouldn't be long now."

Before Penelope could protest, they heard the doorbell ring. They all stood up, looked at each other, and said "Desmond!" then rushed to the door, Penelope winning the race and pausing at the door, holding the latch.

"Why didn't he use his key?" she asked no one in particular.

"He's probably lost it, Pen," said Nigel. "For goodness sake open the door!"

Penelope opened the door. "Oh, it's you," she said, unable to hide the disappointment in her voice. "Come in, Molly. Tell us the worst."

"Don't worry," said Molly, following Nigel and Brian whilst Penelope closed the door. "It's not bad news, just an update."

They all settled in the lounge except Brian who headed for the kitchen to prepare cups of tea for them all, Molly taking the spare 'comfy' chair. Upon Brian's return with the tray of tea and a packet of custard cream biscuits (one of Desmond's top five biscuits), Molly explained that the reason she had decided to call in with this update was just in case any inaccuracies in Desmond's arrival time extended into the afternoon or even later. At least then they would know what progress had been made whilst they were waiting. She recounted her successful mission to Abbey Road and how she was able to plant a time transmitter into Desmond's pocket. She explained the delay mechanism and that they should shortly be getting a signal from it. She also mentioned that when she saw Desmond in New York in 1980 he was wearing trousers that weren't fashionable at that time so they suspected that he may have travelled there from a different time several years before that.

"I wouldn't rely on Desmond wearing unfashionable trousers as an accurate indicator, Molly," advised Nigel, "but the transmitter news is encouraging, isn't it?" he said, looking around for confirmation.

"Yes," replied Molly, "before long we should be able to pinpoint exactly where he is. Then we can go and get him."

"So in the meantime we just have to wait for him to arrive back," said Penelope, confirming that there was nothing else they could do. "Are you in a hurry to get back, Molly?"

"There's not much we can do before the transmitter starts working, so no. Why do you ask?"

"I was just wondering if you could tell me, well us, a little more about when you met Desmond," suggested Penelope.

"Yes, I can, what do you want to know?"

"You said you've met him twice before; tell us about when you met him at Bath."

CHAPTER 24

Middlesham, November 2000

"Gosh!" said Penelope, puffing out her cheeks. "Poor Desmond."

Molly had finished recounting her version of the events of May 1980 and was staring forlornly at the floor. Nigel and Brian remained silent, deep in thought, imagining how Desmond must have felt at the time.

"Why did you leave? Just like that?" asked Penelope, almost accusingly.

"I'm sorry," replied Molly, sadly. "It was getting too serious, and I couldn't commit to a relationship. Because of what I do. I just couldn't see how it could work. I just thought it best to walk away and hope Desmond would be okay. It did trouble me for a long time and there were many times when I almost went back to see him. But I could never be sure that I wouldn't have to leave again and hurt Desmond even more."

"Fair enough," declared Nigel, feeling a little uncomfortable with the atmosphere in the room.

"I'll put the kettle on," said Brian, glad of a reason to leave the room.

"I'll help," volunteered Nigel uncharacteristically, also grabbing at an opportunity make an exit.

Penelope wasn't angry with Molly. She understood Molly's dilemma. She just felt sad for Desmond. Something else was bothering her, however. Molly appeared to be a young woman of no more than thirty and this confused Penelope as Molly's visit to Desmond was twenty years ago. "How old are you, Molly?" she asked.

Molly thought for a second. "I'm not sure, Penelope" she replied. "What you understand as age and how it progresses, linearly, doesn't work like that in my world, in our world of time agents. Our time sits above the linear time that you use. It's in a separate world altogether."

"I see," said Penelope, not seeing at all. "That explains it. So, you don't age like us?"

"Yes, that's part of it. We eventually wear out, but we don't grow progressively older as you would understand it."

"I see," said Penelope, still not seeing. She decided to leave it there as her train of thought was interrupted by Nigel and Brian bringing in further refreshments. "So what happened when you met him in New York?" was her next question.

"Oh yes, what happened when you met him in New York?" repeated Nigel.

"Yes," said Brian. "Did you get back together?"

"Of course not," answered Penelope, demonstrating her understanding of the sequence of events. "That was before she met him in Bath."

"Yes," said Brian. "I knew that," realising his error.

They settled back into their respective seats and leaned forward in anticipation of Molly's next instalment of the story. However, Molly wasn't about to divulge much.

"I can't really go into too much detail now. As you know, I met Desmond and Chuck and we chatted whilst the day unfolded. Although he was a little confused and forgetful, Desmond impressed me with his honesty and his determination to do the right thing. But I don't want to say any more except that Mark Chapman didn't shoot John Lennon, nobody did."

"So John Lennon is still alive?!"

"Yes, well sort of," she confirmed. "I'll explain later. But don't mention it to anyone else for the time being, I haven't even told my time agents the full story yet. Now, if you don't mind, I'll be heading back to Bill's control room in Hamburg. I want to make sure I'm there for when the transmitter starts working."

"Of course, yes. Go find Desmond, Molly," Penelope advised.

CHAPTER 25

Northwest London, February 1967

Chuck was driving through heavy rain. It was the morning after the incident at Abbey Road. The windscreen wipers were overworked but still just about managing to keep the rain away from the windscreen. He was in a dilemma. He had spent the night pondering his situation and he was worried. He had run over Desmond, probably badly injured him, and also made him disappear. And then he'd done a runner. He was not happy with himself.

Over the years he'd managed to remain undetected by the time people. He wasn't sure how he had managed it and so had assumed there was some kind of glitch in their detection system. He had had a few adventures including an encounter with Elvis in the forties. He was only going to ask for the young Elvis' autograph but somehow managed to almost run him over. If it wasn't for the swift action of a passer-by, who appeared from nowhere, the history of popular music would have taken a huge diversion.

The whole incident had frightened him considerably. In fact, it frightened him to such an extent after that he decided not to attempt any time travelling for a while and he settled in America, getting a job at CBS studios in New York whilst working towards gaining his helicopter pilot's licence.

He'd met with Desmond three times; at the Shea Stadium,

the Ed Sullivan Show rehearsal, and outside of the EMI Studios at Abbey Road, although technically speaking the last one wasn't really a meeting as such, more of a collision. He had planned to be at the EMI studios for the same session as Desmond and was really looking forward to seeing the making of a significant part of one of his favourite songs. He also knew that a lot of celebrities were going to be there as well as The Beatles, and he was hoping to add a few autographs to his collection. He was annoyed at arriving too late for the session but that quite often happened. His time travelling wasn't always accurate. Afterwards he thought that he might try again and arrive earlier and avoid running Desmond over. And then he thought that there was no guarantee of exactly when he would arrive and anyway, Desmond had already been injured and had disappeared. He wasn't sure exactly how it all worked but maybe it would mean there would then be more than one Desmond. And that would be very confusing.

As a fellow Beatles fan, he was interested in Desmond's travels and was able to track him on the equipment in his van. His van, the van he had acquired, was fitted with some kind of radar which indicated where and when a time traveller, such as Desmond, was going. It turned out to be a real stroke of fortune the day he happened upon the Transit van when he was out walking near Wembley Stadium on the day of the Live Aid concert in 1985. He just happened to notice that a Transit van he was walking past had its keys in the ignition. Not one to miss an opportunity of getting something for nothing, he glanced around to see if the owner was nearby. He saw no one so opened the unlocked door and clambered inside. There he found not only a radio playing, alongside some sort of monitor which he later found out was a tracking device, but also a shoulder bag. On closer inspection he discovered a radio in the bag; a small radio with 'Rave FM' written on it. After fiddling around with the radios and experiencing a blinding flash of light, he found that he had miraculously transported himself to a different time and place. It took him a while to convince himself what had happened, but he eventually realised that he was seeing the Rolling Stones performing at Hyde Park in 1969, sixteen years before he jumped into the van. After this incident he slowly began to teach himself how to time travel to roughly where he wanted to go, and to get back, just by ensuring a suitable record was playing on the radio.

He had spent a restless, uncomfortable night in the back of the van, tossing and turning on his makeshift bed and pondering his situation. He decided to put a tape into his cassette player, newly 'acquired' during a brief visit to 1978 where he attended the launch of Paul McCartney's 'London Town' album. He had wired it up to the time radio with a connecting switch which he ensured was set to off when he didn't want to time travel when playing cassettes. He was sure the switch was off when he collided with Desmond but somehow Desmond had disappeared, presumably time travelled. He could only think that Desmond must be wired differently, somehow more susceptible to the influence of the time radio, even if it wasn't connected to the cassette player. The time radio was equipped with its own switch for activating time travel but he hadn't used the radio since arriving and he hadn't bothered to turn the switch off.

The tape he was playing was the same one he had on the previous evening when the accident happened; John

Lennon's 'Imagine' album, so his guess was that Desmond was somewhere in 1971, hopefully still alive. He had tried his tracking device several times to see if he could pick up a signal from Desmond but with no luck. He considered trying to follow Desmond to wherever he went, using the radio whilst the 'Imagine' album was playing. Then he thought better of it. *What if Desmond was dead?* he asked himself. *What if he was badly injured?* How would he cope with that?

CHAPTER 26

Tittenhurst Park, Ascot, March 1971

"I'm back, John," said Desmond. He was standing with Dr Jasper between two of the white pillars in the substantial front porch of the Lennon residence. Lennon had answered the door himself. Desmond's left arm was encased in plaster supported by a sling, just visible under his jacket. It was a different jacket to the one he was wearing when he first arrived at the Lennon residence. This one was a white safari-style jacket kindly donated by Dr Jasper to replace the tired-looking black jacket, torn and dirty as a result of the accident, currently draped over his right arm. He was also wearing a pair of purple flairs or 'loon pants' as Dr Jasper referred to them, also courtesy of the good doctor to replace his torn suit trousers.

"How are you feeling, Desmond?" Lennon asked.

"I feel fine under the circumstances. I've got a broken ulna apparently," he announced rather proudly. "I've also got a couple of broken ribs and a bit of concussion. That's probably contributing to my memory loss, TGA. Did I get all of that right, Doc?" he asked, turning towards Dr Jasper.

"Absolutely, Desmond," the doctor replied.

Lennon invited them in, but Dr Jasper declined, explaining that he had better get back to his hospital as he had a number of patients to see that afternoon. He jumped in his car and started the engine. It was a Ford Cortina, which Desmond thought was rather an old car for a doctor to be driving but it was in very good condition. Desmond accepted the invitation and walked in ahead of Lennon.

"Good of you to use the front door this time, Desmond," said Lennon.

"Thanks," replied Desmond. "John, some things have started coming back to me," he continued. "Can I ask you about them? I'm sure you can fill in a few blanks."

*

"Do you know anyone called Nigel?" asked Desmond. They were back in the same white room where Desmond had first appeared. "He's a friend of mine I think, as is Penelope and Brian."

"I had a friend called Nigel in Liverpool. He used to be in the Quarrymen. But that would be a different one."

Desmond carried on remembering things. More and more came back to him as he spoke to John Lennon. "John Lennon," he stated. "John Lennon, Paul McCartney, George Harrison, and Ringo Starr. The Beatles."

"Yes, I've told you all that though," said his host.

"Yes, I know, but this is different. I'm actually remembering you. Yes, yes, The Beatles! I've seen you, in Hamburg, and New York!" He was growing more and more animated the more he continued. "I went to the studios at Abbey Road in London. I spoke to you!"

"Seems unlikely, Desmond," said Lennon, trying to throw some realism into the conversation. "Although, as I said before, there is something familiar about you. Maybe I have spoken to you. Maybe it was at Abbey Road."

All of a sudden, the door burst open and in came Yoko. "There's a man at the gate," she announced. "He says he's a friend of Desmond. He's called Chuck." They both looked up.

"Tell Robert to let him in, Mother," said Lennon. "This could be interesting. Does the name Chuck mean anything to you, Desmond?" he asked.

"Kind of sounds familiar," he answered, scratching his head. "I'm sure I've met a Chuck before but it's not an uncommon name. I may know lots of Chucks."

"Well, we're about to find out," said Lennon as the door swung open and in walked Yoko, closely followed by a man of about forty wearing a baseball cap, dark glasses, and a bemused expression.

"Chuck," stated Yoko by way of an introduction. "He knows who I am."

"And I know who you are," said Chuck, turning towards John Lennon in an excited tone of voice. "You're John Lennon," he announced as if providing the correct answer to a competition question, "formerly of The Beatles," he added superfluously.

"And I'm Desmond," said Desmond, not wanting to miss out on the introductions.

"I know," said Chuck. "We met in America." Chuck went on to explain they he had lived in the States for a while, a few years ago in the early sixties, and how he had met Desmond whilst working on the 'Ed Sullivan Show' and then again the following year when The Beatles played at Shea stadium (although Desmond had met Chuck at the 'Ed Sullivan Show' *after* the Shea Stadium concert). He also said that he had attempted to be at the EMI studios at Abbey Road when Desmond was there in 1967 for the Sgt. Pepper recording session with the orchestra.

"So I *was* there," said Desmond. "And America? I was really in America?" he asked. Something else was also troubling Desmond, something wasn't right when Chuck had said about meeting him in the sixties, but he decided to keep quiet about it for the time being. He was sure he was born in the sixties, 1960 in fact, and he thought he knew he was forty years old. When John Lennon had been talking about his life and The Beatles, he hadn't mentioned any dates as such, he referred to how long ago things were, but no actual dates. Desmond had therefore just assumed he was talking about the nineties. *This is obviously something to do with my head injury,* he thought.

Chuck was previously unaware of Desmond's memory loss but soon realised that this was probably a result of the accident and that he was partly responsible. He also couldn't help but notice the sling Desmond was wearing and the scars around his eye and on his forehead, indicating that he was also physically injured. Chuck reasoned that he wasn't fully responsible as he remembered that Desmond did actually walk out into the road without looking and, had it not been himself passing at that particular time, it could have been someone else. He had, however, continued to wrestle with his conscience after driving off following Bill and Matt's visit to the scene of the accident and as a result had decided that he must keep searching for Desmond. He had eventually turned the radio switch on whilst playing the 'Imagine' cassette and managed to transport himself to Tittenhurst Park. Something that Bill and Matt had been unable to do as they hadn't, up until that point, been able to pinpoint where and when Desmond might be.

"This is crazy," said Lennon. "You mean to tell me that

you were actually in Hamburg and New York to watch us play? And you were in the orchestra at Abbey Road after all? How did you do that, Des?" he asked, adopting the less formal version of his name which seemed to please Desmond. "Maybe you're a journalist or photographer, assigned to cover The Beatles."

"No, I work for the Inland Revenue, I'm a taxman," said Desmond, surprising himself and pouring cold water on John Lennon's attempt at arriving at a plausible solution as to how these things could have happened.

Lennon shrugged and turned his attention to Chuck. "So you're here to collect Desmond, Chuck." It was more of a statement than a question. "How did he get here? 'Cos I found him in a heap on the floor, over there."

"Er, not sure," answered Chuck. "I heard he'd been involved in an accident, and no one could find him." Which wasn't entirely untrue. "So I've been driving around looking for him." Which wasn't true at all. "I guess he must have somehow found his way into your house. You know, in his confused state."

"I'll get Robert to review security. If Desmond can get in undetected, next time it could be someone wanting to kill me," said Lennon.

"I can't imagine why anyone would want to do that, John," said Desmond. "After all, you were in The Beatles," he added, as if being a Beatle would somehow make him immortal.

"There's some crazy people out there, Desmond, you never know what's around the corner," replied Lennon. "You could have been some mad man with a gun."

"Oh now you're being paranoid, John," came back

Desmond. At this point a worried-looking Chuck sat down beside Desmond.

"I think we need to talk," he said quietly in Desmond's ear.

"Do we? Okay then," whispered Desmond, looking down at his feet.

At this point they heard a telephone conveniently ring outside of the room. Robert appeared stating that someone called Klaus was on the line for John. Desmond was relieved to see that Robert had discarded the hammer.

Lennon walked towards the door, closely followed by Yoko. "My old friend Klaus Voorman. Do you remember him, Desmond? You may have met him in Hamburg. He plays bass on the new album."

"Rings a bell," said Desmond.

Chuck and Desmond were now alone in the room. "Why are we talking about the sixties as if it was yesterday?" demanded Desmond of Chuck in a loud whisper. "I'm very confused. What year is this?"

"1971."

"It can't be 1971," stated Desmond, categorically. "I'm forty years old. Look at me," he said, pointing both hands towards his face. "And what was all that about just now, when you said, 'I think we need to talk'?"

"You really don't know, do you? Where do I start?" Chuck asked himself. He took a deep breath. "Right, Desmond, you're a time traveller. The year you're normally living in is the year 2000 and, as I mentioned, this is 1971. You're here because I ran you over outside of the EMI Abbey Road Studios by mistake when you were there in 1967 when 'Imagine' was playing on the cassette player in my van which is attached to my radio. The radio is the thing that transports us through time. I don't really understand it but that's what happens; the radio transports you through time to somewhere, sometime when the record that was playing was popular, or in this case being created. I don't know why it transported you rather than me, but it did. I've been worried about it ever since. I did a bad thing in driving off when I was confronted by your friends Bill and Matt but then I couldn't bear it any longer. I had to try and find you, which I did. That's why I'm here now. We're going to get you back to where you're supposed to be, somehow. Your memory has obviously been affected by the accident and you're in a very confused state. You can't even remember that John Lennon gets murdered in 1980."

Just at that point, an earth-shattering point as far as Desmond was concerned, the door swung open and Lennon returned, alone. Desmond was frantically trying to take it all in. His first thoughts were that Chuck had gone nuts. But then something connected. Chuck's news had somehow reconnected a synapse and an explicit, semantic, and episodic memory was reborn. He clearly recalled the morning of December 9th 1980 when his housemate, Winston, burst into his bedroom at 7 o'clock in the morning to announce that John Lennon had been shot dead.

"Shit! You're right, Chuck, he gets shot."

"What are you talking about now?" demanded an exasperated John Lennon.

"Oh nothing, John," said Chuck, attempting to rescue the situation. He was thinking on his feet. "We were just discussing the JFK assassination. I think it's time we were going, isn't it, Desmond?" He gave Desmond a gentle nudge.

"Oh, yes," said a still-shocked Desmond. "I've taken up enough of your time, John. You've been very good to me. Thank you so much." He extended his good arm and shook Lennon firmly by the hand. "Sorry about your rug," he added, glancing towards the bloodstains. "Oh Yoko! Say goodbye to Yoko for me. And Dr Jasper. Thank the doctor again. And thank him for the jacket and trousers."

"I will, Desmond. It's been good to talk to you, especially about The Beatles. I didn't think I wanted to talk about it but I've enjoyed it. Maybe we'll meet again sometime in the future."

"Or the past," said Desmond.

"What do you mean?" asked Lennon.

"Oh, Desmond's still a bit confused," said Chuck by way of dismissing Desmond's comment, clearly thinking it would be a step too far to start explaining about their ability to time travel.

Lennon appeared to accept Chuck's explanation. "I'll get Robert to show you out to the gates," he said as he walked towards the door and gave a shout to Robert.

Robert and Yoko appeared, Desmond got up from the settee, grabbing his old jacket, and they all made their way towards the front door. As they walked out on to the porch, Chuck produced a small book and a pen from his back pocket.

"Before we go, can I just have your autograph, please, John?" he asked to which John readily obliged. "And you, Yoko," he added, moving along to Yoko and offering her the book and pen. "Put it on the same page if you don't mind." Yoko also obliged and passed the book on to Robert. "Oh, not you, Robert," said Chuck, snatching the book out of his hands. "No offence."

Robert appeared not to take offence and after a further brief round of goodbyes he escorted Desmond and Chuck along the long driveway towards the gates. At the end of the driveway Robert opened the gates and bid them farewell. They had walked just a few steps when Desmond turned and did something that would have an impact on the delicate nature of their timeline and the timeline of popular music in the twentieth century.

"Robert!" he shouted. "John gets shot in December 1980. In New York," he added. Something was telling him he probably shouldn't have revealed such information, but he couldn't remember what.

Chuck was looking a bit shocked at Desmond's decision to reveal the fate of John Lennon to Robert. He thought Desmond probably shouldn't have done it, but he also didn't know why.

"Well Desmond, that was a bold move. Do you think it will make any difference?"

"I don't know, but I just felt I had to do something. But what if it makes no difference? What if he doesn't tell John what I said? Or John takes no notice? Is there any way we can go there; to New York in 1980 and stop it happening? Can we use your cassette player or radio?"

"Phew! I … er, maybe," was Chuck's tentative reply. "But first let's get back to the van. We've got a lot to talk about. I've also got food there. You must be hungry. I am."

Although Desmond had had a snack at the hospital, courtesy of Dr Jasper, he realised he was hungry again and agreed that they should get back to the van straight away.

*

"Right Chuck," began Desmond, "start talking," he demanded.

Just remind me what happened to me. How did I get here?"
They were sitting in the front of the white van munching on
Chuck's sandwiches, having made the short walk from the
gates of Tittenhurst Park.

"I ran you over in the van. It wasn't my fault, Des. You just
walked out in front of me outside of the EMI studios. And you
ended up here, at John Lennon's house. I came here to get you
home."

He showed Desmond the radio and cassette player. "This
is it, Desmond. This is what will get you home."

"Or get us to New York," interjected Desmond.

"Or get us to New York, possibly," said Chuck.

Ensuring the time radio switch was off, as he didn't want
to risk any further complications, he then rewound the
'Imagine' tape that he still had in the player and pressed the
'Play' button. As soon as the opening broken C chord started
playing, Desmond recognised the song.

"Of course, 'Imagine'. Yes, it's 'Imagine', Chuck,"

"I know, Desmond, it's my cassette," he confirmed.

"This is 'Imagine', yet John's only just working on it now.
Tell me more," demanded Desmond as the music continued
in the background.

"I will, but let's find a pub while we're talking. I could do
with a drink."

Chuck decreased the volume, enabling them to talk more
easily and started up the van. He then gave Desmond an
account of his own experiences of time travelling. How he
had happened upon the Transit van one day in 1985 (he
didn't actually use the term 'stole' and Desmond didn't
enquire further) in which he learnt to time travel using
basically a trial-and-error technique and how he almost ran

over a young Elvis.

He parked the van in the road on the same side as, and just beyond, the Nag's Head public house, a few minutes' drive from Tittenhurst Park. He continued talking whilst doing this, recapping on his previous meetings with Desmond in New York and also filling in a few details of the events at Abbey Road including his meeting with Bill and Matt following the accident. All of that brought Desmond up to date and he awaited the next question or comment. It was more of a statement.

"I'm tired, Chuck, I'm so tired."

Chuck was a little disappointed that there was no further reaction to his revelations about time travel but understood that Desmond must be exhausted. "No problem, Des, I've got blankets and cushions in the back." A useful addition to the furnishings and equipment of the transit van that Chuck had cause to use on many occasions, both as a time traveller and during his peripatetic life in general.

They made their way around to the rear of the van and Chuck opened the doors. Desmond was pleasantly surprised to find a neatly stacked pile of blankets and a bundle of seven or eight cushions of various colours and sizes stacked towards the front end. He climbed in, took off his patent leather shoes and safari jacket, then quickly organised a sleeping area. He had left his old jacket in the front of the van along with the transmitter in the right-hand pocket.

"I'll leave you to it, Desmond," said Chuck. "I'll leave it unlocked in case you need to get out and join me in the pub. It's still only early evening, a bit early for me to sleep. I'll see you later. I'll try not to disturb you when I get back." Desmond gave Chuck a wave as his head hit the cushion. For the time being he had forgotten about visiting New York and he was asleep within seconds.

CHAPTER 27

Control Room, Hamburg, 1960

Back in the control room Bill and Matt were anxiously awaiting Molly's arrival in time for when the transmitter started working. A few hours had passed since Molly had left and although she could have returned from Cavendish Crescent earlier, she decided there was no point and that she might as well come back in 'real time' as they would still have had to wait for the transmitter to commence transmitting. They were sat hunched over the control panel staring at a screen as if it would speed up the transmitter. Molly drew up a chair behind them and joined them in staring at the screen.

"Not long now," she reassured them, checking the time readings on her hand-held device. And just at that moment the screen lit up. It was showing a location and time, converted into linear time for easy reading on the screen. The time coordinates converted to 17th May 1971, 16.00 hours, and the location coordinates indicated that the transmitter was somewhere just outside of Ascot, England, at Tittenhurst Park; at that time the home of John Lennon and Yoko Ono.

"Okay, let's go get him," said Bill. "Looks like he's gone to see John Lennon if my knowledge of Beatle dwellings in the 1970s is correct."

"Ready when you are," said Matt.

"We can't," said Molly

"What?" said Bill and Matt incredulously, turning towards Molly.

"We can't," she repeated. "Not yet anyway. Think about it. I went to 1980's New York and met with Desmond. We've learnt that in his current timeline, in his real time, he hasn't gone to New York in 1980. Okay, we know that he could possibly go there in his future, that is after we return him to his real time, but, as we know when I saw him there, he was injured, most likely as a result of the accident."

"And if we bring him back before he gets there ..." continued Bill.

"He won't get there," Matt finished.

"So this is what we're going to do. One of us, one of you two," Molly waved her finger between the two of them, "is going to stay here. Yes, Bill, you stay and monitor the transmitter. Matt and I will go to Ascot to check on Desmond. We'll need to do a Time Transportation Capability Test, a TTCT. At least then I'll be able to provide an update for Desmond's friends, which will hopefully be positive."

"So I'll stay here then," said a disappointed but unsurprised Bill.

"Thanks Bill," said Molly. "Obviously I can't personally check on Desmond because I don't meet him until he gets to New York, but he has never met Matt. So we just need to make sure he doesn't see me or at least interact with me. After that we just need to continue to pick up the transmitter signal. Wherever he goes from New York we'll need to be able to find him."

"But how did he get to New York in the first place? And if he managed to get there, maybe he can get himself back home." Bill posed some logical questions, answers to which

Molly had already been considering.

"Good question, Bill. When I saw him in New York he was with someone called Chuck. They mentioned about travelling in a Transit van." She looked towards Bill with raised eyebrows. Bill's face turned a whiter shade of pale at this revelation.

"So maybe Chuck has some means of time travelling," said a mischievous Matt. "Any thoughts, Bill?"

Somewhat annoyed with Matt for what he considered to be unnecessary stirring, Bill took a deep breath whilst considering the probable chain of events. "Yes, yes, let's get it out in the open. Let's assume this Chuck person stole my van and has used it for time travel. He's possibly the same Chuck that Desmond and I met in New York in 1964 and 1965 and, as we've discussed previously, the same person who ran Desmond over in Abbey Road in 1967. Chuck has obviously met up with him again, wherever he went to after the accident, and is about to transport him to 1980's New York. And the reason we haven't been able to trace Chuck, or at least the van, is because it has the location shield activated, which I usually kept activated to avoid interference as the timelines can be fragile as we know. Is that about it? I'm sorry, Molly. It won't happen again."

"Thank you, Bill. A good summary," said Molly. Matt could barely keep the smile from his face. "And the reason we can't rely on Desmond getting back on his own, even with Chuck's help, is that we just don't know how badly he's been hurt. We all know that the accident, particularly when it's combined with the amount of time he may be away, could have a big impact on Desmond's ability to get back. And assuming he can get back, his arrival point and time may not be as accurate as we would like. So ideally we want to transport Desmond back ourselves but we can't do that from 1980's New York. Because I didn't know about this situation when I was there, I left him and Chuck where they were. Which means if we're not able to intervene, we will need to track him closely using the transmitter. Matt, do you think Chuck will recognise you if he sees you when we go to Ascot?" she asked. "I assume he saw you when you and Bill went back to the scene of the accident."

"Very briefly, but we weren't there long, and it was dark," he answered. "I'll wear a hat."

"Brilliant!" interjected Bill.

"He mustn't see me as he doesn't meet me until New York," said Molly. "It will distort things too much. We just need to get close enough to Desmond to carry out the test."

Molly proceeded to explain about the TTCT. Neither Matt nor Bill had carried out such a test, so she considered it part of their education. She retrieved the test kit from somewhere between the many layers of her dress. It was small and light and was contained within a leather zip-up file no bigger than a man's wallet. She explained that the testing device, similar in appearance to that used in security scans at airports, detects changes in the person's cellular composition and gives an indication of their ability to time travel. All they needed to do was scan Desmond with it from head to toe, ideally without him knowing. In order to protect the timeline, the less Desmond has to question anything, the better it will be for all concerned.

"So let's assume he's with Chuck and somewhere nearby there'll be a white Transit van. Matt, if you can somehow distract Desmond so that he doesn't see me, I'll try and do the scan from behind him," she concluded.

She then said she needed to work on the test kit for a while to calibrate it in readiness for Desmond. An hour later she announced that she was ready.

"Right let's go," said an impatient Matt.

Molly set the appropriate dials and off they went.

CHAPTER 28

Near Tittenhurst Park, Ascot, March 1971

Molly and Matt arrived in the vicinity of Tittenhurst Park, a couple of hundred yards down the road from the entrance. Unfortunately for them, subsequent to Molly programming in the coordinates, Chuck had driven to the pub, and the Transit van in which Desmond was fast asleep, was now a twenty-minute walk away. They had emerged from a small, wooded area onto the road leading towards Tittenhurst Park in one direction and the Nag's Head in the other. Molly checked the readings.

"Looks like he's moved," she said, still studying her device which she had calibrated to receive data from the transmitter. She thought about entering the new coordinates and travelling to Desmond's location instantly, but the walk would do them good, she had decided, and there was always a slight risk of their appearance at a new location being spotted despite the device's safeguards. She certainly didn't want any further complications to the situation. Matt agreed and they set off to find Desmond.

As they approached the pub, they spotted a white Transit van ahead of them just beyond the Nag's Head pub.

"Look!" said Matt, pointing to the van. "Do you think that's it?" It was the third white Transit van they had seen during their walk and this time Molly's response was more encouraging.

"Could be," she said.

Matt donned his disguise, a black baseball cap. They decided to cross the road where they glanced left towards the van as they passed it and saw there was no one in the driver or passenger seats.

"He's not there. Is he in the pub do you think?" asked Matt.

Molly paused and checked her device. "He's in the van. Look," she said, showing Matt the reading indicating they were within a few feet of Desmond.

"He's in the back of the van," confirmed Matt. "Shall I go and knock on the door?"

"I think you'll have to but let's go and have a listen first, to see if we can hear anything."

They crossed the road to the pavement and crept towards the van. Facing each other they each pressed an ear on the side of the van.

"Someone's sleeping," said Matt, picking up the faint noise of snoring. "Can you scan him from here? Through the van?"

"Not really. We wouldn't get an accurate enough reading. We really need to get up close."

"Okay," said Matt. "I'm going to knock on the door and get him outside. Hopefully Chuck won't be there but if he is I'll make sure he doesn't recognise me."

"And how are you going to get him out?" Molly asked. "If someone knocked on my van door while I was sleeping, I wouldn't feel like being helpful."

"Ah, you're forgetting, Molly. I have a natural charm. Get the scanner ready."

Without an alternative plan to get Desmond out of the van she decided to let Matt carry on and use his natural charm.

She retrieved the test kit, took out the scanner, and made her way around to the front of the van where she would be out of sight. Then, when Matt and Desmond were talking, she would creep up behind Desmond and carry out the scan.

Bang! Bang! Bang! she heard, the shock of which made her stand upright and almost drop the scanner. It was Matt's attempt to wake Desmond by banging on the rear doors, prior to using his natural charm. She quickly gathered her thoughts together along with the scanner and peered around the front of the van. She next heard Matt order Desmond out of the van.

"Outside, outside quickly!" he shouted as the doors opened.

Surprisingly, she next saw Matt and Desmond appear on the pavement to the side of the rear door. Desmond, without shoes and jacket, had his back to her and was scratching his head in the manner of someone who had just been woken from a deep slumber. She decided to act quickly and crept up behind Desmond who was now starting to ask Matt what the problem was.

"Where's the nearest pub?" Matt asked.

Desmond stood motionless; his head tilted slightly to the left. Being motionless was useful to Molly as it meant a better scan would result. It was done in seconds, and she slowly crept backwards towards her hiding place at the front of the van just as a dumbfounded Desmond nodded towards the Nag's Head, a matter of thirty yards away. She was about to dip out of sight when she saw a figure turn out of the pub and walk towards them. She then heard Desmond ask Matt, "Is that it? Is that why you woke me up and got me out of bed? To ask me where the nearest pub is?"

"Er, yes, sorry, I didn't see it there," she heard Matt mutter.

As Matt answered, he turned to look at the pub and saw the figure ambling towards them with a puzzled expression on his face. He quickly realised it was Chuck. Molly had slipped around to the other side of the van and approached the rear from the road. She managed to catch Matt's attention without being seen and, with her head, beckoned him in her direction.

"Thanks Desmond. Bye," said Matt abruptly and shot around the side of the van to join Molly.

Molly locked her arm in his and they marched speedily across the road. They didn't look back, they just kept on walking away from the van and the Nag's Head. Chuck had now reached the van and was peering down the road with Desmond looking over his shoulder.

"Who was that?" asked Chuck.

"No idea," said a still bemused Desmond, scratching his head and watching the man walk in the opposite direction to the pub with a woman who seemed to have appeared from nowhere. "He wanted to know where the nearest pub was."

"There's one right here, Desmond. Where have you sent the poor man?"

"I know, Chuck. I can see it actually. It's right there: the Nag's Head. He obviously chose not to go there. It was like he got spooked and took off. Maybe it was something to do with you. He turned to look at the pub and must have seen you. And how did he know my name? He called me Desmond. This is all very strange."

"You're right, Desmond, that is strange. Let's go after them, and find out who they are," said Chuck.

They both peered down the road again, but this time saw no sign of Matt and Molly. Their resolve to find them didn't stretch further.

"They've gone, Chuck. I think I'll go back to bed."

"Okay," said Chuck. "I think I'll go back to the pub. I only came out to see how you were, and there you were talking to a stranger. Good night, Desmond, I'll see you later."

Desmond bid Chuck a good night and climbed back into the van whilst Chuck made the short trip back to the Nag's Head.

*

Matt and Molly had turned off the main road and hurried down a side road, walking as fast as they could without breaking into a trot. They dare not look back.

"So that was your natural charm, Matt," said Molly as they carried on walking. "I'm glad I haven't been on the receiving end of that!"

"It worked though, didn't it?" he replied, in defence of Molly's critical assessment. "And did you like the question? 'Where's the nearest pub?' That threw him completely."

Molly had to agree that asking a ridiculous question somehow stunned Desmond long enough for her to carry out the scan.

Both were looking for the earliest opportunity to turn away from the side road when Molly spotted a narrow pathway up ahead on the right. They quickly headed down the pathway and had a quick look around to ensure no one was approaching. Molly dug out her device into which she punched a series of digits and they disappeared, heading back to Hamburg.

*

The following morning at nine o'clock precisely Desmond stirred. He'd had a good night's sleep and had settled quickly following the disturbance from the stranger asking directions to the nearest pub. Apart from answering a brief call of nature in the early hours, which involved a short journey to a suitable bush, he had slept undisturbed for a further twelve hours. He didn't even stir when Chuck rolled into the back of the van at closing time.

Chuck was still fast asleep, but Desmond was anxious to get moving. "Are you awake?" he asked. "Chuck, are you awake?" he repeated.

"No!"

Ignoring Chuck's response Desmond asked, "When are we going to leave for New York?"

"After breakfast," came the muffled reply from under Chuck's blanket.

Fifteen minutes later they were on the road heading into Ascot on the lookout for a suitable cafe. Having located one, a typical 'greasy spoon' near an industrial estate on the outskirts, they both ordered a large fry-up and discussed their next move.

"Don't you want to go home, Desmond?" asked Chuck.

"Yes, but I'm not quite sure how to get there. I know I live in Middlesham, Cavendish Crescent actually. I also know I need to get to the year 2000 but I can't remember exactly when. Do you know how to get there, Chuck?"

"Sorry Desmond. I know how to time travel, and I can get back to where I came from, but unless I know the date you came from it's going to be very difficult. If the song we choose is near enough from the time you want it will somehow find the right time we're looking for, but it's a big risk."

"Okay, so let's worry about getting me back home when I remember a bit more," said Desmond. "I'm sure it'll all come back to me soon. In the meantime, let's go to New York. I really think we should make sure John doesn't get shot."

"In that case, let's get back to the van and get the radio fired up," said Chuck with a degree of enthusiasm.

Chuck had parked the van amongst other similar-looking vans, a couple of trucks, a few HGVs, and a skip. They jumped in and Desmond sat on his suit jacket that he had discarded the previous day in favour of the white safari jacket.

'I won't be needing this anymore," Desmond said, pulling the jacket out from under him. He then opened the door and threw it into the skip, conveniently located adjacent to the passenger door.

Chuck turned on the radio and stared at it for several seconds.

"Go on then," said Desmond. "Let's go."

"Are you sure you want to do this, Desmond? We could be causing big problems."

"Yeah, it can't be that bad, right? Let's do it."

Chuck fiddled with the control knob for about ten minutes, causing Desmond to become increasingly impatient.

"Yes! We're off," said Chuck at last as 'Don't Stand So Close To Me' emitted from the speakers. "Fasten your seatbelt." And after sixty seconds they had left 1971 and were off to New York, or so they believed.

CHAPTER 29

Control Room, Hamburg, 1960

Like an aircraft executing a perfectly smooth landing, Matt and Molly gently reappeared in Bill's apartment outside of the control room.

"You're back," said Bill unnecessarily, emerging from the control room. "How did it go?"

Molly recounted their adventures at the Nag's Head, including the use of Matt's natural charm to lure Desmond from the van. They were sure they managed to remain undetected, and no harm would be done to the timeline.

"Sounds like it was a close encounter but great news that you weren't spotted," said Bill. "When do we get the test results?"

"As soon as I've downloaded the data into the computer," Molly replied, holding up the test kit. "If you'll excuse me, I'll go do it now."

Bill stepped aside to allow Molly to enter the control room and position herself at the computer. He took the opportunity to ask Matt about something on his mind. "Well done, Matt, seems like you've done a good job in distracting Desmond. Did you get a good look at the van? Was it in good condition? I didn't really look at it when we saw it at Abbey Road and, to be fair, I didn't know it was my van at the time. Was there a dent where it hit Desmond?"

Matt smiled at Bill's concern over his van. "I wasn't really looking at the van much, but I didn't notice any major damage. And apart from a scratched head and arm in a sling, there was no major damage to Desmond either, considering he'd been run over; in case you wondered."

"Oh yes, of course. I was about to ask about Desmond," said Bill, sheepishly.

"Right," said Molly, in what could be described as an upbeat tone as she emerged from the control room. "I have the result of the scan. Let's all sit down." She motioned towards Bill's table and chairs. When they were comfortably sat around the table she continued. "As we know, Desmond was injured as a result of the accident. The scan shows a few changes from the Desmond that originally travelled to Abbey Road compared to when we encountered him after the accident and there may even be some memory loss. It appears that we lost track of him because there was such a sudden change. As we're aware, it's only certain people who have the ability to travel in time. They have to have a certain make-up to their composition, their brain waves, their general aura. The same applies for our ability to track them; our tracking equipment only works on people with those qualities. Any major change affects their ability to travel, and it also affects our ability to track them. This is what has happened to Desmond although the accident didn't prevent him travelling to 1971. His distorted signal obviously impacted on the quantum pathways, and he was sent there even though he wasn't even in the van. The impact combined with the song that was playing was enough for him to be seized by the zero-point field."

"But it didn't get Chuck," said Bill.

"No," replied Molly. "The cassette player must have been somehow connected to the radio in your van, Bill. As Chuck was presumably not intending to travel, we can only assume it wasn't supposed to be connected, otherwise he wouldn't have been playing the cassette. As I said, it must have been Desmond's altered condition that caused him to disappear to somewhere else, which as we now know was John Lennon's house in 1971."

"So why haven't we been able to trace Chuck since he stole my van?" asked Bill. "Do you think he's had an accident too?"

"No, he's probably had the shield switched on when in the van, but he must also be one of those small number of people that have some intermittent immunity to the tracing waves. Anyway, he's not necessarily compatible with time travel. Admittedly he must have some of the qualities, otherwise he couldn't have travelled at all. As far as we know though, he's only travelled with the van, and the shield must have been off when he visited Elvis. That must have been one of his earliest trips."

"So you think that was Chuck?" Bill asked, having already made the connection with the white van.

"I think we all know it was Chuck, Bill," confirmed Molly.

"So what are the chances of Desmond getting back to his correct time?" asked Matt, attempting to bring the conversation back to its original theme.

Molly had already anticipated the question. "Well, we know Desmond has since travelled to 1980's New York but that was in the van, with Chuck, which is different from travelling under your own steam, so to speak, but at least we know he can travel which is good. Having said that, after seeing the data, I think he could possibly travel on his own, but I wouldn't want to risk it. Not at the moment anyway. There's more chance of something going wrong and he could end up in the wrong place and time. Whatever happens, we need to get him home, back to the year 2000 as soon as we can, but we'll have to wait until after his 1980 visit to New York. It's safe to assume that Desmond and Chuck will make the journey to New York tomorrow. By 'tomorrow', I mean tomorrow in the 1971 timeline that Matt and I have just visited. That means that Desmond would have been away from Middlesham for up to two days in his real time, depending on when they leave for New York. That only gives us a maximum of one further day to get him back."

"Wow!" interjected Bill. "This is beginning to get a bit complicated. Even for my large brain."

"Well if your large brain had remembered to lock your van, we wouldn't be in this situation," said Matt.

"Fair enough. Do you think there's a chance we can get my van back?" Bill asked them both.

"We should get your van back, Bill," said Molly, giving Bill a glimmer of hope. "We should also see it as an opportunity to get some control over Chuck who has been able to do as he pleases and is no doubt unaware of the possible damage he is doing.

"If we get my van back he won't be able to travel by the sound of it," said Bill.

"Possibly not," conceded Molly.

"Molly," said Matt. "What happened when you met Desmond in New York then? We haven't heard much about that. Also," he continued with his next question, "what happens next? Have we got a plan for getting Desmond home? We can't rely on Chuck getting him back and Desmond seems to have gone rogue."

"I do have a plan, Matt," she replied, ignoring the question about what happened in New York, "and it will get Desmond home. It also involves getting Bill's van back. I'd also like to tell Nigel, Penelope, and Brian about the plan and that's where I'm headed next. Anyone coming?"

CHAPTER 30

Middlesham, November 2000

Molly allowed some real time, from Nigel, Penelope, and Brian's perspective, to pass before she made her return to Middlesham, this time accompanied by Bill and Matt. In the hour since she had left and returned to Hamburg, they had decided to get the Monopoly out, agreeing that it would keep their minds occupied. Penelope and Nigel had the usual exchange about cheating. Nigel promised not to cheat and declared himself banker. Penelope and Brian were too apathetic to argue, deciding that the predicament surrounding Desmond was more important.

"Don't be ridiculous, Nigel," said Penelope, "you can't fine Brian for moving the wrong piece; he obviously thought he was the Scottie dog."

"Well, I don't see how you can confuse it with the top hat; they're completely different."

"I'm not paying a fine, Nige," interjected Brian forcefully. "I never agreed to your fine system, and any rule changes—"

"Enhancements," interrupted Nigel.

"… have to be unanimously agreed," continued Brian.

"Well Desmond would have voted for it."

"Well Desmond's not here. And I think he would have voted against it. What do you think, Pen?"

"He would have voted against it. Brian, put Nigel's Scottie

dog back where it was and make your move with the top hat," ordered Penelope. "Then it's your go, Nige."

Brian complied and Nigel grudgingly agreed to have his go. He was about to roll the dice when the doorbell rang.

They all stopped and looked at each other. "Desmond," they said in unison.

This time, before rushing to the front door, Penelope moved the curtain aside and peered through the window. "It's not Desmond. It's Molly and she's brought a couple of friends," she said with an air of disappointment.

"I'll get the door," said Brian.

"Nige, you get a couple of chairs from the kitchen. And put the kettle on while you're there," ordered Penelope.

Nigel was about to protest but then thought better of it. He knew there was no point in arguing when Penelope was in her organising frame of mind.

Brian led Molly into the lounge. Bill and Matt followed her in like a couple of security personnel. Nigel joined them, dragging two folding chairs behind him.

"You've met Bill before," said Molly with a wave of her right hand towards Bill. "And this is Matt, who you've heard about," she said, waving her left hand in his direction.

They exchanged greetings and all took their seats, Molly in the spare comfy chair and Bill and Matt taking the kitchen chairs.

"We've got an update for you," began Molly, "and Bill and Matt have also come along to share the news."

"Where's Desmond?" asked Penelope, cutting to the chase, anxious for further news.

"The good news is," began Molly, "the transmitter has worked, and we have located Desmond. He's in 1971, near

John Lennon's house. Tittenhurst Park, Ascot."

"What's he doing there?" asked Nigel.

Before Molly could answer, Brian put forward his suggestion. "He's obviously gone to visit John Lennon. Why else would he be near John Lennon's house?"

"Yes, he probably has," agreed Molly. "We've deduced that he must have been transported there as a result of the accident. He couldn't have decided to go there himself as he was hit by the van which was no doubt playing a song from that era and the quantum pathways were somehow distorted by the impact and he was seized by the zero-point field."

"So why haven't you brought him back?" asked Penelope, unfazed by the technical jargon. "Is he too badly injured?"

"Not necessarily," Molly answered. "He is injured but he can travel. In fact, he's about to go to New York. Remember when I said that I saw him in New York, you know, with the arm in a sling? Well, he's about to go there from 1971, with Chuck who's also in 1971 with him. We have to let that play out otherwise it will cause complications with the timelines. We also have to wait until he gets there in our real time. We can't jump ahead of what the transmitter is telling us but hopefully it won't be too long."

Penelope was processing the latest response from Molly. "So, he's not alone in 1971? Is that a good thing? I suppose it is. And he can't come back here until after he's been to New York in 1980. Okay, I think I understand," she concluded.

Molly went on to update them all on her trip with Matt to see Desmond in Ascot, 1971. She confirmed that Chuck and the van were there with Desmond and that he was sleeping in the van when they encountered him. She explained how, between them, they were able to carry out the TTCT. She also advised them that the test result indicated some change to Desmond's cellular makeup which made it imperative that she and her time agents should be there to transport him back from wherever and whenever he goes after New York. She also reminded them that they could lose some of the accuracy of Desmond's arrival time owing to the change in Desmond, but she was confident they would get him back. She didn't expand on the need to get him back within a day of his arrival in New York, feeling that there was no need to cause additional anxiety to an already difficult situation.

"So, what happens next?" Nigel asked, giving Penelope a break from asking the questions.

"It's simple," Molly continued. Matt looked up and waited earnestly for what was coming next, having been patient since Molly first mentioned the plan back in Hamburg. "We just monitor the transmitter and when Desmond and Chuck leave New York, wherever they go we synchronise our arrival for the same time as them."

Molly's concern over the different timeline that Desmond was about to find himself in was still nagging at the back of her mind, but she decided to remain silent about it. She felt that now wasn't the time to burden them with further doubts about Desmond's situation. Bill and Matt were also still unaware of the alternative timeline, and she knew this had to be rectified soon.

"I wouldn't be surprised if they went on some other time exploration trip," Molly continued. "Who knows?"

She actually had a vague inkling that Desmond and Chuck would be travelling somewhere else before attempting to get Desmond home. She could recall no factual evidence of this, it was more of a hunch based on vague memories of their conversation back in 1980, but felt that, by saying this, it would prepare Desmond's friends for him not being able to come straight back to Middlesham. "The test shows that Desmond's memory may be affected, and his brain waves are indicating a confused state so he may not even know where or when to go, even if he does want to get back. We'll make sure we bring him straight home from wherever he goes."

"Is that it?" asked Matt. "I was expecting something much more elaborate."

"More or less," answered Molly, "apart from, you know, the van and Chuck." She was attempting to be discreet about the supplementary task: regaining Bill's van and preventing Chuck from carrying out further disruptive time travel expeditions. She felt it unnecessary to tell Desmond's friends about Bill's carelessness in having his van stolen by Chuck. "I'm also considering whether or not we also need Bill or Matt there in New York, just in case something goes wrong. It can't be me because I'll already be there, and we can't risk a time loop."

"I'll volunteer to do that bit," said Matt, anxious to get one over on Bill and keep in Molly's good books.

"I think it's better if I do it," said Bill, "I know him better."

"We'll see, it may not be necessary anyway," said Molly non-committedly, although secretly she was thinking that someone needed to be there to monitor their next journey; to make sure they travelled back further in time before attempting to get home. "Now we need to monitor the transmitter so that we know when they leave 1971 and also, more crucially, when they leave 1980. One thing to bear in mind is that Desmond, in his confused state of mind, may not remember Bill and if that's the case there's no guarantee he'll even trust us to get him back. That's why I think we'll need the three of us there, wherever he goes, just in case."

"So we'll grab hold of him! Me and Bill can take an arm each and you, Molly, will operate your device," suggested Matt.

"I was thinking more of a verbal persuasion, Matt, but if necessary I suppose we'll have to use a more physical form of coercion," responded Molly, somewhat deflating Matt's enthusiasm. "Does anyone have any questions?"

"If Bill or Matt are going to New York, why don't they just bring him home from there?" asked Nigel, jumping in before Penelope could ask a question.

"Because I'm already there in that timeline. We can't disrupt it any further by changing things again. We have to let them do what they did, uninterrupted." Molly hoped that the explanation would be sufficiently plausible to satisfy Nigel's inquisitiveness.

Penelope raised her hand as if she was back in the classroom, such was Molly's authoritativeness. "So how long before the transmitter tells us they've left for New York? I don't really understand. Do we have to wait as long as they do before they go there?"

"No, but we do," said Molly, referring to herself and her time agents. "The transmitter only works in linear time. So, we have to wait for them to sleep, get up, and decide to go to 1980. That doesn't mean you have to wait though. We'll go back to 1960, track the transmitter for the next twelve hours or so, or however long it takes. Then we can come back here in your real time with an update, let's say half an hour from when we leave. Does that make sense?"

"Because that's all in the past," proffered Brian, happy to get in on the conversation. "In theory I suppose you could spend years in the past waiting for the transmitter signal but still come right back here now."

"Yes, in theory," came in Bill before Molly could answer, wanting to make himself useful.

"But there's no reason why it shouldn't be more than a few hours. Once they've rested and are ready to go, I'm sure they'll be off," added Matt reassuringly.

"How do you think Desmond will react when he realises it's you who brings him back, Molly?" was Penelope's next question, shifting the focus of the conversation.

"I'm not sure. It'll have been twenty years, in his time, since we met in Bath. He may not be too bothered."

"I think he will, Molly. Try not to get his hopes up," Penelope warned, "seeing as you're not likely to be around afterwards."

"Okay, I'll be careful. The important thing is to get him back safely."

"I wish I could come with you," said Penelope suddenly. "I've known him a long time and even if he is confused, he may be prepared to trust me rather than the three of you when you try to get him home. No offence."

"Yes, well you can't, Pen," said Nigel. "Only Desmond can time travel and you know it. And I've known him longer so if anyone should go with them it should be me."

"I disagree." It was Brian's turn to get in on the discussion. "Me and Desmond are closest, so it should be me."

"Don't be ridiculous," said Penelope for the second time that afternoon, this time to Brian. "We can't all go!"

"Pen, none of us can go. We can't time travel," said Nigel, bringing the discussion back down to earth.

"Well, that may not be entirely true," said Molly. A statement which caused everyone else in the room, including Bill and Matt, to turn quizzically towards her.

CHAPTER 31

En route to Manhattan, New York,

somewhere between 1971 and 1980

Desmond and Chuck experienced a flash of light when the sixty seconds of 'Don't Stand So Close To Me' had passed. If Desmond's brain had been fully recovered, he would have recalled that he always arrived at his new destination instantly. However, on this occasion that wasn't the case. Instead, they experienced a few seconds of a sensation of travelling at an incredible speed, seemingly passing through different shades of light, coupled with a feeling that they were about to crash and die at any point. They then came to a sudden stop following an almost instant deceleration. And the light had gone; it was pitch black.

"Wow!" said a shocked Desmond. "I don't remember anything about my time travelling but I thought what we've just experienced might have rung a bell. What happens next?"

"That doesn't normally happen, Desmond." Chuck was as shocked as Desmond. He searched in the darkness for the internal light switch above the windscreen, switched it on, then sat motionless, staring into the void through the windscreen. "I've no idea where we are."

The radio was silent, 'Don't Stand So Close To Me' had stopped abruptly, as soon as they vanished from 1971.

"What shall we do, Chuck? You're in the driver's seat. Try the lights," Desmond suggested.

Chuck did as suggested. The dipped headlights shed no light on the predicament they faced. Literally nothing was visible ahead of them. Chuck next tried the full beam headlights. Again nothing. He switched a few more switches, the functions of some he wasn't sure but tried them anyway in the hope of something happening. Instead, all he managed to do was to turn off the locater shield. Next, he grabbed the winder for his window, this model of the Transit van being dated long before electric windows.

"Wait Chuck! Don't open it! We could be sucked out into nothingness."

Chuck stopped and stared at Desmond. "Really? I hadn't thought of that. I'll just open it a little bit and see what happens. If it's just a little crack, we won't fit through and I'll get ready to shut it straight away."

Desmond nodded his agreement at the flimsy plan and Chuck proceeded to open the window. Nothing. Feeling more confident, Chuck then opened his door.

"What are you doing, Chuck?" said Desmond in a mild panic. "You can't get out. There's nothing there! You'll disappear into nothingness, and I'll be stuck here on my own. At least with you here I've got someone to talk to."

"Don't worry, Des, I'm not going anywhere. Just thought I'd see what was below us."

He leant out of the door and had a look below then craned his neck to look behind the van. "Nothing there." He closed the door, wound up the window, and stared at the radio.

"While we're here, and assuming we'll eventually get moving," began Desmond after a couple of minutes of silent contemplation, "let's discuss what we're going to do to stop John from being shot. We know that his killer is Mark Chapman and he had made contact with John earlier in the day when he had asked him to sign the LP he was carrying." Desmond again surprised himself with his recollection of the events from the various accounts he had read and seen. He deduced that his memory was still gradually returning, bit by bit. "I can't remember all of the events, but I think the LP he was carrying was recent; probably released a couple of months earlier."

"'Double Fantasy'," said Chuck.

"No, I really think it happened, Chuck. So, what if we wait outside the entrance to the Dakota for Chapman to arrive, or see if we can spot him, as he may already be there of course."

"Okay, so let's assume we see him," said Chuck, attempting to bring some practicality to the situation, "what are we going to do then? Ask him if he would mind not shooting John Lennon?"

"Maybe. It would certainly freak him out a bit, hopefully enough to change his mind."

"But what's to stop him returning another day? He might even decide to shoot us instead!"

"Mmm … you're right, Chuck. Perhaps we need to think this through. What if we take a different approach and speak to John instead?"

"Desmond, imagine how that would make John feel; to be approached by two strangers who tell him he's about to be shot. He'd probably get us arrested."

"No, he wouldn't, he knows us," protested Desmond. "We only saw him yesterday."

"That was nine years ago, or it will be if we ever get to

1980," Chuck reminded him.

"Oh yes, that's right. I keep forgetting about this time travel business. Of course, that's why we're going there. We know the future, or the present as we normally call it when we're not in the past, we've been to the past and now we're on our way to the future of the past we've just been to which is still the past of our present. Right, it's clear in my head now. So, what else can we do?"

Chuck was silent for a moment while he worked out Desmond's analysis. He nodded to himself. "Yes, I think you've got it, Des. Now, 'what else can we do?' you ask. What if we get him arrested somehow?"

Desmond was also silent for a moment while he thought it through. "Yes, good idea, Chuck," he said, breaking the silence, "but how will we do that? We can't just ask the cops to arrest him, they'll just think we're a couple of troublemakers. And anyway, he'll just deny everything and walk away after they've spoken to him. Then he'll come back another day and shoot John Lennon."

"You're right, let's think about this further."

They both sat there in an identical classic thinking pose, their thumbs and forefingers forming a rest for their chins. For a few minutes they had forgotten about their predicament. They had no idea when or if they would ever get out of the darkness that surrounded them. For all they knew, their discussions about how they would handle the situation in New York could be redundant.

"Okay, this is what we do, Chuck," said Desmond, unable to think any further. "We either shoot him, Mark Chapman that is, or we wait until he's about to shoot John and we pounce on him. You know, catch him red-handed, then security and the cops will take over. What do you think?"

Chuck couldn't get past Desmond's first, extreme, idea. "Shoot him! How do you suppose we're going to do that?"

"Yes, I see what you mean. We'll need a gun and I'm not sure how to get one."

"Do you really think you should be handling a gun in your condition, Des?"

"Oh yes, I was thinking you would do the shooting as you're more capable at the moment."

"We'll have to go for the pounce I think," continued Chuck, moving the subject away from the shooting option. "It's risky though. Not only do we have to get close enough, we also have to get the timing right. No good pouncing on him after he's fired the gun."

"Good point. The sooner we get there and case the joint, the better. Let's go!"

Chuck smiled at Desmond's choice of words. "Yes, we need to case the joint, but we have to get there. We're stuck, we can't go anywhere, remember?"

"Oh, put the radio on. And find 'Don't Stand So Close To Me' again. That should do it."

"Why didn't I think of that?" replied Chuck, surprised at Desmond's assertiveness and the simplicity of his suggestion. He did as suggested, and soon found the song on the radio. After sixty seconds there was a loud creaking noise. They lurched forward, stopped, then started again. This time they kept going and sped up to breakneck speed and the lights reappeared. There was a final blinding flash and they emerged in New York. The date was 8th December 1980.

CHAPTER 32

Cavendish Crescent, Middlesham, November 2000

Unbeknownst to Bill and Matt, Molly had been working with other members of the Time Peacekeeping team on experimental time travelling equipment. The equipment consisted of a quantum accelerator, wired into a long, chunky cuff bracelet, which compensated for a lack of time travelling capability, potentially allowing a non-traveller to travel in time. Development had reached an advanced stage and it had already been used to successfully transport a junior time agent to the 1950s and back. This trial had the safety net of the time agent being able to transport themself back should anything had gone wrong but, apart from a few minor accuracy issues, everything went smoothly. They were now in a position to try it out on a normal human – a human without time travel capability. Although the opportunity which now presented itself to Molly came a little earlier than she had anticipated, it did seem to her that it was too good an opportunity to miss. And if she was able to use the equipment on three humans at the same time, this would accelerate the trial process. The reason for commissioning the development in the first place was for situations where a time traveller, for whatever reason, loses the capability to travel. Exactly the situation Desmond could find himself in if his injuries or an extended stay impacted on his time travel capability.

"So we're taking Desmond's friends with us?" was Matt's question after Molly had explained about the quantum accelerator.

"Is that wise?" asked Bill. "We've had enough trouble with Desmond as it is."

"We *are* in the room," Penelope protested. "I think we should have a say in this."

Nigel and Brian nodded in agreement whilst looking towards Molly for reassurance.

"But you were just saying you wouldn't want to go," said Bill

"That was before we knew about Molly's bracelet," replied Penelope. "I was just thinking aloud. I didn't really expect to be able to go. Nor did Nigel and Brian," she advocated on their behalf. Nigel and Brian again nodded in agreement, happy to let Penelope do the talking.

"Why have we not heard of this before, Molly?" demanded Bill.

"We didn't want to worry you about it, Bill. I knew you would be keen to get involved and probably want to try it out, but I really couldn't risk trying it until we were sure it worked."

"Well, I would have liked to have been involved," said Bill with a little hurt in his voice, "but I don't think I would have tried it on three at once."

"Oh, let's give it a go. I'd be happy to risk it on three," said Matt.

"We're still here," Penelope reminded them.

Molly turned towards Penelope, Nigel, and Brian. "What do you think?" she asked, diplomatically. "I think it will be a great opportunity for you. You can't go to New York as I'll need to go with you, and, as you know, I'll already be there. But you can go to the next destination, once we know where and when it is. Then you can help us get Desmond home."

"Well I'd like to give it a go," Brian was the first to confirm his intentions.

"So would I," said Penelope, not wishing to miss out but secretly still harbouring doubts.

Despite Nigel's earlier insistence that it should be him that goes rather than Penelope, his expression betrayed his feelings now that it was being suggested that all three of them go to meet Desmond. "On second thoughts, I think I'll stay if you don't mind. Someone should be here in case Desmond comes back, and I've got to work tomorrow."

"We're not going tomorrow, Nige," answered Brian, "if we're going, we're going today. Am I right, Molly?"

"Yes Brian. When Bill, Matt, and I leave in a few minutes, we'll time our return for about half an hour later. Don't forget, Nigel, that however long it takes us to find Desmond, we can return here any time from when we leave, and you can do the same."

"Okay, let's all go," decided Penelope, ignoring Nigel's reluctance.

"Great!" said Molly.

"Great!" said Bill and Matt, slightly less enthusiastically.

Molly explained what would happen next. She would call back home and pick up the equipment while Bill and Matt returned to Hamburg. No one knew exactly where 'home' was for Molly, and no one felt inclined to ask. She would then join Bill and Matt and wait for the transmitter signal. Bill, she had decided, would travel to New York to keep track of Desmond and Chuck as soon as the signal came through.

When Bill had left for New York she would return, with Matt, to Cavendish Crescent where she would ensure the quantum accelerator bracelets were fitted correctly before they all left to find Desmond.

"Gosh, how exciting!" Penelope was now completely sold on the idea.

Nigel appeared to have overcome his doubts and was also now feeling more confident about their time travel, as was Brian.

"See you in half an hour then," said Molly. "Bill, Matt, come on. I'll fill you in on New York when we get back."

CHAPTER 33

Manhattan, New York, December 1980

"Are we there yet, Chuck?" asked Desmond, glad to be back in daylight and gazing through the windscreen down West 73rd Street. It was 10.45 a.m. and the van had arrived on the left-hand side of what turned out to be a fairly quiet stretch of road at the rear of the Dakota Apartments, the much busier Central Park West being thirty yards behind them. "Looks like we managed to escape from our stay in the black hole or whatever it was," he added.

"I think we're here, Desmond," said Chuck, staring at the dashboard. "New York, and I'm assuming it's the day John Lennon is due to get shot."

"What do you think it was, Chuck, the darkness? You said that hasn't happened before. It's as though we got stuck part way here. But where were we?"

"I don't know. Maybe we just got stuck in the time tunnel."

"There's no such thing as a time tunnel, Chuck," said Desmond immediately. "It's more about the quantums," he added, surprising himself again with his recollections.

"How do you know that and what do you mean by 'the quantums'?"

"I'm not sure, I just know it's not a time tunnel. Someone must have told me."

"Well, at least we're here, never mind how we got here. Maybe the stop on the way is something you can ask your time buddy about if you ever see him again."

Chuck had filled Desmond in on the details of the accident and how Bill and someone called Matt had come to ask him questions and how this panicked him, resulting in him driving off to avoid risking losing his van.

"Good idea, I'll ask Bill. Now shall we go and have a look around?" Desmond was becoming impatient to 'case the joint'.

Chuck had a quick check of the van controls, noticed that the locater shield had been switched off, and switched it on again. *Can't be too careful,* he thought to himself. "Out you get, Des," he said as he fiddled around in the glove compartment. "Just making sure I've got everything we need."

They stepped out of the van, Chuck locked it up and they made their way towards the main street behind them. On Central Park West they turned to the right alongside the imposing Victorian Renaissance-styled exterior of the Dakota Apartments.

"Here it is, Chuck," said Desmond, recognising the iconic building from the many accounts of Lennon's death, gradually returning to his memory.

It was a cold, crisp, winter's day. The street was busy with traffic and pedestrians. Desmond, having left his safari jacket in the van, was feeling the cold, his good arm wrapped around his body clutching his upper left arm still in its sling as they strolled towards the corner of Central Park West and West 72nd Street. They walked in silence, looking out for anyone who could possibly be Mark David Chapman. Neither recalled exactly what he looked like, but they figured their best chance of seeing him was to look for a man with an LP under his arm. They both gazed up at the impressive facade of the building as they reached the corner and turned right down West 72nd Street towards the arched entrance, just over halfway along the eastern side.

As they approached, they were watched by Molly Parks from the window of a cafe on the opposite side of the road, just down from the Majestic Hotel. The alert she had received back at her headquarters had indicated that John Lennon's timeline was about to be compromised. It came from a static position somewhere in the 1970s which was unusual. Her subsequent journey on the way to 1980's New York had not gone smoothly. There had been a delay, a delay which caused her to briefly become suspended in a void between timelines. She had been heading for the timeline in which former Beatle John Lennon was murdered at 10.50 p.m. on 8th December outside of the Dakota Apartments. The timeline in which she eventually arrived, after extracting herself from the void by restarting her travel device, was a different one. This timeline had followed a different path. It started in 1971 following a visit from Desmond Jones to Tittenhurst Park in Ascot. There were several 'nudges' during the visit that had eventually led to a new timeline being created, the most prominent one being Desmond's comments to Lennon's handyman Robert, warning him of Lennon's pending murder in 1980. As Desmond and Chuck had also found, the fracture in the timeline wall was of such magnitude that both they and Molly had passed through it.

She took a sip of coffee from her huge yellow cup and continued to watch as a woman of about 30, bespectacled with longish light brown hair and carrying a rectangular bag over her shoulder, approached from the left of the arched entrance to the Dakota. She paused in front of the guard box next to the entrance and the doorman emerged. She then spoke to him for a few seconds. He returned to the box and briefly picked up the phone.

Molly deduced from the signal she was receiving on her device that the person who had sparked the original warning signal on their way to New York was one of the two men who had paused on the other side of the entrance to the Dakota. The signal she was now receiving, however, was not a warning signal, it was merely indicating that there was someone there who didn't belong in this time.

As the doorman made his call, Desmond caught Molly's interest as he appeared to call out to the woman with the bag over her shoulder. The woman smiled briefly and held her bag closer as the doorman emerged from his box and beckoned her into the building, passing through the gates at the rear of the archway. Molly recognised her as photographer Annie Lebovitch who was on her way to photograph the Lennons.

"Why did you say that, Desmond?" asked Chuck. "There must be people going in and out of here all day."

"Yes, but did you hear what she said? I'm sure she mentioned John and Yoko to the doorman. Something about photography. So, I just asked her if she was going to see John Lennon. I thought she might be able to introduce us, or rather reintroduce us. Then we could warn him about ..."

"Well you certainly spooked her Des," said Chuck, not really noticing that Desmond had stopped mid-sentence. "I'm not surprised she ignored us. She probably thought you were some kind of weirdo. Anyway, I thought we had decided to pounce on Chapman and get him arrested rather than approach John."

Desmond had stopped talking and stopped listening. His attention had been caught by a man a little further down the street, leaning against the wall of the building. He was holding an LP in his left hand and was staring at it intensely. In his other hand he held a book.

Molly's gaze followed Desmond's, and her focus also stopped at the sight of the man with the LP. *That's him*, she told herself, *Mark Chapman*. She ordered another coffee from the inquisitive waitress, hanging around at her table in a prime spot by the window, then she re-focussed on the scene across the street. There were a few other people hanging around near to the Dakota entrance; a bearded man with a camera, a young couple chatting and occasionally glancing towards the arched entrance, no doubt waiting for a glimpse of, or even an opportunity to chat to the former Beatle, John Lennon.

"Chuck, Chuck, do you think that's him?" asked Desmond, patting Chuck several times on the arm whilst nodding down the street towards the man with the LP. "Shall we pounce on him?"

Chuck took in the scene a little further down the street. "I think we should just wait and observe," was his reasoned response. He glanced across the street towards the cafe where Molly was sitting. "Let's go over there and grab a coffee, I'll treat you. I always carry a few dollars around with me as I never know when I'm going to be back in the States. If we get a table by the window we can observe, you know, just see what's going on for a while, while we decide how we're going to approach the situation."

"Good idea. We can case the joint from there."

Molly watched as they made their way across the street to the cafe. The large single window made it an ideal place to view what was going on. The wrought iron table and chairs were not the most comfy, but the bright yellow cushions, matching the cups, added some degree of cosiness. The walls, white, adorned with large images of coffee pots ensured that no one could be mistaken as to what sort of establishment this was. *This*, she thought, *could be an ideal opportunity to speak to them about what they're doing here.* The cafe wasn't busy. Apart from Molly there were only a couple of occupied tables. There was a vacant table to her right, next to the entrance. Desmond and Chuck entered the cafe and immediately sat at the table, Desmond with his back to her and Chuck to his right. The waitress, dressed in a bright yellow dress, appeared from nowhere at the same instant they sat down. She took their order of coffee and cakes whilst they made themselves comfortable. Chuck found a pencil in his pocket and scribbled something on a napkin which he then slid across to Desmond. 'I think Stevie Nicks is behind you' it read.

CHAPTER 34

Control Room, Hamburg, 1960

Bill and Matt sat huddled around the main screen waiting for a signal from the transmitter whilst Molly sat at a small screen in the corner making calculations.

"I can't believe they haven't left 1971 yet," said Bill. "Why is the transmitter still saying they're in Ascot? By their linear time it's halfway through the next day."

They had been studying the screen in shifts, waiting for the transmitter to indicate that Desmond had moved to 1980, but nothing had happened. After a twelve-hour wait, they all reconvened in the control room to decide what to do in the event that no signal was received.

Molly joined them, having completed her calculations. "It's not moved. The transmitter. The calculations show that it's been in exactly the same place for at least the last few hours without moving an inch, which means Desmond isn't wearing the jacket. It could mean they've wandered off somewhere and left the jacket behind, or there was always the chance that he didn't take it with him to 1980. We'll give them a bit longer but then I think we'll need to send you, Bill, to New York with a new transmitter. Then Matt and I will get back to Cavendish Crescent with the bracelets." She nodded towards a rucksack on a chair in the corner. "There is a minor problem, however. It's a different 1980."

Bill and Matt looked at one another then looked back at Molly for an explanation.

"What I haven't told you is that when I was in New York, I had passed through a fracture on the way and ended up in a different timeline. Things got very mixed up around then and although the warning I had received related to a possible interference with John Lennon's timeline, which ended in 1980, both Desmond and I had passed through the fracture and ended up in the same place, which wasn't where we were supposed to be. I had to keep a very close eye on things because in that timeline John Lennon is still alive. He wasn't murdered by Mark Chapman."

"Wow! How will Bill get to the other 1980?" Matt asked with genuine concern. "I know time agents have done it before, but it sounds like it could be treacherous."

"Thanks Matt," said Bill. "So how do I get to another timeline, Molly?"

"Well, it can be treacherous," said Molly, failing to calm Bill's increasing nervousness. "But it can be done. It involves precise timing though. As we know, we move between times in an instant but what you will have to do is cross the timeline partway through that instant."

"How will Bill manage to do that?" asked Matt.

"You'll have to slow down the process, Bill, using a device," Molly replied.

"Not another device!" said Matt.

"Yes, another device. It's a very complex piece of equipment which pauses the quantum reflex. It will enable you to locate a passage through to alternative realities caused by split timelines. We have to calibrate it to pause at the right point which, in your case, Bill, will be just over halfway to

1980. As the timeline you want to get to started in 1971, that's eleven years from now. The device will indicate the correct passage. You then just need to make sure you head that way. Coming back is less complicated. You just go back to a time before the split in 1971. When you travel forward again, you'll be on the original timeline."

"I see," said Bill. "Seems straightforward enough. This passage you talk about sounds a bit like a tunnel, a time tunnel."

"There's no such thing as a time tunnel, Bill, as well you know. It's a passage. Just make sure you choose the right one, otherwise you'll end up somewhere else," warned Molly. "The worst-case scenario is that you end up in a time void, but let's not go there."

"Yes, let's not," agreed Bill.

"Of course, there is a possibility we could still trace them without the transmitter, but I don't want to leave too much to chance."

"How do you mean?" asked Matt.

"Well, I didn't know at the time, but the warning I received to prompt me to visit 1980 couldn't have come from Desmond. We know we can't pick up his signal because of his altered state, so it must have come from Chuck. For some reason, perhaps by accident even, he must have switched off the shield in the van. Otherwise, I wouldn't have received the warning, would I?"

"So by sending Bill with the transmitter we're doubling our chances of locating Desmond. Yes, I see. Definitely worth the risk of sending Bill."

"Thanks Matt," said Bill.

"You're welcome. So how long are we going to give it

before Bill goes?"

Molly delved into her many layers of dress and produced another small, rectangular black box. "I have the device right here. I can calculate the calibrations, show you how it works, and you can then go when you're ready, Bill."

"How many more devices have you got under there, Molly?" asked Matt.

"I like to be prepared, I am the Time Peacekeeper," she reminded them.

"So how did John Lennon not get shot?" asked Bill, returning to Molly's earlier revelation. "Was Desmond actually involved in John Lennon's survival?"

"You'll see," she replied curtly, not wishing to divulge more details at this stage. Bill and Matt knew better than to press Molly for more information.

"Okay, let's do it," said Bill, getting back to the task in hand. "And I'll meet you at … well, wherever they go next."

Molly and Bill sat huddled together for the next half hour while Molly did her calculations and gave occasional instructions to Bill. Matt continued to monitor the screen for signs of a signal from the transmitter which, unbeknownst to them, was still lying abandoned in a skip.

"Right, I'm almost ready," said Bill. He was holding the device, staring at its tiny screen. "I just need to change into my disguise."

"We'll leave you to it then," said Molly, beckoning Matt to follow her out of the control room, picking up the rucksack on the way. "See you after New York, Bill. Good luck!" She closed the door behind them, leaving Bill to depart for an alternative timeline, dressed as a hippy.

"Come on, Matt, let's get back to Middlesham."

CHAPTER 35

Manhattan, New York, December 1980

Desmond's eyes darted from side to side as if this in some way might enable him to see the lady behind him; the lady who Chuck seemed to think was Stevie Nicks. He hadn't noticed her when they walked in, his gaze remaining on the other side of the street just in case he missed something.

"Who's Stevie Nicks?" he asked, his memory still failing him in some areas.

"Never mind. Maybe it'll come back to you later when you get a chance to have a look. I'll get her autograph before she goes though."

"Sorry to disappoint you, but I'm not Stevie Nicks," said the lady behind Desmond, having overheard their brief conversation, "but I'm happy to give you my autograph."

"Oh, er, yes okay then," said Chuck, taken a little by surprise.

He dug out his autograph book from his pocket, found a blank page, and handed it to Molly along with a pen he kept close to the book, half hoping that he would see Stevie Nicks' autograph appear. Desmond had turned his chair sideways so as not to appear rude to the lady who apparently looked like Stevie Nicks, *whoever she is*, he thought. He noticed the name 'Molly Parks' as she handed the book back to Chuck and this stirred a faint memory, but he couldn't place her so decided that perhaps she looked like somebody he knew. *Maybe I do know Stevie Nicks*, he thought to himself.

"Do you mind if I ask why you're here?" she asked as their beverages and cakes arrived.

Desmond thought this seemed rather nosey, coming from a complete stranger, and he immediately adopted a defensive attitude. "Only if you tell us what you're doing here, Molly Parks," he countered.

Chuck raised an eyebrow, taken aback by Desmond's show of assertiveness.

"I'm here to keep an eye on you two. I look after things and there's something I need to look after today."

Desmond and Chuck looked at each other, both trying to make sense of Molly's cryptic statement.

"And what is it you're looking after exactly?" asked Chuck.

Molly decided to come right out with it. She knew that at least one of her two companions were not from this time.

"Let's not beat about the bush. At least one of you is a time traveller and as you're together I guess it's both of you. You've come here to prevent John Lennon from being murdered. Am I correct?"

"Yes!" answered Desmond who was too shocked to answer any differently.

Molly went on to explain that her job was to maintain the timelines and prevent additional parallel timelines opening up where possible, as well as looking after her time agents and working on a number of research and development projects. This they seemed to accept without too much doubt as they were both familiar with the concept of being able to time travel, even if they didn't understand it. Chuck was looking a little worried, however, as he was thinking that someone had finally caught up with him after all his time travel escapades. He made a mental note to himself not to divulge any unnecessary information to this Stevie Nicks lookalike. Desmond, on the other hand, was fine with it as he could remember very little about his travels prior to arriving in John Lennon's house.

She then went on to tell them about the timeline they were in, that they had passed through a fracture and crossed into an alternative timeline, an alternate existence. They had no real understanding of alternative timelines and fractures but were able to make some sense of this as it seemed to explain the break they had experienced on their journey to 1980.

"So what's the difference," asked Desmond, "between the two timelines?"

"John Lennon is still alive. If we follow this timeline linearly, up until before the future, John Lennon is still making music."

"What do you mean 'before the future'?" asked Chuck.

"I mean as far as linear time has got. The future hasn't happened yet. Well, your future hasn't."

"Yes, yes, never mind that, Chuck, it's all too confusing to think about at the moment but Molly said John Lennon is still alive. How about that!? So, Mark Chapman doesn't murder him. There's no need for us to be here!"

"Unfortunately, I think there is … sorry I don't know your name."

"I'm Desmond. And this is Chuck, but you know that already as you heard me call him Chuck."

"Yes, I did," confirmed Molly. "Hello Desmond and Chuck. I'm Molly."

"Yes, you are. You're Molly. How did I know that?"

Desmond asked.

"Because you saw my autograph and you've already referred to me by my name a couple of times."

"But I know you. I know you from somewhere, I'm sure. I've had an accident and lost a lot of memories. But they're coming back."

"We've never met," confirmed Molly, "but time can be funny like that."

"So why do we need to be here?" asked Chuck, getting back to Molly's earlier point. "If Mark Chapman doesn't murder John Lennon, there's nothing for us to do."

"We are meant to be here, aren't we, Molly?" said Desmond. "I don't know why I know this but sometimes a time traveller is there to ensure things happen to maintain accuracy of the timeline. Maybe Bill told me."

"You know Bill?"

"Apparently. I think so anyway," confirmed Desmond.

"Okay," said Molly, parking this information. "And yes, you're right by the way. I'm pretty sure you're meant to be here. Mark Chapman's intentions haven't been affected by the split in timelines. You need to prevent him from killing John Lennon."

"Right," said Desmond thoughtfully. "So we still need to pounce on him, Chuck. Or you do, more accurately. I've got a bad arm."

Chuck was about to protest but his attention was drawn to the other side of the street where some activity was taking place. The man with the beard who was carrying a camera was approached by the man they concluded was Mark Chapman. Desmond, Chuck, and Molly watched as the two men chatted. The bearded man, Molly informed her companions, was probably Paul Goresh, a man who was well acquainted with John Lennon as a result of his regular stints outside of the Dakota, waiting for a chat or the opportunity to take pictures.

"Mark Chapman is asking him about John Lennon," she informed them, having thoroughly researched the events of the day. "He's just wondering if he thinks he'll be coming out of the apartment so that he can sign the album."

Molly had decided that the best course of action was to let the day play out. She had deduced that this timeline must be governed by determinism, so whatever actions Desmond and Chuck took were supposed to happen. She explained to Desmond and Chuck what was due to happen for the next few hours.

They decided to work a rota system for keeping watch on events across the street, just to ensure things happened as expected. They each took in turns to go outside for fresh air and exercise whilst the others stayed in the cafe for food and drinks. The next point of interest which Molly had correctly predicted was a radio crew arriving to interview Lennon.

"He's from RKO Radio," Molly reliably informed Desmond who was still sat to her right on the next table whilst Chuck was out for a stroll. They watched them enter the building through the archway, stopping to chat to a fan apparently asking them about its most famous resident.

They chatted until Chuck came back a half hour later. Desmond asked questions about Molly's job with Molly providing information about suitability for time travel and how it was important that time travellers should only be away for a limited amount of time. This didn't seem to register with Desmond, that he might need to get back home before too long, perhaps because he wasn't quite sure exactly when in the year 2000 he needed to go.

"I think I'd like to go on another adventure with you, Chuck," he stated as Chuck took his seat next to Desmond. "You know, when we've dealt with all this John Lennon business. I'm getting better; my memory is coming back, and I think by the time we've been somewhere else I might even know when exactly I need be in the year 2000. And Molly, I know you said we've never met but I knew a Molly once, I'm sure of it. It obviously can't be you though, can it, because I know it was a long time ago and you're quite young?"

Molly was about to explain the difference between the way age works in her world and the linear age process that Desmond was familiar with, when Chuck drew their attention to another Lennon-related incident across the street.

"Look, look!" he called out enthusiastically, pointing to Mark Chapman shaking the hand of a young boy of about five years old, accompanied by a woman holding the child's other hand. "That's Sean, John's son, and their nanny. That's what you told us would happen, Molly. You are clever!"

"It's already happened. Well, in a different timeline, but it seems to be the same so far. All I had to do was read up on it."

"It's still impressive, Molly," said Desmond. "You're cool!" Desmond wasn't usually one to use the word 'cool', but it seemed fitting. Molly smiled and made a mental note to find out more about this man she found to be both likeable and intriguing, a stranger until a few hours ago.

"Thanks, Desmond," she said. "Keep watching because I think you'll find that the next point of interest will be John Lennon signing Mark Chapman's copy of the LP."

"Would that be a good time for Chuck to pounce on him do you think?" Desmond asked.

"I think it may be better for you to do it later," suggested Molly, "if indeed a pounce is the right option. John has an appointment at The Record Plant, and it would be a pity to disrupt too much of his day."

"It would be more of a pity if he got shot while we're here stuffing our faces," Desmond countered.

"He won't get shot now, Desmond. Everything has panned out as expected so far. It's better if things stay closer to the way it happened in the other timeline. It's your choice though. You're supposed to be here, I'm not."

They watched and waited. Annie Leibovitz left the building at 3.30 and about an hour later John and Yoko appeared. They saw Lennon sign the LP, then, after their car failed to turn up, watched them jump into the radio station's car, cadging a lift to the recording studio.

"That's it now until 10.50 tonight," said Molly. "You need to prevent the murder by then. I can't interfere so I probably won't hang around."

Desmond looked a little disappointed at this news but decided to concentrate on the job in hand. "We'll have a chat with John before Chapman gets to him," he suggested. "You know, warn him somehow. Hopefully he'll remember us and take us seriously. That way you may not have to pounce but we'll need to keep an eye on Chapman."

"Sounds okay to me," said Chuck, seemingly relieved that he may not have to pounce on Mark Chapman.

"Sounds good to me too," added Molly, although concerned about a lack of a proper strategy. "You two work out your plan, I'm going for a walk in Central Park before it gets too dark. I'll be around here somewhere, just in case, but I'm going to keep out of the way. It's been great meeting you."

They said their goodbyes and Molly left the cafe while Desmond looked forlornly on. "I wonder if I'll ever see her again," he said.

CHAPTER 36

Middlesham, November 2000

At 6.00 p.m. Molly, armed with the rucksack of quantum accelerator cuff bracelets and Matt, rang the doorbell of number eight Cavendish Crescent. They had arrived in Desmond's porch, not wanting to alarm Nigel, Penelope, and Brian by making a sudden appearance in the living room, even if the device had allowed it. Brian let them in, and they took their usual seats.

Molly told them that they had received no signal from the transmitter and that they had sent Bill to 1980. She then picked out one of the bracelets from the bag on the floor by her feet.

"This," she declared, "is the quantum accelerator bracelet. Who wants to try it on first?"

"Me, me! Please, please, me!" cried Penelope, again raising her hand like an overly enthusiastic schoolgirl.

Nigel and Brian couldn't compete with such enthusiasm and conceded that Penelope was going to be first so sat back and watched the demonstration. The bulky bracelet was six inches long and about half an inch thick, full of wires and circuits covered in black plastic and a small screen. There were four clips, spaced out along the length opposite a hinge which enabled the bracelet to be opened and then clipped into place on Penelope's left wrist. Along the length there were a series of buttons and dials which, Molly explained, needed to be used in a specific order. She next handed Nigel and Brian a bracelet each and helped them attach them securely to their wrists.

"As soon as we know where and when to go, Matt and I will program the coordinates and synchronise your equipment with my device. It's probably best if we all hold hands."

Nigel took Penelope's hand. "What are you doing, Nigel?" she asked, pulling her hand away. "She means when we actually travel."

"Oh yes, of course. I'm just a bit nervous," Nigel replied sheepishly while Brian giggled.

"Yes, when we travel, Nigel," confirmed Molly. "Because the concept, and the equipment for that matter, is new, holding hands will give us an extra layer of security in case of any discrepancies in the data or any equipment malfunctions. I'll set a ten-second delay on the device before we all hold hands."

"I see," said Nigel. "Is that likely to happen then?"

"I'm sure it'll be fine," Molly reassured him. "It's just a precaution. Now, Matt will explain what happens when we get there and how we'll get back."

"Yes," said Matt, happy to get involved. "We'll all arrive together. Then Molly and I will quickly assess the situation. Hopefully Desmond will recognise you all and be happy to see you. Then, as soon as we can, depending on the situation we're in, we bring Desmond back with us. We'll all travel together, holding hands." He looked towards Nigel. "Not now, Nigel," he added.

"What about Bill?" asked Brian. "Won't he be there with us?"

"Yes, Bill will be there, but he has another task to complete so he'll travel back separately." She went on to tell them the story of Bill's van and how Chuck stole it from him. "So Bill will be reclaiming his van and delivering Chuck to … somewhere."

"Oh, I see," said Penelope. "So, if Bill hadn't had his van stolen, none of this would have happened."

"That's right, Penelope," answered Matt. "I've already reminded him of that."

"Yes, Bill is fully aware of that," said Molly, "but now he's got the opportunity to get his van back and confront Chuck who we're pretty sure was also the autograph hunter who almost ran over Elvis."

"And now we just have to wait for the signal to see where they go next," continued Matt. "As before, the transmitter only works in linear time, so Molly is going to go back and wait for the signal for a few hours then she'll come straight back here."

Nigel, Penelope, and Brian sat in silence for a moment, taking in all the news and contemplating the fact that they were really going to travel in time.

Nigel was next to speak. "So how long will you be, Molly?" he asked.

"I'll come back in fifteen minutes. It'll give Matt time to get you all fitted up and prepared. See you soon." She went out into the hall, closing the door behind her.

*

Exactly fifteen minutes later she came back through the door. "Right. I know where we're going. I've got a feeling you're going to love it!"

CHAPTER 37

Manhattan, New York, 8 December 1980

Bill arrived in West 73rd Street shortly after Molly left the cafe. He was directly in front of the transit van, pleased that the time travel mechanism's built-in people detector had worked and there was no one around. He was wearing the hippy disguise he wore to Abbey Road with the addition of a blue greatcoat he had grabbed as he prepared to leave Hamburg which he felt would shield him from the cold. In addition to the outfit, he felt confident that the wig and dark glasses made him practically unrecognisable. He tried the door of the van, just in case it was unlocked with the key inside. Unfortunately, Chuck proved to be more security conscious than Bill so he resigned himself to the fact that he would have to wait a little longer to reclaim his van.

His instructions were to plant the new transmitter on Desmond without him knowing. He knew he shouldn't interact with either Desmond or Chuck as he wasn't supposed to be there. The problem of ensuring that Desmond's next journey was back in time before 1971 before trying to get home was his main concern, and he wasn't sure exactly how he was going to do that.

He moved out from the front of the van, intending to make his way along towards Central Park West. He stopped abruptly when he saw Desmond walking towards him. He quickly did an about-turn and walked in the opposite direction, crossing the road after a few steps. He took cover behind a small truck parked a little further along and chanced a peek towards the Transit van where he saw Desmond lean into the passenger door and pick up a white jacket. *Good to see you, Desmond, old friend,* he thought to himself whilst fighting back the urge to run over and give him a hug. For a split second he also thought about taking the opportunity to get his van back but quickly dismissed the thought. *All in good time.*

Desmond quickly put on the jacket and made his way back up the road. Bill gave him a few seconds before following him from the other side of the road. *So, Desmond's got a new jacket. Probably explains the transmitter signal still coming from 1971. He's obviously left his suit jacket there.*

Bill reached the corner of Central Park West and West 72nd Street and leant against the wall of the Dakota Apartments whilst surveying the scene. He watched as a figure emerged from the cafe across the street and join Desmond who had stopped outside of the Dakota. *And there's Chuck,* he confirmed to himself. He continued to watch as they approached the bearded man with the camera who was still hanging around several hours after Molly had recognised him as Paul Goresh. He watched while they had a quick word with him before they posed together for a picture. *Typical Desmond,* thought Bill, *can't resist having his picture taken.*

The next few hours passed very slowly from Bill's point of view. It was a cold December evening and he wished he had timed his arrival for later. Molly had briefed him on the series of events up until the time Lennon arrived back from the recording studio much later in the evening, so he was pretty sure nothing of importance was going to happen until then.

She hadn't expanded on any detail, just told him to let it happen and remain calm.

He watched as Desmond and Chuck walked down West 72nd Street away from him, deciding nothing was about to happen for a while. There was no sign of Mark Chapman either, from what Bill could see. *Maybe nothing happens,* he thought. *This is a different timeline after all.* He quickly crossed the street and headed towards the cafe next to the Majestic Hotel.

*

"There must be a bar around here somewhere," said Chuck, who had persuaded Desmond to go for a drink.

They walked for a few minutes before spotting a bar on the corner up ahead of them on the right. "I guess it'll be alright to have a drink," said Desmond, "seeing as nothing is going to happen until John gets back from the studio."

The entrance to the bar was right on the corner with a large window either side stretching briefly along the two streets it straddled. Red, imitation-leather-clad booths were lined up against each of the windows opposite the right-angled bar. A few of the booths were occupied but they had no trouble finding an empty one. Chuck ordered two Buds from the bar.

"Don't worry, Des, it's all going to be okay." Chuck could see Desmond was getting nervous as the time to act was approaching.

"How can you say that, Chuck? We don't really have a plan and we're running out of time. I don't understand. Molly seemed to think we're somehow going to stop the shooting, but she's left us to it. What if Chapman turns nasty when we approach him? He's got a gun, remember. Maybe we should just leave."

"And allow John to get shot? We're meant to be here, Des. Molly said so. It's already in place."

"Okay, I guess you're right. Let's discuss exactly what we're going to do."

They sat and talked, ordered food and more beer. At the same time Bill, ensconced in the cafe, ordered cakes and coffee. Molly had finished her walk in Central Park and had decided to return to the cafe and wait. She hardly noticed the hippy figure sat a couple of tables away as she took her seat at the table near the door. Bill noticed her, however, and became a little edgy. He had to remain anonymous so decided to leave. *I'll wait by the van until it's all over*, he decided. *I doubt if anything much is going to happen anyway. I expect Mark Chapman changes his mind and comes to his senses in this reality.*

He made his way out of the cafe without attracting any unwanted attention. He breathed a sigh of relief once outside and then thought about his impending task; how to plant the transmitter on Desmond. He thought that perhaps he could somehow attach it to the van but didn't want to risk it falling off. *I'll wait and see*, he thought whilst turning down Central Park West.

*

At 10.30 p.m. Desmond and Chuck were finishing their drinks and preparing to exit the bar. They had decided that Desmond would approach John Lennon as soon as he got out of the car upon his return from the studio. Chuck, they had agreed, would hang back and keep a close watch on Mark Chapman, ready to pounce should he need to.

Molly had been asked to leave the cafe fifteen minutes earlier as it was closing. She was waiting outside. It was cold and she had things to do back in the world of time travel control. She knew that this timeline played out with John Lennon surviving and there was nothing left for her to do. The threat to the original timeline didn't materialise as they ended up in the parallel timeline. She was in two minds whether or not to hang around or to head home. After all, she had no emotional connection to the situation. But she did take a liking to Desmond. *Maybe I'll find out a bit more about him at another time*, she thought to herself. She decided to walk around the block, perhaps hanging on until after 10.50 when the next significant incident was due to occur. So she started walking down West 72nd Street. She felt it best to avoid the Dakota entrance to prevent any unintentional interference.

She reached the junction of the street with Columbus Avenue and turned right. As she passed the bar on the corner, Desmond and Chuck emerged and walked the other way, back up West 72nd Street towards the Dakota. Molly looked over her shoulder as they walked away without seeing her. *They'll be fine*, she thought.

Desmond and Chuck made their way slowly towards the Dakota, keeping a look out for what could be John Lennon's car as well as trying to spot Mark Chapman among the occasional vehicles and pedestrians. They saw both as they reached the Dakota. Chuck held back a few yards as planned while Desmond carried on towards the entrance. Lennon was emerging from a black limousine just as Chapman came into view from across the street. Desmond froze. He was supposed to call out to Lennon, to attract his attention, to warn him that Mark Chapman was about to shoot him. Then something clicked. It all came back to him.

Molly, Molly, of course. How could I forget her? I don't know how but she's exactly the same as when I met her all those years ago, when I was twenty. It's the same person. I've got to find her.

He turned towards Chuck who was waiting for Desmond to attract Lennon's attention. *What's he playing at? He's left it too late!* Chapman had crossed the street and was heading straight for Lennon, gun in hand. Desmond was feet away, to his left. Chapman ignored Desmond who was still facing Chuck and aimed the gun towards Lennon. Desmond suddenly remembered why he was there. He turned back to see Chapman, about to fire.

"WAIT!" Desmond shouted. "Don't do it!"

Chapman, temporarily put off guard, turned the gun towards Desmond and squeezed the trigger. Desmond closed his eyes, waiting to die. He heard a gunshot followed immediately by a second shot. The first one seemed to come from behind him. He opened his eyes and turned towards Chuck who was holding a smoking handgun aimed past Desmond towards Chapman. He immediately turned back towards Chapman who was lying injured on the ground, holding his right shoulder, his gun having skidded across the ground towards the security guard who calmly picked it up. He quickly realised the series of events. He also realised he was still alive. Chuck had shot Chapman in the shoulder a fraction of a second before Chapman fired at Desmond, sending the bullet from Chapman's gun heading harmlessly towards the sky.

"Let's get out of here, Desmond," said Chuck calmly, but with a sense of urgency as he pocketed his gun.

Chuck walked quickly towards a silent Desmond, gently coercing him along the sidewalk. They walked past a shocked John Lennon who was leant up against the arched entrance of the Dakota clutching Yoko who had rushed out of the car.

"You're welcome, John," said Chuck as they hurried past. Lennon nodded, almost imperceptibly, before rushing into the Dakota with Yoko, aided by the security guard.

CHAPTER 38

Manhattan, New York, 8 December 1980

Sirens wailed as they approached the corner of the Dakota and turned left along Central Park West. Desmond was still in shock, but Chuck remained remarkably calm. They walked quickly along the side of the building, the busy traffic heading towards them. They turned down West 73rd Street towards the van.

Moments before he heard the shots from the opposite side of the Dakota, Bill was leaning nonchalantly against the side of his Transit van. As the shots rang out, he looked to his left and right like a startled animal. He quickly surmised that the shots must in some way be connected to the John Lennon situation but before he could take any further action, he saw Molly about twenty yards away down the road. She had been heading towards him on her stroll around the block when she stopped suddenly on hearing the shots. Bill regained his composure and darted across the street before she could spot him and crouched behind a parked car. He watched as she stood for a while before continuing along towards the van. At this point Desmond and Chuck turned the corner and also headed towards the van.

"Wh ... where did the gun from?" were Desmond's first words since the shooting.

"Oh, I, er, borrowed it from someone. I like to carry a

gun. I keep it in the van," Chuck replied. "You never know when you might need it. Fortunately for you I was carrying it. I'm a bit like your guardian angel, aren't I, Des?"

"Says the man who ran me over," Desmond pointed out. "But thanks Chuck. Thanks for saving me. And John. You saved John Lennon."

"Well we both did, Des. You shouted, to stop Mark Chapman shooting John. That was brave."

"Yes, that's true. We both did well."

"But what happened, Des? You were meant to go straight to John Lennon before Chapman got there. Why did you hesitate?"

"I suddenly remembered everything. About Molly and everything. I think my memory has come back. Maybe it was the pressure of the situation, I don't really know."

As they reached the van, they saw Molly walking towards them. Bill peered out from the cover of the car, watching as they converged at the front of the van.

"Molly! We saved John Lennon! We did it. Chuck shot Mark Chapman. And I helped."

"Yes," said Chuck. "Des distracted Mark Chapman enough to stop him shooting John. He nearly shot Des though."

"Yes!" said Desmond excitedly. He was recovering rapidly from the shock of it all. "That's when Chuck shot Mark Chapman. He saved my life."

"Well done. I knew you'd do it. I mean, I literally knew. But you *shot* him, Chuck? I didn't see that coming."

"And I remember you, Molly," said Desmond, changing the subject. "I mean I remember everything."

"I'm sorry Desmond, as I've said, I haven't met you

before today, not yet anyway."

"Oh, oh I understand. You haven't met me yet. But you will. What are you doing here anyway? I thought you'd gone."

"I'm going now. I just thought I'd have a little walk while you sorted everything out. I'm off now though. Things to do. Where are you two going anyway?"

"This is our van," explained Desmond, pointing to the van next to them. "It's how we got here."

Bill had not had his van stolen until later in the eighties, so Molly had no reason to question the appearance of the Transit van. "I see, right. Off you go then, and take care. Oh, one more thing. You said you thought you knew Bill earlier. That'll be because I've decided to assign him to you when you start time travelling. And Chuck—"

"Never mind about me," he said hurriedly, opening the passenger door. "Come on, Desmond, let's leave Molly to get on with her time stuff." He then bundled Desmond into the van before he could protest.

"Goodbye Molly," said Desmond sadly, before Chuck firmly closed the door and made his way around to the driver's door.

"Well goodbye then," said Molly waving at them through the window. She then turned and strolled up the road.

Bill watched in desperation as Molly walked away and as soon as he thought it was safe to do so, crossed the road towards the van. Whilst listening in on the conversation, all he could think about was the transmitter and how he was going to get it planted without anyone seeing. He also had no idea whether Chuck was going to try and get Desmond home straight away or go somewhere else. He had to act, and quickly.

He ran straight to the passenger door and jumped in. He had reasoned that nothing he did now was going to change the events of this version of 1980. "Hi Desmond, Chuck," he said as he muscled Desmond across to the middle seat.

They took a couple of seconds to compose themselves before they both said, "Hi Bill."

"How did you know it was me?" he asked, removing his wig and glasses.

"We've seen that look before," replied Desmond, eyeing him up and down. "And what the hell are you doing here? It's good to see you by the way," he added.

"Two reasons. I've come to get my van back and also to ensure you get back home, Desmond. I was supposed to plant this transmitter on you as you appear to have left the last one in 1971." He held up the transmitter and placed it in the well next to the gear stick.

"Your van? This is your van, Bill? And why the transmitter?" asked Desmond.

Bill went on to explain about Desmond's injuries causing him to become untraceable and how his ability to travel may also be affected. He told him about the transmitter being planted in his suit jacket by Molly.

"Molly was there? At Abbey Road? Wow! She was right there behind me." He contemplated this for a moment before remembering what happened to the suit jacket. "I dumped it. The jacket. I didn't need it after Dr Jasper gave me this one," he said opening up the jacket to show Bill. "And the van. How did you get Bill's van, Chuck?"

"Your friend Chuck here stole it from me in 1985 when I was inspecting the 'Live Aid' preparations. That's right, isn't it, Chuck?"

"Yep," acknowledged Chuck, sheepishly. "But I didn't know it was your van. I just found it with the keys in. It was like it was saying 'take me away,' so I did. I've had a good run though."

"Okay, never mind the van," Desmond interrupted, "what are we going to do next?"

"We need to go back in time before we get you home, Desmond," said Bill.

"Well, that's fine with me. But why?"

"It's to do with the alternative timeline we're in. We have to go back to before it split, then we can go forward on the original timeline. It's a bit like a fork in the road. You go back past the fork then you'll go forward on the right road. Got it?"

"Yes, I think so. Chuck and I thought we'd like to go on one more trip anyway." He thought for a moment. "How about the Cavern Club? In 1961 when it was all happening."

"That sounds good, Desmond, we just need to get the right tune on the radio," said Bill.

"Do you want to do that, Bill?" asked Chuck. "I guess you'll want to drive anyway."

"Okay. I'll come around to your side."

Bill jumped out of the van and closed the door. Chuck immediately started up the van and sped off down West 73rd Street before Bill could react. He stood at the side of the road, watching in disbelief as the van sped away.

"Not again!" he said.

CHAPTER 39

Liverpool, England, 5 November 1961

"Oh don't worry, Desmond. Bill will find us; he left his transmitter with us." Chuck held up the transmitter which he had picked up from next to the van's gear stick. "I'll take it with us," he said, and put it in his pocket.

Desmond hadn't stopped berating Chuck since they left Bill standing by the roadside in 1980. He recalled that Bill had said something about his ability to travel being affected by the accident. Without Bill, he was worried that he may not get back at all.

"We can always try and get you home using the van if not," Chuck continued.

"The van is not always that accurate, Chuck, as we know. What if I arrived back before I left? There would be two of me!"

Desmond's point about the accuracy of the van appeared to be evidenced by the fact that they had arrived in Liverpool with nothing happening at the Cavern. They had made their way from where the van appeared, in a side street, to Mathew Street a few blocks away. On arrival at the East entrance to Mathew Street, the home of the Cavern, they made their way along the narrow street, overshadowed by several four-storey buildings, towards the Cavern, the entrance to which was towards the far end on the left. They passed The Grapes pub on the right; a favourite hangout of The Beatles, Desmond pointed out to Chuck. Unfortunately, it was closed, being 11.00 a.m. in 1961 which was probably just as well as neither Desmond nor Chuck had any old, English cash.

They reached the Cavern, number ten Mathew Street, and stood back admiring the original entrance, with the posters advertising The Beatles and Gerry and the Pacemakers among others. Above the double black doors was the curved writing on the rectangular sign; 'Cav' on one side of a record and 'ern' on the other. An iconic sign that was to remain for many years. Desmond had visited the 'new' Cavern in the nineties and was grateful for this opportunity to see the real thing.

"Where is everybody?" asked Desmond, suddenly realising that there were very few people around.

"Erm, it's a Sunday, Desmond," said Chuck. It must be closed. Looks like we've landed on the wrong day."

"Well, that's disappointing, Chuck. It must be that van of yours. I mean Bill's. So we're not going to get to see The Beatles at the Cavern."

They stood in the middle of the road staring at the closed doors as if that would change things. "That is disappointing," agreed Chuck.

Desmond walked up to the entrance and knocked on the right-hand door. No one answered so he gave the door a gentle push and was surprised to find that it opened. He looked around at Chuck. "Shall we?" he said.

Chuck didn't need to consider for long and they both crept through the door, closing it behind them after Chuck found the light switches on the wall of the passageway leading to the top of the steps. They followed the steps down, turned to their left at the bottom, and found themselves in an empty

Cavern Club.

"Wow," said Desmond. "It's small. And it smells of disinfectant."

They looked across at the arches where, on a weekday, crowds of young Liverpudlians would congregate, unable to get a seat. The chairs were stacked at the far end on their left, leaving most of the floor empty in front of the tiny stage, set in the arched area to their right.

"That's where it all happens, Des. Just imagine it," said Chuck, nodding towards the stage.

They moved to the middle of the floor and gazed silently at the stage. There were two microphone stands at the front and speakers either side at the back. Chuck grabbed a couple of the chairs, and they resumed their gazing whilst seated. Then they heard a noise from the top of the steps. Someone had entered the building and banged the door shut behind them. They could hear footsteps slowly clattering on the stone steps descending towards them. Desmond and Chuck stared at one another.

"Who's that?" whispered Desmond.

"We'll find out any second now," came the reply.

A man in his mid to late twenties appeared at the entrance wearing shiny shoes and a smart suit.

"Oh, good morning," the man said, in what Desmond considered to be a posh accent. "I'm Brian Epstein. How do you do." He offered his hand. Desmond and Chuck stood up and shook the proffered hand. "And you are?"

"Desmond, Desmond Jones actually. And this is Chuck." Desmond pointed at Chuck as if to avoid any confusion.

"Oh, right. I'm supposed to meet someone called Paddy here. I'm arranging a visit for Thursday to see The Beatles.

Are you anything to do with them? Or Paddy?"

"No, we're just here to meet someone. Paddy said it would be okay. He must have forgotten to mention it to you," Chuck lied. "I expect he'll be here soon. Here, have a seat. We'll wait outside."

Chuck grabbed Desmond by his good arm and moved towards the steps.

"Oh, okay then," said Brian Epstein. "But don't leave on my account."

"No that's fine, Mr Epstein," said Chuck, not wishing to bump into Paddy. "Come on, Des."

"Let's stay and have a chat with Mr Epstein," said Desmond. "We haven't seen him for a while." Desmond walked towards the back of the club and picked up another chair.

Chuck stood and watched, conceding that they were not about to leave after all.

"So," began Desmond. "I expect you're thinking of managing The Beatles. Do you need any help?"

*

A couple of minutes earlier Molly, Matt, Nigel, Penelope, and Brian arrived safely in the tiny band room at the side of the stage. Molly had calculated the exact coordinates according to the transmitter which appeared to be a matter of feet away. They had held hands and stood in a circle in the lounge of number eight Cavendish Crescent before Molly had activated the bracelets using the master control.

Nigel, Penelope, and Brian stood with a look of surprise and shock on their faces but before anyone could speak, Molly held a finger to her lips, indicating that everyone should remain quiet. She extricated her hands from the circle and peered around the doorway of the band room where she spotted Desmond and Chuck talking to someone. She quickly deduced that they were talking to Brian Epstein and the nature of Desmond's question about managing The Beatles was enough to make her act quickly.

"Wait here!" she said to the others and stepped out on to the stage.

Brian Epstein was about to ask Desmond how he could possibly know he was going to manage The Beatles when Molly appeared.

"What? Molly! How?" said Desmond, abandoning his conversation with Brian Epstein before it had started.

"Good to see you, Desmond," she said, holding out her arms towards him.

Desmond ran towards her, stepped the few inches on to the stage, and they kissed.

"I never expected to see you again, you know, after New York," he said. "I know it was only like a few hours ago but it's great to see you too."

"Desmond, I haven't seen you for twenty years," she replied

"Oh, of course. That was the old Molly."

"If you like. But I'm here now. We've come to take you home."

At this point Penelope appeared on the stage, being unable to hold back any longer. Molly took a step back while she rushed up and hugged a bewildered Desmond. It was all too much for him, unable to formulate a suitable question. He just said, "Pen? How?"

Next to appear were Nigel and Brian together, entering the stage as if returning for an encore, causing Desmond to almost faint with surprise whilst receiving a joint hug. Finally, Matt appeared and introduced himself.

"Good to finally meet you, Desmond," he said, shaking his hand. "I've heard a lot about you."

"Matt's one of my time agents, like Bill. We've all been working together to find you and get you home."

"Where is Bill, by the way?" asked Molly.

"Don't worry, I'm here," came a voice from beside the stage. "Despite the best efforts of Chuck." Bill entered the crowded stage, having transported from 1980 just as the others had left the band room, and bowed to the audience of Chuck and Brian Epstein who had been watching transfixed while the big reunion was going on. "Keys please, Chuck."

"Sorry Bill, couldn't resist," said Chuck with a smile, digging out the van keys from his pocket and tossing them to Bill.

"Let's get you home then, Dessie," said Molly. "Sorry we didn't get to see The Beatles but I'll make it up to you."

"Yes, that's partly why I came," said Brian.

"And me," said Nigel.

Penelope gave them one of her looks.

"But mainly to bring Desmond home," said Brian. "Isn't that right, Nigel?"

"Yes, of course," agreed Nigel, not wanting to incur any disapproval from Penelope.

"How did you get here?" asked Desmond, finally regaining the ability to speak.

Nigel, Penelope, and Brian held up their wrists with the bracelets attached.

"All will be explained," said Molly, aware that Brian Epstein was still observing all of this. She felt that he had already seen enough, and she wanted to prevent any further reason to cause an additional timeline. "It's time we were leaving. Follow me everyone. Not you, Brian," referring to Brian Epstein. "You wait here if you don't mind."

A bewildered Brian Epstein nodded and sat back down, waiting for Paddy. "Good to meet you all. Whoever you are. Perhaps we'll meet again someday."

"We will," said Desmond.

Molly led the way up the steps, leading Desmond by the hand. The others followed with Bill and Matt bringing up the rear. They emerged into a cold November day almost exactly nineteen years from their next destination.

"Right," said Molly, "this is what we're going to do next." They had found a quiet part of Mathew Street, which wasn't a problem on a Sunday in 1961. "Chuck, you take Bill back to the van and decide where you would like Bill to take you. Matt, you go with them just in case Chuck gets any ideas about taking the van." Chuck was about to protest but realised there was no point in arguing with Molly.

"Goodbye Des," said Chuck, hugging Desmond. "Sorry about running you over and all that."

"No worries, Chuck. It's been great. Thanks for saving my life."

Nigel, Penelope, and Brian all looked at each other, wondering how Chuck had saved Desmond's life.

"We'll ask him later," said Nigel, speaking for all of them.

Chuck, Bill, and Matt then made their way down Mathew Street towards the location of the Transit van.

The others watched silently as they left then Molly said, "Desmond, you need a Time Transportation Capability Test to see if you are okay to travel."

Desmond turned back towards her, looking a little concerned. Firstly, as there seemed to be a possibility he couldn't travel if he failed the test, and secondly, he didn't know what Molly was talking about.

"Don't worry, Desmond, you've had one before," said Molly reassuringly. She pulled the TTCT device from between the layers of her dress and quickly proceeded to scan Desmond before he could protest. "Mmm," she said, the tone of which worried Desmond slightly. "You're still not quite back to normal which is probably due to your injuries from the accident. You've also been away from your proper time for quite a while. Better put on one of these just to be safe," she added, pulling out a time travel cuff bracelet from another part of her dress. "I brought a spare with me just in case. Give me your arm."

Although he didn't understand it, Desmond was happy to comply, confident that all would be explained in good time. She expertly clipped it around his good right wrist.

"Right. I think it's time to get back to Middlesham," said Molly. She checked her device and individually calibrated the four bracelets.

"You can hold my hand again now, Nigel," said Penelope.

CHAPTER 40

Middlesham, November 2000

"Right then! Round one: Entertainment," said Murray the quizmaster.

There was an extra team at the Admiral Nelson this week. 'Le Beats' had temporarily split into two in order to accommodate the extra team members. Desmond and Penelope were joined by Molly and Chuck. Nigel and Brian had acquired Bill and Matt. After much discussion, Nigel had decided that this way was the best way to split the teams.

*

"Well, here I am," said Desmond, ninety minutes previously, after safely arriving back at the house, "with a little help from my friends."

He had been updated on everything the others knew, starting with Chuck running him over at Abbey Road. Desmond and Chuck had also given their account of everything they could remember from Desmond's arrival at Tittenhurst Park in 1971.

Chuck had arrived in Cavendish Crescent minutes after the others, accompanied by Matt, having decided that Middlesham in the year 2000 was as good a place as any for him to settle down. On the way to the van back in Liverpool, he had explained to Bill and Matt that he had no permanent place of residence and he liked the idea of settling down in

Middlesham. Desmond was delighted.

Bill had arrived a few minutes after Chuck and Matt, having had a few errands to run. Desmond opened his front door and was greeted by Bill holding a small package.

"Bill, you're here!" said Desmond. "Come on in and join the party."

"Thank you," said Bill, handing Desmond the package. "This is for you."

Bill followed Desmond into the lounge where Desmond tore open the yellow, padded envelope. The rest of the room, having greeted Bill, were curious to see what he had brought him, and crowded around Desmond.

Inside the envelope was what looked like a leather-bound book or diary. The inscribed front cover read: 'The Extraordinary Adventures of Desmond Jones'. He opened it. It was in fact a photo album which contained seven photographs, each covering one of the certificate-size pages and each featuring an image of Desmond. The first was at the Kaiserkeller in Hamburg, taken by Astrid, the next at the Shea Stadium, New York, by Linda Eastman. The third one was at the Ed Sullivan rehearsals, taken by Chuck, and the fourth was at Abbey Road Studios with a couple of Rolling Stones in the background, taken by Pattie Harrison. The fifth featured John and Yoko outside of their Tittenhurst Park home with Desmond superimposed on to the background. Bill confessed that with no one taking a picture of him there, that was the best he could manage. The sixth was one of Desmond and Chuck, taken by Paul Goresh, outside of the Dakota Apartments, and the seventh, taken from the side of the stage at the Cavern, was secretly snapped by Bill before announcing his arrival there.

Desmond gave Bill a big hug, "Thanks Bill," he said. "Thanks for everything."

*

Everyone was impressed by the efforts of Desmond and Chuck to save John Lennon, and shocked at and grateful for Chuck's use of the shotgun.

"Let's fill in more of the detail at the pub," Desmond suggested after the initial discussions. "We can all do the quiz! And I can buy you that drink I owe you, Bill."

"After all you've been through, Desmond?" said Penelope. "Are you sure you want to do the quiz?"

"Yes, he'll be fine," answered Nigel before Desmond could respond. "You can stay, can't you?" he asked, turning to Chuck, Molly, and her team. "Yes of course you can," he answered on their behalf.

Before leaving for the pub, where they had decided to eat by way of celebrating Desmond's return, Molly had taken Desmond into the hallway. "I'm staying, Desmond," she said.

"What?"

"I'm staying."

"What? Where?"

"Here. In the year 2000. If you want me to that is. I wasn't sure how you would feel after last time. You, know, when I left abruptly. It won't happen again."

"Yes, yes stay."

"Well, in that case, I thought I'd get a place of my own and see how we get along. In the meantime, Brian says he'll put me up in his spare room. We can start again, Desmond, from where we left off in Bath."

Desmond was so happy. "That sounds perfect," he said.

*

"Well done team," said Nigel, congratulating himself along with Brian, Bill, and Matt.

Nigel's team, 'Le Beats volume 2', had won the quiz convincingly, with 'Le Beats' finishing in fifth place. Desmond wasn't bothered in the least. Molly and Chuck had done their best, but their lack of general knowledge left Desmond and Penelope with too much to do and they couldn't compete with 'Le Beats volume 2'.

On the way back, walking arm in arm with Molly, Desmond had a thought. "There's one thing I don't understand about New York, Molly."

"Only one thing?"

Desmond carried on regardless. "If you travelled to 1980 a few years ago, that was before we went there, before I started time travelling, before I caused the split timeline in 1971 … wasn't it? How could you have been alerted a few years ago, long before I went there?"

"Well Des, I was working in 1995 at the time, but the future had still happened, up until 2000. The alert was for 1980, twenty years ago but only fifteen years from where I was. Think of it as a time bubble!"

"Whatever you say, Molly," said Desmond, not understanding a word of it.

EPILOGUE

Live Aid, Wembley Stadium, North London,

13 July 1985

"They're halfway though their set now, John, we're on in five minutes."

"Five minutes? Christ, has anyone seen Yoko?"

"She's gone to her seat at the side. Don't worry, she's with Linda. Let's just run through what we're doing, one last time. It's all one's we know."

"One last time, Paul, how many more one last times are there going to be? Maybe we should have rehearsed a bit more, it's been sixteen years!"

John and Paul were getting anxious.

"Just the one, John. So, we start with 'I Saw Her Standing There', then we do 'Sgt. Pepper', then George does 'Something', then it's 'Money'."

"Hooray! One for me to sing," interrupted John.

"Two for you, 'cause we finish with 'Twist and Shout' remember. But before that it's 'Let It Be', got it?"

"Got it. Where's Ringo?"

"He's here, don't worry," said Ringo as he walked into the makeshift dressing room on cue. "Okay let's go."

They stood up. John, Paul, and George with guitars in hand, Ringo holding a pair of drumsticks.

"Where are we going, boys?" asked John.

"To the toppermost of the poppermost, Johnnie," replied a chorus of the other three Beatle voices.

*

Deep into the crowd, Desmond was beside himself with excitement. He turned to Molly, his girlfriend of three months, who had brought him back through the fractured timeline to 1985 as a birthday treat. He wept tears of joy as his heroes shuffled on to the stage. And then he heard Paul McCartney's famous introduction to 'I Saw Her Standing There'.

"One, two, three, four ..."

The End

Printed in Great Britain
by Amazon

86665602R00159

ABOUT THE AUTHOR

Michael lives with his wife in Exeter in Devon where he was born and raised. He worked for many years as a Learning & Development manager. His interest in music and the Beatles in particular started in the 1960s and continues to this day. He plays guitar and piano and has written the occasional song. He also enjoys playing golf and is a keen follower of Exeter City Football Club.